BURNING FOR ALEXANDER

LUCY LENNOX

ISBN: 978-1-954857-71-1

Cover Art: Najla Qamber | Qamber Designs
Cover Image: Wander Aguiar
Editing: One Love Editing
Proofreading: Jodi Duggan

BURNING FOR ALEXANDER

I came to Legacy for a fresh start—to outrun my past and forget the anonymous man I fell for online.

But now all I see is Alex Marian.
The bane of my existence. Firebug. Reckless bar owner. Walking disaster.

It doesn't matter that he's the sexiest man alive. Or charming. Or kind.

He's entitled, spoiled, rich, naive—everything I hate.

He's also young and untouched—not that it's any of my business.

The townspeople say he's the sunshine to my grump.
What they don't know is that worrying about him keeps me up at night.

He's the match, and I'm the gasoline—and the way he looks at me says he knows exactly what kind of fire we'd make together.

But Alex Marian might just be worth the burn.

AUTHOR'S NOTE

It is not necessary to read *Rescuing Dr. Marian* before enjoying *Burning for Alexander*, but if you do, please note that Foster Blake and Tommy Marian haven't arrived in Legacy yet when Alex and Judd begin sparring in *Burning for Alexander*.

Special Thanks to Mary S. for suggesting the name Kaidee, short for Katherine, and to Saralina D. for suggesting the name Elias for use on characters in this story.

Final note: I know small-town Montana fire stations do not have as many firefighters as I have gifted Legacy FD with. ***waves fictional wand at you*** Let's just pretend. M'kay?

1

ALEX

IF THE ACCIDENTAL conflagration had occurred at any other time, it wouldn't have been a problem. We'd have put it out with a wet bar mop before anyone was the wiser and gone on with our lives.

Unfortunately for me, tonight was not my night.

So when the fire started, it happened to be at the exact same moment our town's new fire chief walked into my restaurant with the sheriff.

"What the actual fuck?" the angry man in a navy blue Legacy FD fleece asked again, glaring at me.

He stood too close, wedged behind the bar, wielding my two-hundred-and-fifty-dollar Amerex fire extinguisher... which he'd just discharged all over my beautiful, hand-carved bar as if he had no idea the effect potassium citrate and acetate had on burled walnut.

I ignored him and called through the opening behind the bar to the kitchen. "Karim, please grab some clean, damp cloths and dry cloths. Quickly!"

Chemical solution came close to dripping from the edge of the bar as I lunged to stop the flow with the towel tucked into my back pocket. "Fuck. *Fuck*," I muttered under my breath. "Can you please move? I have to clean this before it gets all over everything."

The man reached for the small bottle lying next to the charred remains of my napkin and straw holder and held it up.

It was the sanitizing spray Tavo had been using, too close to the Bacardi 151 float I'd been flicking a lighter on. The combination of the two had caused the flaming kerfuffle in the first place.

The grumpy fire chief nudged me back with a fingertip to the shoulder. "You will not touch anything."

I ignored the odd twinge I got from feeling his finger on me. The older man was sexy as fuck, no doubt about it. Thick, wavy hair that was more salt than pepper, dark eyes that seemed happiest pinning people like bugs on a board, and broad shoulders. Most of all, a commanding presence.

But so far, it seemed like he had the personality of a meat grinder.

He continued with another soft poke. "This is now a crime scene, and disturbing it is a violation of—"

"Crime scene?" I barked out a laugh. "Guy, it's a small mishap at best."

"Your 'mishap' appears to be deliberate arson, and as such, I will be doing a full investigation."

I opened my mouth to tell him just how ridiculous he was

being when I remembered the first time he'd come in here a few weeks ago. "Wait, is this about the day we met? About me not knowing who you were? Is this some kind of retaliation for my bad memory?" Hopefully, my voice didn't sound as high-pitched and unhinged as I felt. Annoyance and incredulity bubbled up, and I wanted to deck the man. "I told you, we've never met before!"

And I could say that with certainty because the man was sex on a stick. I would've wanted to climb him and beg him to do dirty things to me. But now that it turned out he was an asshole, maybe it was a good thing we'd never met.

His jaw clenched. "We've met. More than met, in fact. And if you want to pretend otherwise, that's your decision. But, no, this has nothing to do with our previous... encounter. It has to do with fire safety. *Public* safety."

"When exactly did we meet?" I asked, letting Karim take over the cleanup from the other side of the bar while I kept the chief's focus turned slightly away. The less "evidence" of this minor incident, the better. "Because I'd remember you with all this..." I waved my hand to indicate the whole of him. "Bluster and general assholery."

His eyes widened and then narrowed. "Three years ago in Amsterdam. Ring a bell?"

I thought back to the only time I'd ever been to Amsterdam. It was during a layover from France on the way to meet the rest of my family in Iceland. But that had been more like eight years ago because I'd been at Château de Pommard finishing my level three WSET qualification.

Before I could tell him any of this, Sheriff Westland approached and made eye contact with the frothing fire chief.

"Chief Kincaid, I'm sure this was nothing but an accident, and since you were so quick to react, there's not much harm done other than a ruined... whatever that was," he said, nodding toward the melted napkin caddy.

"And the finish on my bar from the K-class extinguisher," I muttered under my breath.

Chief Kincaid made a growling sound, clearly directed at me. I kept my eyes averted and tried to look innocent as a lamb.

"I need to know who started the fire so I can write it up," Kincaid said. "Arson or not, it was still a careless fire in a restaurant and needs to be reported. Also..." He met my eyes, cold blue searing into me. "No more fiery drinks."

"That's not fair!" I cried. "We're known for the Slingshot Flame. People come from all over to try it! You can't just take it away from us. Besides, I have a fucking fire effect permit—"

He shrugged. "Not anymore. Consider it revoked as of now."

Nerves coiled in my gut.

The Slingshot Flame was talked about in hotels, campgrounds, and Airbnbs all over the area.

I'd only been running Timber for two and a half years, and I was counting on this summer's tourist traffic to help solidify my place on the map. Timber couldn't afford to lose one of the things that made it unique and fun. It was hard enough sustaining a restaurant under any conditions, but in a very small town with large swells and dips, thanks to the fickle tourist population, it was impossible to know what might bring about the end of a place's popularity.

I took a deep breath and dug deep, searching for any shred of patience and respect I could find for this asshole.

"Chief. What can I do to get the permit reinstated?"

"Fuck-all," he growled.

Sheriff Westland sighed and shook his head. "Let's all just calm down. I believe de-escalation is called for here. Alex, I agree with Chief Kincaid." He held his hand up at the angry fire chief's smug expression. "But I think it'll most likely be a temporary permit suspension while you and your crew undergo more rigorous training and submit to a full safety inspection."

Kincaid's eyes were smoking embers, and if the sheriff hadn't been fully hydrated, the man might have incinerated on the spot. "I believe I carry the decision-making power for the Legacy Fire Department, Elias, do I not?" His voice was cold as he addressed our friendly sheriff.

Sheriff Westland's golden retriever aura didn't hide the fact that he had teeth like any other good dog. "Of course you do, but I don't believe you've been in Legacy long enough to see the bigger picture. Maybe I can explain it to you back at the station. And maybe Alex, here, can make us a stack of pizzas to take to your crew while we're at it?" He lifted his eyebrows at me.

If it had been anyone other than the sheriff, I probably would have told him where to shove my gourmet pizzas. But it wasn't. And I owed Elias Westland a lot for his support over the past three years. "Absolutely. That sounds like a good idea," I said quickly, moving around Chief Asshat to inform the kitchen to get started on the order.

The sound of the two alphas faking cordiality faded as I moved deeper into the kitchen. "Juni, sorry to do this to you, but I'm going to need an assortment of ten pizzas, garlic knots, and a variety of salads for the firehouse as soon as we can get them ready."

Her steely eyes glinted at me. "You tell that posturing piece of sh—"

"I got it!" Deena said, pivoting to the prepared dough mounds on a tray in a nearby rack. "Karim will put together the salads, right, Karim?"

He nodded and moved past me to the sink before washing his hands.

After everyone settled down, Juni, my head chef, glanced up at me with a reluctant nod. "You did good."

That was all she said, but enough of the kitchen crew heard it, as tuned in to her as they were, that the room filled with nods and murmurs of agreement.

I blew out a breath and glanced back out the kitchen door to see if anyone was close enough to hear. "Did anyone see Tavo? The sheriff or the fire chief?"

Juni shook her head. "No way. That kid bolted, just like you told him to. He's probably tucked away deep in the library by now. Maureen will look out for him, don't you worry."

She was right, but I still worried. Our kitchen assistant was a young man with the weight of the world on his shoulders and enough legitimate stress distracting him to have accidentally sprayed accelerant at the drink I was making. As soon as I realized what was happening and who was walking in the door of the restaurant at the worst possible time, I'd shoved him toward the kitchen with a hissed "*Run.*"

The last thing we needed was nosy law enforcement officers, including an asshole fire chief with something to prove, getting up in our business.

The kitchen staff hustled, working well together as a team, and got the order out as quickly as possible. There was a silent understanding in the kitchen that the sooner we got rid of the LEOs, the sooner everyone could take a deep breath and relax.

Poor Tavo didn't turn back up until almost closing time, much later that night.

"You okay?" I asked, spotting him behind the dumpster after I tossed in a bag of trash. As soon as he stepped into the beams of safety floodlights on the back of the building, I saw how scared he looked.

"Alex, I'm so sorry! I promise it was an accident!"

I held open my arms. "Oh, honey, c'mere. We're okay. I promise."

He raced across the remaining yards of asphalt and launched himself into my arms. His small frame wasn't enough to even make me stumble. Poor thing needed some meat on his bones, as my great-great-aunt Tilly would say.

Tavo's body was racked with sobs I was fairly sure weren't just about the fire at Timber, so I held him tightly until he was ready to let go. When he pulled back, his eyes were shimmery. "Can I... can I still, um, stay with you? Because I'll understand if the answer is no."

I rolled my eyes and grinned at him. "Don't be ridiculous. Of course you can. Come on."

I turned to head toward the old wooden stairs leading up to the place I called home over the restaurant. Unlike my friend Maddox, who lived over his family's hardware store in town in a residence resembling an actual apartment, I lived in more of a rabbit warren.

The building was an old timber roadhouse that had been around for almost a hundred years. Over time, it had been added onto like a LEGO house with rooms originally built to expand the kitchen, store beer kegs, bulk food supplies, pool tables, and various other things as the mood had struck various owners over the years.

My place was a motley collection of little rooms forming the interconnected and finished attic spaces of the add-ons. Thankfully, it meant Tavo had a tiny room to himself—one just large enough to fit a simple twin bed and small wooden dresser.

Unfortunately, the rooms were connected by narrow passageways that made sharing the living space a challenge at times. Once we made our way upstairs, Tavo ducked into his room and waited for me to do my nightly bathroom routine before taking his turn. I moved into my bedroom to throw both dormer windows wide open and let out the stuffy heat of the day.

I flicked on the large box fan and set it in one window to create some airflow, and then moved back out of my room to the small kitchen in search of a glass of ice water. The stress of the day began to melt away as I moved through my nightly routine.

It wasn't until I was setting tomorrow morning's alarm on my phone after slipping into bed that I saw the email notification from the Legacy Fire Department. I clicked it open to see the "Official Notice of Permit Suspension."

As my eyes scanned down the page, my anger began to simmer and then boil over.

> *Incident involved ignition of alcohol-based sanitizer aerosol in proximity to open flame being used for bar drink presentation. Resulting fire involved napkin holder and was extinguished with in-house Class K extinguisher. Preliminary cause determined to be procedural negligence and failure to adhere to fire safety protocols. Referred for code compliance review.*

I was going to kill that overreacting motherfucker. Before taking a moment of maturity to catch my breath and calm down, maybe even sleep on it the way a professional adult would have, I hit the Reply button and gave Legacy's new fire chief a piece of my fucking mind.

2

———

KINCAID

IndexEcho: *Now that you've passed your ICS-100, what else should we talk about?*

DrunkenPoet: *You told me identifying details were off-limits, so I'll have to get creative. What's your favorite wine and why is it Sauvignon Blanc?*

IndexEcho: *Sorry, more of a beer guy. Wine's too rich for my blood. Fave beer is Summer Song made near where I grew up. You?*

———

Subject: Re: Official Notice of Permit Suspension
Dear Fire Dom Kincaid,
Thank you for your prompt and wildly proportionate response to the recent incident.
While I appreciate your detailed retelling of how a flaming

orange peel met a rogue spritz of sanitizer and briefly terrorized a napkin holder, I feel compelled to point out a few things:

The "procedural negligence" was, in fact, me attempting to provide an entertaining, Instagram-worthy drink presentation to paying customers—something you might know about if your job involved serving people instead of scowling at them.

The fire was extinguished immediately using equipment I purchased, installed, and trained my staff to use.

No injuries occurred, unless you count my emotional trauma from watching you drench my walnut bar in potassium salt foam like it was a county fair pie-eating contest.

So while I admire your commitment to the "kill a mosquito with a sledgehammer" approach, I respectfully request you un-suspend my permit before I decide to bill the Legacy Fire Department for damage to my bar's finish.

Warmest regards (pun very much intended),
Alexander Marian
Owner, Timber

I STARED at the email on the monitor in front of me while my coffee cooled on the desk. "What the actual fuck," I grumbled under my breath. "Is he insane?"

A voice shouted through my doorway from somewhere in the hall. "Chances are yes, if you're talking about McMasters, Chief."

Cody McMasters fired back. "Fuck you, Javi!"

Back in Philly, I would have snapped, "Knock it off!" But I hadn't been in Legacy long enough to start being a hard-ass with my crew.

"Who's refilling air canisters right now? Wasn't that supposed to be you, Sujo?" I called out.

"Yes, sir," he said. "But if you're asking the state of someone's mental health, Tiff's the one you want to ask. She's pretty clued in to people like that."

I grunted. The last thing I needed was to ask Javier Sujo's girlfriend anything. I'd only met her once, and my ears were still ringing from her bubbly questions.

After leaving the site of the incident at Timber yesterday, Sheriff Westland had cautioned me on "raising a stink" with Alex Marian. "Or any Marian, for that matter," he'd added. "They're big money around here. The Legacy equivalent of the Kennedys. I'm not saying they're above the law. No way. I'm just saying, go easy. Be sure before you pick a fight with someone over something that looked like a fairly minor accident."

"The United States sees fatalities every year from restaurant fires, Elias," I'd informed him. What I hadn't added—because it wasn't relevant—was that the number was three. For a country of three hundred and thirty-five million people. Not bad odds. But still greater than zero.

And the number of fire- and smoke-related fatalities on my watch *would* be zero if I had anything to say about it.

At least from here on out.

I stood up from my desk and moved out of my office to the large open bay where the crew was working on various tasks in and around Legacy's two largest rigs. "Lieutenant Pope," I said, spotting the woman I wanted to talk to. "Got a minute?"

The deceptively small woman turned from where she was currently polishing the chrome bumper of the nearest rig and lifted her eyebrows before standing up. "Sure, Chief. Let me wash up?"

I nodded and returned to my office. When she came in and took a seat, I leaned forward over the desk. "First of all, thank you for coming in early and finishing up that certification paperwork. I know it's a pain in the ass."

Kinsey shrugged, the cut muscles of her shoulders and biceps standing out in the navy tank top she wore. "Gotta be done, right? At least most of it's online now."

"Agreed. When you were in Chicago, did you ever see a fire that started from a cocktail at a bar or restaurant?"

She pursed her lips in thought. "Well, yeah, I guess. I mean, we had this one club that got crazy one night, and the bartender went all Tom Cruise in *Cocktail*, you know?"

I squinted at her. "You know that movie?"

She laughed and shook her head, setting her dark brown ponytail swinging across her shoulders. "No, man, but I've seen the GIF, right? Anyway, I guess the bartender was showing off and decided to arc the high-proof shit that he lit up with the lighter. So the flame arced, too, and set a bunch of Cinco de Mayo decorations off. Shit burned up this wooden beam over the bar, and if a quick-thinking barback hadn't gotten the extinguisher out quick enough, it would have reached the shelves of spirits behind them. Why do you ask?"

"They lose their flame effect permit?"

"What? No. They fired the bartender who did it. Turned out his blood alcohol was almost as high-test as the Bacardi 151. Club owners were pissed. If the cops weren't swarming around, they woulda beat the shit outta the guy."

In addition to being savvy and experienced, one of the highest-ranking firefighters on the crew, Kinsey was a social person, outgoing and friendly. Chances were, she knew exactly why I was asking.

I pushed off the desk and stood back up. "Okay, let's go. We're going to follow up on the Timber fire, and I want you to accompany me for the origin and cause investigation."

She stood up and brushed off her dark uniform pants before tucking her tank top in a little more neatly in preparation for pulling her button-down uniform shirt back on out in the bay. "Sounds good. Just crossing t's and dotting i's?"

I reached for my tablet as well as my travel coffee mug. "Depends on what Alex Marian has to say for himself this morning," I grumbled.

ON THE DRIVE over to Timber, I paid close attention to my surroundings, still trying to memorize directions and street names.

Spring was finishing up for real this week. Mountain snowmelt ran fast in the roadside ditches, and the air was damp and sharp with the scent of thawed earth and new grass. Patches of green were creeping up the hillsides, and the peaks on the horizon wore only ragged collars of snow now, clouds drifting lazily around their shoulders.

Through the windshield, Legacy's landmarks appeared in sequence—the farmers market's hand-painted sign propped against a wall for touching up, the library's front steps swept clean after winter's grit, the gas station where two old-timers leaned against the ice chest, jackets already discarded on a nearby bench in the mild warmth. I slowed for the turn onto Founder's Row, where the hanging baskets had just gone up, spilling bright pansies and trailing ivy toward sidewalks still damp from an early morning sprinkle.

Up ahead, Timber's broad front windows caught the pale sunlight, its carved wooden sign etched with the now-familiar *Timber — Artisanal Pizza & Curated Wines*. Even from here, I could imagine the scent of yeast and woodsmoke from the ovens, the warm murmur of customers inside.

The place was too familiar already. Not only had the mayor

and sheriff brought me here after our interview, where Alex had acted like he'd never seen me before, but I'd also made the mistake of coming in to grab takeout my first night in town, not realizing the postcard mailer in my welcome packet was for the same place. Again, Alex hadn't even given me a second glance, looking right through me as if he hadn't bailed on me that night in Amsterdam.

The shock of seeing him again had hit me like a backdraft. For three years, I'd carried the memory of that night—the way I'd convinced myself to find someone, *anyone*, to have sex with. To get past my hang-up on the memory of someone I'd lost to the cruel trickster of time and fate.

I'd found the attractive stranger sitting at the hotel bar, flirting with the bartender enough to convince me he was into men and possibly looking for action. He was sexy and relaxed. Didn't seem to take himself too seriously. The perfect one-night stand to get someone else off my mind for at least a few hours.

After talking and flirting over a round of drinks, we'd made arrangements to head upstairs together after I visited the men's room and he signed the bar tab. I'd looked forward to exploring his body and enjoying the feel of him doing the same to mine. It had been a long time since I'd been with someone sexually. Even longer since I'd been touched by someone truly interested and attentive... unless you counted the attentions of the medical personnel at Ramstein for several months after my accident, which I did not.

But when I'd come out of the bathroom, I'd spotted the guy tonsil-deep with another man in a dark alcove.

"What the fuck?" I'd almost blurted. But I'd quickly taken the rejection as a sign. Wrong man, wrong night. Hell, wrong city, maybe.

Regardless, it had left me with a decidedly bad taste in my

mouth for the sexy stranger who was now the subject of my next incident investigation.

When I'd spotted him here in Legacy, leaning casually behind the bar with that same damn smile but muscles significantly more defined and hair cut into a deliberately messy style, my chest had gone tight. Attraction had slammed into me, raw and inconvenient —and strangely stronger than before—only to be doused in an instant by his blank look. No recognition. No flicker of familiarity. Just a polite, distracted brush-off, like I was any other stranger wandering in for pizza.

The burn of it hadn't faded. That whiplash from wanting him to wanting to *strangle* him was still with me every time I saw his face.

I felt the familiar curl of tension in my gut as I pulled into the large lot behind the restaurant, the unwelcome combination of disliking someone you also wanted to fuck. Thankfully, I'd brought reinforcements. Someone to help me remember I was a professional and this was a job.

Kinsey had been quiet on the short drive, taking the opportunity to review the necessary steps involved in an origin and cause investigation. My lieutenant was driven to move up to captain as soon as possible, and I wanted to make sure I was giving her ample opportunity to get the relevant experience she needed.

When we stepped out of my vehicle and began walking around to the front, she finally spoke up. "I've been meaning to ask, what brought you to Legacy?"

I thought about what to say. *I needed a gay-friendly place to live that wasn't on the East Coast, where my shitty past didn't want to let me go, or on the West Coast, where the man I'd once loved happened to live. No, I'd gone to the state that he'd dreamed about. Pure coincidence, really.* Definitely not appropriate to discuss with a member of my crew. *This is far enough away from my past that I can breathe.* Also not something I wanted to share.

"I was looking for a nice place to live that had an opening for chief." I shrugged. "Saw this listing in the forums online and reached out."

She kept talking. "Your chief back in Philly wasn't close to retirement or anything? What about another station nearby?"

I side-eyed her. "You ask a lot of questions."

One of the things I'd learned about Kinsey Pope early on was that she wasn't easily intimidated by me or anyone else. My accusation didn't stop her.

"No offense, but you don't seem like the type to settle down in small-town Montana," she said.

"What type do I seem like?" I asked, glancing around the large outdoor seating area that already had a smattering of customers, even though it was still early and the weather carried a spring chill.

Kinsey shrugged. "Dunno. The city type, I guess."

I couldn't help but bark out a laugh. "What in the hell makes you say that? I grew up in Point Marion, Pennsylvania. Tiny place not far from the West Virginia border." I dug deep and found my country drawl. "Weren't nothin' but a country boy once upon a holler."

We entered the restaurant to the sound of her chuckle. She turned back to me with a grin. "Just returning to your small-town roots, then, huh?"

I flashed her a grin. "I figure there's gotta be possum around here somewhere. That's all I need to feel right at home."

It was bullshit, of course. I'd spent the first twelve years of my life there, but my teenage years had been spent at a foster care group home outside Philly.

"Well, well," Alex Marian said, glancing up from the reservations computer at the host stand. "If it isn't Captain Compliance. Welcome back. Today's special is a gourmet pizza just for you called the Flaming Overreaction, a molten-hot pie piled high with fiery Calabrian chiles, roasted red peppers, spicy soppressata, and a drizzle of chili-infused honey. Just the right amount of heat to set off your taste buds—without, you know, calling in the fire marshal." He finished his little spiel with a wink.

Something about that wink set a torch to my cardiac rhythm, but I refused to take the bait. "Lieutenant Pope and I are here to ask you a few questions for the origin and cause investigation into yesterday's incident."

Alex's teasing grin dropped. "You're joking."

I narrowed my eyes at him. "I don't joke about fire safety."

He glanced at Kinsey and back to me. "He's not joking, is he?"

Kinsey folded her arms in front of her chest, trying to look serious. "Fire safety isn't a joke, Alex. You know that."

"Yes," he snapped before turning to me. "In fact, I do know that. I've cleared brush lines and fire breaks bigger than your goddamned rule book, run irrigation at 2:00 a.m. to keep a wildfire from jumping the road, and spent more than one harvest season praying the hills wouldn't go up like matchsticks. I've done the hot work permit dance, babysat barrel toasters with an extinguisher in hand, learned the difference between a Class B and a Class K before I knew my fucking alphabet, and evacuated a tasting room full of wine-drunk bachelorettes without losing a single pair of Louboutins to the stampede. So believe me when I say this isn't my first flaming rodeo."

His fiery response didn't help my jacked-up heart rate, but I refused to let him see any reaction. I tried to look as bored and professionally distant as possible. "Sounds like what you're saying is you have a history of attracting fires."

His eyes widened comically. Before he could open his mouth

to excoriate me with vitriol, an attractive woman stepped around him, shoving him backward until he was looking at the back of her long, dark waves.

"Hi, you must be Chief Kincaid," she said, offering a killer smile and her slender hand for a shake. "I'm Ella Marian, Alex's sister. I can assure you he's been involved in many... flaming rodeos, but he was only responsible for one of them."

"Ella!" Alex squawked. "What the fuck? Are you trying to get this place shut down?"

Kinsey murmured something under her breath that sounded like, "We aren't actually talking about rodeos, right?" But I was too keyed up to pay much attention.

"Seems like something I ought to know about, Mr. Marian," I said, leaning around his sister to see the irresponsible restaurant owner himself. "You being *prone* to setting fires, that is."

Alex lurched at me, as if going for my throat, but his sister elbowed him in the gut.

"*Oof.* Fuck, El. Jesus." Alex heaved in a breath. "You and I both know he's being unfair, and now you're making the situation worse."

I shook my head. "Not possible. And it's not unfair, it's the NFPA 921. Not only is it a code requirement, but this investigation report is also required for your insurance claim. The faster you allow us to proceed, the faster we'll be out of your hair."

Alex's hands tightened into fists. "Insurance claim for what? It was over in two seconds. The damage totaled forty bucks after I was able to clean up the chemicals!" He took a deep breath in through his nose, held it, and let it out in a controlled exhale. "It will cost me more to replace the Class-K extinguisher you deployed unnecessarily."

I opened my mouth to snap at him again, to put him in his place for daring to talk back to someone who had the power to shut this place down. But then I remembered the young lieutenant standing next to me.

This behavior wasn't professional. And it wasn't like me. I prided myself on my professionalism. Hell, back in Philly, some of the crew called me Ice Man and made jokes about the steam that came from having me with them on a job. The last thing I needed was for this pissant to get under my skin.

I stood up straight and looked down my nose at him, doing my best *I don't give a shit* impression. "We can come back with an administrative warrant for the origin and cause investigation if necessary. Let us know how you'd like to proceed, Mr. Marian."

Ella cracked a brittle but relieved smile. "He'll comply. What do you need?"

Before Alex could bite out a response, she cheerfully clapped a hand over his mouth. "Why don't we all have a seat over in the corner of the bar area where it's nice and quiet, hm?"

I nodded and followed her to the table, taking a seat before glancing down at my tablet and opening the report template. "I'm going to need to talk to the staff witnesses," I said, while finger-typing the basics into the first few fields.

The momentary silence surprised me. I looked up to see a flash of nerves or... guilt in Alex's eyes. It was only there for a moment, and then it was gone.

"Just me," he said, tilting his chin up defiantly.

I tilted my head and waited for him to elaborate. He didn't. "That right? You were the only employee who witnessed the..." I wanted to say *inferno* just to provoke him, but I reminded myself to be professional. "Incident."

He swallowed and nodded. "Yes, sir."

Motherfuck, how that word did something to me coming out of his mouth. I stared at the man for a beat too long before deciding to play nicely. "Fine. We'll start with your interview, then. Can you tell us exactly what happened?"

And damned if Alexander Marian didn't start blinking rapidly and lying his pretty mouth off.

It was a sight to behold. Pink cheeks, teeth scraping across full, abused lips as he stopped to think up the next part of his story, and the tiny little scratch of one fingernail on the tiny freckle of his opposite hand.

He was sexy as fuck, but up until now, I thought maybe he knew it. Now? Now I saw a side of him that was entirely unexpected. The previously brave trash-talker was hesitant, unsure, and stammering.

As he relayed a tale of pouring the rum at the same time he was trying to light the alcohol on fire *and* sanitize the bar with a flammable spray, even Kinsey's mouth opened in disbelief. Not only would it have been impossible for him to do all three things simultaneously, but he'd even had more than twelve hours to come up with a more plausible story than "I did it."

Once he was done, the reddish-brown hair at the edge of his hairline was damp with sweat, curling delectably against his temple. He firmed his jaw and glared at me defiantly.

"Okay," I said, typing the details into the tablet. "Let's go over it one more time. Can you tell me exactly what happened from the beginning?"

Before he could sputter and wail, claim the repetition unnecessary, I leaned into his personal space and forced him to meet my eyes. "And this time, cut the shit, Marian."

3

ALEX

IndexEcho: *If you could move anywhere, where would you go?*

DrunkenPoet: *Probably Montana. They say it's the last best place.*

IN MY DEFENSE, I didn't know the fire chief had the power to arrest someone. That was my bad.

"For the last time, he didn't arrest you, the sheriff did," Ella muttered, not looking up from her phone as she read my mind. "Which of these mug shots should I send to the family chat?"

"It was a tiny fucking fire!" I railed, pacing the old Persian carpet in front of the wide, stacked-stone fireplace in my family's lodge. "Like... like... less fire than Aunt Tilly had on her birthday cake this year. What the fuck is that man's problem?"

"I'm choosing the murder-face one," she continued, tapping the screen. "What did Chief Kincaid even say to you that made your eyes pop out like this?"

I ignored her. "You can't arrest someone for a minuscule accidental fire that only damaged my own damned property!"

My sister flicked our grandmother's colorful afghan to cover her outstretched legs on the overstuffed sofa. "Westland arrested you for malicious mischief. You're lucky he didn't also cite you for disorderly conduct. Kincaid wanted him to throw the book at you. It's only because you looked horrified the minute you slung the man's iPad across the bar that he kept the charge to a misdemeanor."

I flapped my hands in the air. "I'll buy him a new tablet. I told him I would! It was an *accident*."

"Chief Kincaid is right. You sure do like to throw that word around," she said with a snicker. "Accident, my ass."

"Why are you so calm right now?" I shouted. "He could revoke my business license! The man has it out for me."

"All you have to do for the fire stuff is to complete mandated staff training, submit to additional random safety inspections, and keep yourself out of trouble. He didn't even charge you for lying in your testimony, or whatever that incident report interrogation was. It's the malicious mischief that's going to fuck you up if you're not careful."

"So I'll pay a fine. Big deal. But if I can't get the fire chief off my back, it's going to be a problem."

My cousin Lennon, who was quiet as fuck on his chattiest day, glanced up from the tattered paperback he was reading on a nearby armchair. "You'll get farther with sugar cubes than a crop," he murmured before going back to his book.

What the fuck? "I don't know what that means," I said.

Ella finally glanced up from her phone. "He's talking about catching flies with honey. Try being nice to the new fire chief. Charm the man. Maybe then he'll stop having it out for you and start giving you the benefit of the doubt."

She tossed her phone on the sofa and stood up. "I'm in the mood for shitty mac 'n' cheese. Who's in?"

Lennon's hand shot up, and I grudgingly agreed that I could go for a little toxic orange powder. "As long as you don't tell a single soul I ate it," I muttered, following in her wake toward the kitchen. "Because I will deny it to my dying breath."

"Stop with the chef snobbery," she said with a laugh. "Even Sam eats Kraft Mac sometimes."

When we entered the large, sprawling lodge kitchen, the two of us immediately fell into the familiar rhythm of cooking together. Our dads had forced the three of us to contribute to the family meals from a young age, and we'd also grown up around our uncle Sam's restaurant since it was part of our family's property.

Ella, our sister Mattie, and I knew our way around a kitchen. I'd gotten so good at making quick, custom pizzas for everyone, I'd discovered a kind of meditative effect from it. So when I'd decided to leave Napa and start my own thing in Montana, I'd had an easy time deciding what that would look like.

I'd grown up on a vineyard, the only son of a winemaker. Wine and pizza were my life, but they were also my peace. My anchors. They were an integral part of what family meant to me. And now they were my passionate career pursuit.

A pursuit placed quickly in jeopardy by a new fire chief with something to prove.

"Do you think he's trying to make an example of me?" I asked once the water was on to boil. "Or do you think he was so used to excitement in Philadelphia that he's making shit up here in Legacy to keep himself busy?"

Ella pulled two boxes of mac out of the pantry and reached for the fridge door handle to grab the milk and butter. "Was it Tavo? Is that why you lied to the chief about the fire?"

I sighed and nodded. There was no sense in lying to my oldest sister. She'd get it out of me eventually anyway. And she knew the trouble Tavo was in. "It was an accident, though. Just like I said."

"Maybe you should tell Kincaid," Ella suggested. "Ask him to keep Tavo's name out of the reports."

"Are you kidding?" I squeaked. "The man probably makes love to his fire code rule book every night! No way would he leave a detail off his beloved report."

I didn't want to imagine Judd Kincaid making love to anything, so why that expression had come out of my mouth was beyond me.

"I wouldn't mind him making love to me," Ella said, flashing me a grin. "Man's a snack."

I sputtered. "Ella, what the fuck? How can you be attracted to such an uptight, overblown, by-the-book…" I struggled for the right word. "Fire safety fetishist!"

I winced. Once again, it was unnecessary to sexualize the asshole fire chief. The man was already the personification of sex. If you were into that kind of thing.

I'd like him to be into me.

I gritted my teeth against my inner rogue slut. A part of myself that had no business expressing opinions since I, myself, had absolutely zero experience in the sex department.

Not that I didn't *want* to have any.

I did.

I wanted very much to have quite a bit of it.

But, contrary to my rogue slut's desires, my rogue *heart* was still stupidly and hopelessly devoted to an old flame. And had decided, somewhere along the way, to hold out for romance before giving the cow away. Or whatever.

I was in my Amish virgin era. Against my will and against my better judgment. Unfortunately, I was hung up on a someone from my past, and I worried no one would be able to live up to the comparison.

As steam began clouding over the pot on the stove, I moved to pour in the pasta. "I wish you and the chief well. May your flame of desire ever be doused by his overly generous extinguisher."

"Ew," she said, making a face. "Never mind. You made it weird."

I busied myself with stirring the pot. "He's good-looking. I mean, that's just an objective fact. The... the hair with the barest silver at the temples. The laugh lines around his eyes. And that eye color. Are they silver or blue? IDK, but they're piercing. And of course, he's built. What firefighter isn't? They work out all the time in their fancy gym at the station house, so of course he has muscles for days. Not that I noticed because... ew."

"Ew," she repeated with a smile in her voice I didn't need to turn to see. "Right. Ewwwww."

I nodded. "Exactly. Gross."

"Disgusting."

"It's a good thing his job requires masks sometimes," I added. "So no one needs to look at all that..."

"Perfection," Ella added.

"Exactly."

"Mmhm." She moved around me to pull a bottle of water out of the fridge. "You wanna fuck him, though, right?"

I let out a whimper. "So, so much."

"Same." She sighed.

I turned to face her, putting my hands on my hips. "We can't, though. No sleeping with the enemy. Agreed?"

She placed a hand on her chest and feigned innocence. "He's not *my* enemy!"

"Whatever happened to family loyalty? Marian or die. Huh? What about that?"

She laughed. "Fine. We'll compromise. I'll wait until this feud between you ends before putting the flirt on. Fair?"

The timer for the pasta dinged, so I turned back to reach for it, grabbing the pot holders out of the drawer first. "You already flirted with him earlier today."

"That was before I knew we were at war with the man."

I nodded. "War. Exactly. We're at war, Ella. And Chief Kincaid is the enemy."

SIX WEEKS LATER, the war escalated without warning. And it was all my fault.

In my defense, it was the Fourth of July. Who doesn't love lighting sparklers on the Fourth?

Okay, fine. It was the second of July. But I was practicing.

"Do you have any idea how forest fires start?" Chief Kincaid roared out of his open window as his vehicle came to a loud stop, tires crunching over gravel on the side of the road as the headlights swept across me in the dark. "Because of reckless assholes like you!"

I stared at him in shock. "How... why are you even out here? This is private property."

"Your sister called and said you needed help. That you were trying to light shit on fire. Have you lost your goddamned mind?"

My sister? Ella had ratted me out to the chief? Was she trying to make me look bad so she'd look like an adorable angel in comparison? I was going to murder her. And it was going to be a slow and painful death.

Kincaid pulled an extinguisher from the back of his SUV and strode over, inspecting the remains of a small brush fire a few feet away.

"Okay, now wait a minute," I began, holding up my hands. "Because this was an accident."

His eyebrows shot into his hairline. "Oh, really? That's a shock. You mean it wasn't malicious arson? Good to know, Alex. Good to know."

It was the first time I'd heard the sound of my name in his voice, and it made something smooth and hot slither down my back.

"I was trying to record a light painting for Timber's Instagram," I snapped, gesturing to the camera set up on a tripod nearby. "You know, the kind where you write a message in the air with sparklers while shooting it with a slow shutter speed—never mind. Anyway, it's not as easy as it looks because you have to write the words backwards, and then you have to light the next sparkler before this one burns out, and I—"

"I don't give a single fuck *why* you set the grass on fire, Marian. I care *that* you set the grass on fire!" he roared.

Why was he better-looking when he was mad? And why did my dick seem to like an angry man so much? Maybe I had a temper kink. Was that a thing?

"But it's my grass," I said stupidly. "And it's no longer on fire. I put it out. As you can see."

I gestured at the pathetic area of burned pine needles and brush, wincing a little when I saw just how big it looked from here, maybe five feet long and a couple of inches wide.

"Why in the world would you light sparklers next to the underbrush? Why not do it out there in the open where the worst thing that could happen was a spark falling on fresh, green grass?" He approached the burned area and squatted down, which pulled his pants taut over his muscular ass and made my brain blink out and fizz a little.

"Huh?"

"Are you even listening?"

I cleared my throat and shuffled my feet. "Yeah, and I'm hearing a lot of 'Looks like you did a great job putting out the fire, Alex. Good job!' At least... that's my interpretation of your grumbles. Did I get it right?"

He reached out with a nearby stick and poked at the charred remains of the forest floor. "Why are there drag marks?"

Because there may have been a shrieking, shuffling, panic-induced fire dance involved while I struggled to stomp the flames out?

"Dunno," I said, shrugging for emphasis. "I guess sometimes fire detritus looks like that."

Kincaid glared at me over his shoulder. "Yes, it does. When someone drags a body through it."

My voice reached an octave reserved for devout fans of Jesus and Taylor Swift. "I didn't drag a body through it!"

He sighed and stood up, running his own boot through it to make sure any embers were dispersed. I made an absurd noise of *see?!* And gestured wildly to his own action.

"Drag marks!" I added. "You did the same thing."

He deployed his small handheld extinguisher and sprayed the area down. "Why are you out here alone?"

I glanced at him in the odd, shadowy light coming from his headlights. It was late; I'd had to wait a long time for it to get dark enough for my project.

As much as I couldn't stand the man, I also couldn't help but be distracted by the sight of his uniform shirt straining around his muscular chest. I cleared my throat to disguise the large swallow of drool. "Why are you still in your uniform? It's eleven at night."

He moved back to his vehicle and put the extinguisher away. I found myself following him like a puppy.

"Suspected gas leak out by Haymaker Loop," he muttered.

I leaned a hip against his car and crossed my arms. "And you were still on duty?"

He closed his eyes and inhaled as if praying for patience. "I was buying groceries after work when the call came in. The home-owner requested me specifically. Said she needed to talk to me about the conduct of one of my crew on a previous call."

I barked out a laugh. "Oh my god, you were Kitsoned!"

He closed the hatch and moved closer, standing close enough for me to remember how much taller he was. "Explain," he said with narrowed eyes.

"Maureen Kitson will flick her housecoat at any man in uniform around here. Ten bucks says Cody McMasters threw you under the bus. Mrs. Kitson spent eight months trying to seduce him until he finally figured out how to drop a casual mention of having a contagious and chronic STI. Even that didn't work until he described his... lesions... in gory detail."

Kincaid looked put upon. "And then?"

"And then she moved her attention to the sheriff, only he spun a tale about a long-lost love he's never been able to get over. And then it was Marco's turn, back before he moved over to SERA..."

"I'm going to kill McMasters," he grumbled. "Spent two hours thinking she was just a close talker before she asked me to triple-check the gas smell in her bed."

I couldn't hold back the shout of laughter. "Oh my god, tell me you sniffed her sheets! Please tell me you got into that woman's bed and humored her."

He shot me an annoyed look, but I could see the barest hint of a smile at the edge of his mouth. "Maybe I would have, if I hadn't already discovered she doesn't have natural gas or propane service to her house."

My laughter nearly stole my breath, and tears leaked out of my eyes. "No gas, and she called in a gas leak? What the fuck caused you to stay for two hours?"

"While she didn't have a gas leak, she absolutely did have three smoke detectors wildly out of date. Which she apparently knew since she'd already bought the replacements."

I rolled my eyes. "So you did the Boy Scout thing and installed them for her."

He shrugged. "It was either that or hold the ladder while I tried not to look up her housecoat. And believe me, I'd already determined she was going Scottish kilt-style under that thing."

The laughter returned, only now it made me snort and howl. I doubled over and stomped my boot on the ground. "Stop, stop, I can't breathe."

He took the opportunity to pound me on the back so hard I nearly staggered to the side. "Take it easy, there, Firebug. It wasn't that funny."

When I finally caught my breath, I sniffed and eyed him. "Seriously, why are you out here? I told my sister I had a slight fire incident and stomped it out. I only needed her to bring me a jug of water to be sure it was all out before leaving."

"She said there was a suspected arson in progress at—"

"Shut the fuck up! Are you serious?" I cried.

And then Judd fucking Kincaid grinned a wide grin that transformed his face from the gruff asshole, hell-bent on catching me in a code violation, into the world's most stunning man.

"Of course I'm not serious. She called Javi to ask him to run out here and help, but he called me since it involved a person of interest in an ongoing fire investigation."

"Are you kidding? Is he for real? What the fuck?" I didn't appreciate the fact that I sounded like a dog's squeaky toy since this asshole fire chief came to town, but apparently, I couldn't stop it.

Javier Sujo was dead to me. No more two-dollar refills on his girlfriend's favorite chardonnay.

"The man's just doing his job, Alex. He knew if he came out here as a civilian and something happened, I'd fire his ass."

I tried standing up a little straighter so he'd take me seriously. "Stop following me around. It's harassment."

He tilted his chin as he peered down at me, his body language relaxed enough to be in complete contrast with mine. "Stop lighting shit on fire. It's illegal."

I thought about continuing to fight with him, to try and win. But then my eyes caught sight of the skin on his forearm as he raised a hand to run fingers through his hair. His uniform sleeve was rolled up, and the way the odd light from the headlamps caught on his skin, making it look rough and scarred, grabbed my attention.

My experience in and around commercial kitchens was enough to have had plenty of exposure to minor burn scars. This was more than that. This was something awful.

I'd heard enough horrible fire stories from someone in the firefighting industry to know that most fire injuries came with stories of horrific pain and long, painful recoveries.

Kincaid's damaged skin made me want to reach out, run my fingers along the artifact of whatever he'd gone through that day, if only to soothe him, to *see* him. But I quickly remembered this man wasn't for me. He wasn't mine in any way.

He was a stranger. An acquaintance. An enemy.

"Yes, sir," I said, clearing my throat and throwing a jaunty salute at him. "No more fires. Sounds like a plan. Have a nice night."

After scurrying to my car, I hopped in and peeled out, not bothering to stop in at the lodge on my way past my family's large property. Instead, I headed straight home to my apartment over the restaurant and threw myself in bed.

Images of Kincaid's large presence, his narrowed eyes, and the way his tight body looked in his uniform conspired to keep sleep at bay. Which meant the following day, I wanted to maim anyone who looked at me sideways.

I did a good job holding my tongue and playing happy host to our customers until Chief Fun-Killer walked through the door.

And announced my first "random" fire safety inspection.

4

KINCAID

DrunkenPoet: *I was wondering if you ever want to meet IRL...*

IndexEcho: *Not if, Poet. But when.*

THE LAST THING I wanted to do was see Alexander Marian again so soon. I was still irrationally angry at him for the little sparkler stunt he'd pulled the night before on his family's land.

The man had a huge, filthy-rich family, and he dared to put their gorgeous Montana property at risk? How ignorant could he be?

I'd already heard about the Marian family from the sheriff and various members of my crew. I knew they were from California and had bought the historic Legacy Inn and all its surrounding property over twenty years ago, that they'd brought in enough money to help turn the town's future around, and that Hazel Marian's investment in a tech company here had brought in jobs, too.

The influx of all that cash had apparently solidified Legacy's reputation as a destination worth visiting. Restaurants, art galleries,
and the single ski slope were enough to make tourism a significant
portion of Legacy's economy, and it was thanks in large part to the
financial stability the Marians had brought.

So why would Alex be so careless? It made no sense.

But then again, when I remembered how careless he'd been
with me in Amsterdam, how he'd arranged to come back to my
room with me for the night and then taken a better offer the
minute my head was turned, it made sense.

At the time, I'd wondered if it had been his youth. The man was
clearly still in his twenties, while I was decidedly... *not*. So when he'd
blown me off, I'd chalked it up to immaturity as well as selfishness.
And so far, seeing him in his regular life had proved me correct.

When I'd gotten to the station this morning and had seen an
alert pop up for a standard inspection due, I'd groaned in
disbelief.

Timber.

I'd glared at the alert and clicked through to the details
because this wasn't related to the reports I'd filed after the drinks
fire. It was something else completely.

"Hey, Sujo!" I'd barked after seeing the name on the notes.

Within moments, Javi had popped his head through my doorway. "Hey! I'm gonna have the Untrace incident report on your
desk in an hour, tops, Chief, I promise—"

I'd cut him off with a wave. "That's not what I... wait, what
incident?"

"Dumbass left his mug warmer on and lit a folder on fire
yesterday." Javi had rolled his eyes. "No damage, but I gave the guy
a lecture. It'll all be in my report."

I'd nodded, leaning forward in my chair. "Put that aside for a second and tell me about this commercial kitchen renovation at Timber."

Forty minutes later, I'd found myself back at Timber, sparring with Alex Marian yet again.

"It's already been inspected," Alex said, looking more tired than angry today. "Don't you have a record of it? I want to say it was back in April? Had to be. That's when the renovations were done."

"The suppression nozzle on the vent hood was supposed to be replaced after that inspection," I explained. "This is a follow-up to make sure the work was done and everything is functioning properly for fire suppression. While I'm here, I'll inspect your cleaning logs for the vent hood, test the alarm functionality and the shut-off feature of the wet chemical system, and double-check the location of your extinguishers."

Alex gave me a blank stare. "Any way you can do that without interfering with the running of my business?"

"Absolutely not," I said, flashing him a chipper grin. "Today's Tuesday. Would you rather me come back on Friday or Saturday evening?"

He blinked. "Uh, no? I'd rather you come back never."

"If wishes were horses... Anyway, I'll help myself to the kitchen. Feel free to ignore me and continue doing what you were doing. Unless it involves butane, propane, kerosene, alcohol... or an open flame of any kind."

Alex's cheek flexed as he ground his teeth. "I own a wood-fired pizza oven. There are open flames in my place of work. I will continue to cook with them whether you like it or not."

I pressed my lips together and lifted my eyebrows. "Will you, though?"

He rubbed his face with both hands before looking at me with bleary eyes. "Will you just get on with it, please? Jesus fuck. Less talking, more inspecting."

It was a good sign he wasn't nervous about the inspection. Hopefully, that meant all his ducks were in order and we could both get through this as quickly as possible.

Unfortunately, his ducks were not in a row, but I had to admit that it wasn't his mistake.

"This is the wrong suppression nozzle," I informed him, pointing to the offending part. "It looks like your contractor replaced it with the exact same part."

I saw the fear wash over him, his entire body going rigid in expectation of me shutting him down until he could get it fixed.

"I'll give you five days to get it fixed," I said, feeling particularly magnanimous. "But if it's not..."

He sucked in a shaky breath. "I'll figure it out. It's just there aren't that many... never mind." He blew out a breath and stalked off to the tiny office behind the commercial fridge.

After watching him walk away, dejected and stressed, I climbed down from the ladder, took it back out to my vehicle to store it properly, then took a seat in the truck to type up the report. When I was finished, I made a few phone calls and returned inside to find Alex at his desk.

The so-called office was a glorified broom closet behind the walk-in fridge. Every inch of wall space was crammed with something touting prestige—gourmet food awards, educational certificates, glossy photos of a smiling family at a fancy wine-tasting. Framed printouts of splashy media coverage were lined up on a shelf like some kind of pageant display. Even the desk seemed to brag: stacks of papers teetering next to an open laptop as if he were a hard worker, a coffee mug with a perfect ring staining the blotter like it had been placed there for effect.

It didn't feel like a workspace so much as a shrine—to his pedigree, his family's money, his own need to prove something. All flash and little actual substance. The only thing that seemed to be about him personally, rather than his fancy family, was the scent of him. It wasn't the same cologne I'd smelled on him that night in Amsterdam. It was different. More down-to-earth.

Of course the man smelled like trouble—yeast and firewood and something sweet and tart, like he'd pressed merlot-dipped fingertips behind his ears. Alex Marian was sunshine bottled and shaken over smoke. A scent that made me want to lean closer and investigate more, even when I knew better.

I held my breath to keep from huffing it and knocked on the open doorframe. "I emailed you a copy of the report with the information you need to tell your repair person."

He didn't look up from his laptop. I could see a Google search for fire suppression system installation and maintenance companies pulled up on the small screen.

"And I, uh, included a list of reputable guys who can hook you up," I added. "Good luck."

Before he could say anything, I bolted out of there. Not only did I need to get to my next inspection, but I also needed to get the hell away from Alex Marian before I asked him why he was so tired.

I didn't need to know. Moreover, making nice with a proven liar was not a great idea.

When I got back behind the wheel of my vehicle to head to a cherry orchard fifteen minutes outside of town, my phone buzzed with a call from my closest friend.

"Max," I said, accepting the call against my better judgment. I'd learned a long time ago not to ignore Max Franco. The man was relentless and would just keep calling.

"You owe me one," he said, laughter in his voice. "A big one."

Just the sound of his easy tone helped ease the tension from my shoulders a little. "Oh yeah? How's that? Pretty sure I'm still up on the owing scale, jackass."

"Pfft. How many times you gonna throw that whole 'saving my ass' bullshit in my face? Anyway, my friend Kaidee is coming your way. She's doing a whole summer thing between the Tetons, Yellowstone, and Glacier. She's a schoolteacher and wants to make the most of her break."

"Okay? Does she need recommendations for hotels and restaurants or something?"

"No, dude. She needs a place to stay. Someone to show her around. You'll really like her. And she's single, so, like, go for it."

"Go for it? Does she have your permission to hook her up with random guys? Jesus." I waved to one of our local deputies as I passed some road construction. "I don't need dating help, Max. And I definitely don't want to start something with someone who lives in Philly."

"She lives in Boulder. That's practically next door to you."

I huffed out a laugh. "It's an eight-hour drive."

"Anyway, you don't have to marry the woman. Just have a little fun. Take her out, go for a hike together. Maybe take your mind off work a little bit."

For some reason, the idea of meeting a nice woman didn't appeal to me these days. It was harder to have a quick, sex-only connection with a woman without risking hurt feelings. With men, I could be more transactional. Make it clearer from the start that all I was interested in was a quick release.

I'd stupidly fallen for a stranger on the internet years ago and fucked it up. And even though we'd never met in person, and I'd never even learned his real name, I still compared my connection with anyone I dated to him.

DrunkenPoet.

I gritted my teeth and forced him out of my head for the millionth time.

"Yeah, okay," I forced myself to say. "I'll host your friend, as long as she understands my crazy work schedule. She needs to be willing to be ditched at a moment's notice."

"Yeah, yeah, she's cool. Girl who solo hikes the big peaks isn't afraid of alone time, you know?"

We exchanged a few more words before I arrived at my next inspection site and had to end the call. He promised to give Kaidee my details so she could get in touch with me directly.

By the time I entered the machine shed at the orchard, I'd forgotten all about it. But that night, when I stepped out of a long, hot shower and moved into the kitchen of the log home I was renting so I could reheat leftovers for dinner, my phone buzzed with a message from Max's friend.

Kaidee and I texted back and forth about her upcoming visit, and by the time we'd made arrangements for her to stay in my spare room for a couple of weeks, I was feeling optimistic. She seemed friendly, interesting, and chill, as well as completely fine looking after her own entertainment. She said she looked forward to learning more about my job so she could tell her third-grade students all about meeting a real-life firefighter.

I clicked into her Instagram and saw jaw-dropping photos of vistas, hikes, early wildflowers, and her smiling face. She was beautiful, but not in a cover-model way. More in a girl-next-door way. Something about her felt safe and easy, and I looked forward to getting to know her.

And maybe putting *DrunkenPoet* out of my mind once and for all.

5

———————

ALEX

IndexEcho: *How's the head this morning, sunshine?*

DrunkenPoet: *Broken. How did you know I was drinking?*

IndexEcho: *Late-night haiku about waffles. Hard agree about syrup geometry, BTW.*

———————

"Don't do it," my sister warned, pointing her cocktail straw at me across the bar.

I emptied the rest of my cosmo and held up my glass to toast. "Shall I compare thee to a winter's night? Thou art more frosty and more full of spite. Rough codes do shake the darling buds of May, and firemen's breath doth blow special effects permits away."

My voice was soft and slurry, which perfectly matched the warm numbness moving sluggishly through my veins.

"You did it," Ella said in disgust. "Don't we have a rule about this, Alex? You quote poetry, you owe me a shot."

"Uh, *no*. That rule only applies if I quote lyrics from transformative modern poet Taylor Swift," I said smugly. "I don't make the rules. Mattie does." After a pause, I added, "All you are is mean."

"Goddammit," Ella muttered. "He's throwing it back to the *Speak Now* era. I'm calling Mattie."

Tavo took another sip of his Shirley Temple and giggled as if he'd had any alcohol at all. "I think it's cute. Alex's poetry thing."

Ella shook her head while she held her phone out in her palm, the ringing loud on speaker mode. "Not cute. Pathetic. When Anders Creighton broke up with Alex sophomore year in college, he was on a Fireball shots and e.e. cummings kick. It was not pretty."

Ohhh, e.e. cummings. Love me some e.e....

I sucked in a breath and gave it a shot. "chief kincaid... (if that is your... real name)...your eyes are... two blue... extinguishers... that put out... my spark..."

Ella clapped a hand over my mouth. "No. Be done."

I blew out a breath and slumped. "Anders wouldn't have written me up for a faulty—"

My sister Mattie's voice came over the speaker so loudly I jumped and knocked over my new napkin holder.

"What the fuck, sister-from-hell, I'm asleep."

"You made me knock over the new napkins!" I shouted.

"Oh Jesus," Mattie groaned. "Is he drunk? Is that why you're— fuck, is he spouting *poetry*?"

"*Swiftian* poetry," Ella agreed grimly. "Among others."

Tavo giggled louder. "Oh my gosh, this is amazing."

"Don't worry," Ella added, reaching for the napkins that had spilled across the bar. "Timber's closed. We were having a few drinks to celebrate the Fourth, and your brother got carried away."

"He's *your* brother when he's like this," Mattie muttered.

I heard a man's voice in the background and leaned in to say hi to my future brother-in-law. Before I could say anything, Mattie continued. "Why're you drunk, Alexander the Grape? Is this about your sex life? Ella and I think your dry spell has gone on way too long. You need some stress relief."

I blinked at the phone. "You and Ella were talking about my sex life? Ew."

"No shit, ew," Ella said. "But we're right. When was the last time you got laid?"

Never. Thankfully, I wasn't drunk enough to say that out loud.

"'S been a while," I said instead. "Looooong while," I added with a giggle and hiccup. That much was true.

Tavo leaned forward on his stool, flashing a big smile. "I heard there's a new class up at the rescue academy. They're, like, medics and helicopter pilots and wilderness emergency people." He fanned himself with long, slender fingers. "They say the instructors are even hotter than the students."

"Ew, no," Ella said. "Our cousin Tommy is one of those instructors this summer."

I shook my head. "And no adrenaline junkies, thank you very much."

Been there, done that. I'd fallen for a guy who was stationed somewhere in the Middle East. Worrying about him had been bad enough, but when he'd suddenly gone silent, fear had eaten away at me piece by piece.

Had he ghosted or died? There was no way to know.

I hadn't even learned his name, which meant his disappearance would forever remain a mystery.

"Whose name, Alex?" Tavo asked.

I shook my head at him. "Huh?"

"You said you didn't even have his name. Whose name?"

Fuck. I was drunker than I'd thought if I'd said that out loud.

My sisters both made a sound of understanding, and Ella jumped up. "Time for bed. You're cut off, and we're going upstairs right now."

Tavo offered to finish turning off all the lights while Ella dragged my drunk ass upstairs. When she stood behind me in the bathroom doorway, making sure I was brushing my teeth like I'd promised, she asked, "Do you think that's why you're giving this fire chief such a hard time? Because of your online guy?"

IndexEcho.

"It's not the same thing. *Index* is… *was* a specialist in ARFF equipment and techniques. Aircraft rescue and firefighting in the military is a big fucking deal. They're the ones who put out like… giant military plane fires and explosions and…" I couldn't bear even thinking about it. "Chief Kincaid puts out sparklers," I said, sounding bitter even to my own ears. "Not at all the same thing."

"Still, maybe the chief is bringing up some shit from that time, you know? Might be worth talking to someone about."

She meant my therapist. But I'd already therapied this shit to death. "I'm fine. He just needs to get his nose out of my business and mind his own."

But Ella's idea had merit. Maybe I wasn't giving the new fire chief enough credit. Instead of assuming he was an overly picky asshole, maybe I needed to give him the benefit of the doubt.

What if he was just trying to impress the town until his reputation as a competent, safety-conscious fire chief was well established? For all I knew, he was this much of a stickler for everyone.

In the morning, I'd start asking around.

~

IN THE MORNING, I wanted to die. Unfortunately, I'd agreed to meet my cousins for breakfast at the Pinecone.

"Let's go," Ella said, bustling into my space and throwing the blackout curtains open. "Tavo said everything is fine at Timber, and Juni's in a good mood today. That means we have at least an hour for family breakfast."

I grumbled and groaned until she mentioned our cousin Tommy would be coming. At least the genders would be balanced a little.

Fifteen minutes later, I was showered, dressed, and grumbling my way into Legacy's most popular breakfast spot.

As soon as Tommy saw me, he winced. "You need hydration and electrolytes, my friend."

Technically, Tommy was a doctor and probably knew better than I did, but that didn't stop me from arguing. "I need a few more hours in my bed, is what I need."

My cousin Lennon grunted and shoved a menu at me. "Spinach and banana smoothie, maybe. Eggs and toast if you can handle it."

Sadie hustled over with coffee, already made creamy as fuck but not too sweet. "Juni called and told me to get you an IV of this started ASAP."

The unusually thoughtful gesture by my moody head chef was much appreciated. "Doesn't sound like her," I said.

"She also said not to bother coming back unless you have a healthy to-go serving of my maple bacon and banana nut bread."

I nodded. "There it is."

As my sister and cousins chattered around me, I slumped down and slurped my coffee, allowing the caffeine to hit and the energy of the crowded diner to perk me up.

Sadie came back with more coffee and Tommy's orange juice before asking what we wanted to eat. After she wrote everything down, I reached out and touched her arm. "Hey, have you by any chance had any interactions with the new fire chief?"

"Kincaid? Sure. Nice guy. Handsome, too. He comes in here with the other firefighters."

I shook my head, which was a mistake. Nausea rolled through my gut. "No, I mean... have you had inspections or been cited for any code violations?"

Sadie's face crinkled in thought. "Don't think we have one due for another few months. Health inspector was out about four months ago, though. Why?"

Before I could come up with an answer that didn't reveal my current situation on Kincaid's naughty list, Sadie was called over to help another customer. When she passed by a minute later, she asked if I was doing a food truck at the Slingshot Showdown.

"Oh fuck!" I breathed. "I forgot to apply for my permits. I was in the middle of filling all that stuff out a few weeks ago when Uncle Dante called about Tavo."

"How is Tavo?" Ella asked. "I didn't want to ask him last night and ruin everyone's good mood."

"Fine, I guess. He's been helping out in the kitchen, and when he's not there, he spends time creating these flint and steel kits to sell at the farmer's market. I told him to check with Maddox Sullivan to see if he might want to carry them at the hardware store."

My sister narrowed her eyes at me. "I meant, how's he holding up? Emotionally?"

Our cousin Tommy looked around the table as if missing something. "Who's Tavo?"

Lennon spoke in a low voice so no one could overhear. "Kid from Marian House," he said, referring to the LGBTQ+ teen shelter our uncles ran in San Francisco. "He's hiding out for a while. Staying with Alex."

Tommy waited expectantly for more, but Lennon went back to his coffee.

Ella turned to Tommy. "He fell for the wrong sugar daddy. Found out the guy was married and tried to get out of it. Unfortunately, the guy's obsessed. Doesn't think he should have to give Tavo up regardless of the whole 'wife' thing."

I sighed. "And worse? He's a powerful judge with money and influence."

Tommy's eyes widened in surprise. "How old is this kid?"

"Twenty," I explained. "So legally, he's not a kid anymore. But he ended up at Marian House a few years ago after his parents found him with another boy and kicked him out. His family wound up moving back to Mexico because they blamed American culture for Tavo's sexuality."

"He was at Marian House long enough to finish high school," Ella continued. "Then got a job as a barback at a trendy place in SoMa."

"Where he came to the attention of the judge," I added. "Judge became a regular at the bar, flirted with Tavo, and finally asked him out. Romanced him, made him feel special. Spoiled him rotten—which was powerful, considering Tavo's family hadn't been well-off even before he started living on the streets. I think his mom worked as a housekeeper, and his father was a day laborer."

Tommy nodded in understanding. "Would've been easy to fall for someone who could make your life more comfortable. Plus, the kid was probably desperate for someone to care about him."

Sadie showed up to pass us plates filled with food, and when she disappeared again, Tommy asked, "So he's here in Legacy, hiding from the judge who doesn't like the word 'no'?"

I nodded. "Uncle Dante called and told me the situation. I offered to help. And since the judge in question has access to law enforcement resources, that means keeping Tavo's name out of anything official."

Ella added, "Including fire investigation reports."

Tommy glanced at me and lowered his voice even more. "He here legally?"

I shrugged. "He's a DACA recipient, which means it might not take much to get him sent to Mexico. And if his social security or immigration records ping here in Montana, the judge could find him. So, I can't hire him at Timber. But he's helping out for free in exchange for room and board."

Lennon looked up from the food piled on his plate. "Soon as Tavo upsets the judge, the judge can do any number of things to ruin his life."

Tommy sucked in a breath and nodded. "So we keep Tavo safe. And we don't tell anyone he's here."

I scooped a bite of scrambled eggs onto my fork with a toast triangle. "Thankfully, the judge calls him *Octavio*. So if we all stick to his nickname, it'll help."

Everyone dug into their food as I picked around mine carefully, wondering if my stomach was upset from the hangover or because I was worried Kincaid would learn that Tavo had been involved in the fire at Timber.

I still felt bad about lying. Not because I hated taking the fall for something that wasn't my fault, but because I didn't like lying, full stop.

And for some reason, I especially didn't like lying to Judd Kincaid.

As much as I disliked the man and thought he was overly strict about fire safety and his vaunted "protocol," I also respected someone who took his job seriously and followed the rules.

I didn't want him to think I wasn't the same, because I was.

I'd worked my ass off at my fathers' vineyard growing up. I'd learned the family business and taken in as much information about viticulture as possible, since it had been understood that Alexander Vineyards would be under my management one day.

Ella had always been the adventurous sibling, the kind of person who didn't intend to stay near home. Mattie, on the other hand, was content to stay in the Bay Area now that she had a job in the wardrobe department of the San Francisco ballet. That had left me to carry on the Alexander tradition—the winery in Napa that had been in our family for generations.

But I hadn't been sure I wanted it.

And it wasn't until finding an anonymous confessor online that I'd finally admitted it "out loud."

IndexEcho had encouraged me to follow my own dreams.

Your family loves you. They'd want you to live your best life, no matter what that looks like.

As I left my family at the Pinecone and walked back to Timber to start my workday, I lost myself to memories of the man. The way I'd met him on a random message board five years ago while asking for help with a certification course on Incident Command Systems I had to take on behalf of the vineyard.

DrunkenPoet: *I'm taking ICS-100 and I'm confused about how span of control applies to a small business staff.*

IndexEcho: *Here's how we handled it on airfields with limited crews...*

That one question had led to *IndexEcho* basically hand-holding me through the certification process. He'd been so funny, so calm, so patient, that even when the certification was over, I'd found any and every excuse to keep talking to him. Had a question about wildfire breaks in agricultural settings? I'd ask *IndexEcho*.

Came across an article on aviation innovation? I'd send it to *IndexEcho.*

Over the months, we'd become close enough that I began to confide in him. Things I hadn't told anyone else.

DrunkenPoet: *Do you ever worry about letting your parents down?*

It had taken a few minutes for him to respond.

IndexEcho: *Not really. My parents passed away years ago.*

I'd stared at the screen, stomach tumbling with regret and guilt at being so thoughtless.

DrunkenPoet: *Index, I'm so fucking sorry.*

IndexEcho: *Me too. But please don't be sorry you brought it up. Tell me what's on your mind.*

So, I had. I'd confessed about having incredible parents, about being spoiled with an embarrassment of riches. And still feeling smothered by expectations.

IndexEcho: *You deserve a chance to be yourself without family pressure.*

I'd started to respond that they didn't pressure me, exactly. They loved me and wanted my happiness. But then I'd realized their assumption that I would take over the vineyard was pressure enough.

DrunkenPoet: *I don't want to disappoint them.*

IndexEcho: *Your family loves you. They'd want you to live your best life, no matter what that looks like.*

IndexEcho: *Not everyone wants to be a farmer, Poet. Surely your Mom and Dad know that.*

We'd still been early enough in our online relationship for me not to correct him. I didn't tell him it was a vineyard, not the kind of family agriculture business he probably expected. And I hadn't told him it was two dads instead of a mom and dad. At that time, all I'd known about him was that he was a military contractor working on aviation firefighting equipment somewhere overseas. I hadn't known whether he was phobic or not.

Later, once we'd kept talking and he'd casually referred to a bad date with the word "he," I'd stared at the word in shock and excitement.

He. As in, the date had been a man.

DrunkenPoet: *You're gay?*

IndexEcho: *Bi. That a problem?*

DrunkenPoet: *No. Shit. Sorry. No. I'm gay.*

He'd only sent back a GIF from the TV show *Brooklyn 99* that said "Hot damn." And the grin on my face had made my cheeks ache.

Our conversations had immediately turned flirty and personal, and over the course of the next few months, I'd fallen completely in love with a stranger online.

Unfortunately, he'd still had five months left on his work

contract, which had meant putting off any plans or pressure to meet in real life too soon.

The promise of it had been there, though. A thin, vibrating string of hope and excitement that ran through all our interactions.

IndexEcho: *Poet... the minute I'm stateside, I'm coming for you.*

DrunkenPoet: *Promise?*

IndexEcho: *Nothing will keep me from finding you. Nothing.*

But three weeks before he was scheduled to fly back to the States, he'd failed to answer a simple question about whether he preferred barbecue chicken or pork. I'd been testing ideas for a new pizza recipe for my sister's birthday dinner, and I'd tossed the question out while I'd been creating a shopping list.

After twelve hours, he still hadn't responded.

DrunkenPoet: *Index, you there? Get caught up on a long shift?*

Nothing.

I'd scoured the news for any mention of incidents he could have been involved in. There'd been a mortar strike at Al Asad Air Base in Iraq, a border clash in Syria, and a hotel shooting in Dakar, Senegal, all during the same forty-eight-hour period.

I'd tried so hard not to assume it was the air base strike because that one had resulted in seven deaths and two dozen injuries.

Later, I'd prayed for him to be one of the injuries.

After sending a long string of embarrassing messages, culminating in sobbing and begging that he just tell me to fuck off if need be, but to let me know he was alive, I'd finally given up.

Well, more like Mattie had forced me into therapy over it, and I'd agreed with my therapist's suggestion to close my message board account in an effort at closure.

Closure hadn't come. But I'd finally picked myself up off the pyre of self-pity and done what *IndexEcho* had encouraged me to do. I'd had a hard conversation with Blue and Tristan Marian.

IndexEcho had been right.

My fathers did love me. And they wanted me to live my best life, no matter what it looked like. Even if it looked like buying a crumbly old roadhouse in Montana and turning it into a gourmet pizza restaurant and wine bar.

"There he is." Mali smiled brightly from the host stand when I pulled open the door to Timber. "Alex, there's someone waiting for you at table twelve. Said it's about something related to the vent hood?"

My stomach dropped, expecting it was Chief Kincaid again, here to complain. But when I walked over to the table in the corner, I saw an older woman in Carhartt overalls with short hair, a tablet, and a canvas tool bag.

"Vic Norman," she said, offering me a firm handshake. "I'm here to fix your fucked-up nozzle."

I let out a sigh of relief and grinned wide. "Vic, I could kiss you right now."

Her eyebrows lifted, and a dimple popped. "I charge extra for that."

The memories of *IndexEcho* faded into the background of my mind, where they usually lived comfortably after these four years. And I focused instead on making sure Chief Judd Kincaid would be out of my hair as soon as possible.

So I could get on with the plan of following my dreams.

6

KINCAID

DrunkenPoet: *It's taking all my self-control not to ask for a pic of you.*

IndexEcho: *I'm suddenly hating that I'm a stickler for the damned OpSec rules on this job, Poet.*

I WAS SCANNING through emails at work when I came to a permit request for a restaurant to operate open-flame grilling during an outdoor event next weekend. The person applying for the exemption? Alex Marian on behalf of Timber.

Because of course it was.

"Jesus fuck," I muttered under my breath before barking, "Sujo, get in here."

Javi came hustling in, hair still damp from his post-workout shower. "Yeah, Chief. What's up?"

I showed him the request. "What's this Slingshot Showdown at Sundown?"

He grinned. "Oh man. It's killer. A group of scouts started it like twenty years ago or something, and now it's an annual tradition. You know the mountain's called Slingshot, so the Showdown is basically a massive slingshot tournament. It starts in the morning with different brackets and narrows down to the best of the best by the evening. By the time the final round happens, it's more challenging because of all the shadows on the mountain. You planning on going? You totally should, man. They've got food trucks and live music, crafts and shit. It's a good time for sure."

"I wasn't asking because I'm looking for a good time," I said, trying to retain my patience. "I was asking because Timber is applying for an open-flame permit."

He pursed his lips and nodded. "Yeah. I think they do their Swiss mushroom burgers and stuff like that. Obvi can't bring the pizza oven out, you know?"

"We're on strict fire restrictions right now," I reminded him.

"Yeah, but people gotta eat."

I grunted and hit Reply, referring back to my first email from Alex Marian for help with the wording of my response.

Subject: Re: Application for Exemption Permit

Dear Alexander "Aspiring Arsonist" Marian,

Thank you for your last-minute and wildly optimistic application for an open-fire grilling permit during the Slingshot whatever-the-fuck.

While I appreciate your eagerness to earn a few bucks by endangering the local populace as well as all vulnerable wildlife and personal property, I feel compelled to point out a few things:

The "controlled outdoor cooking" you've proposed is, in fact, you attempting to operate open flames during peak fire season where a single spark could ignite half the county—something you might

*understand if your job involved preventing disasters instead of
creating them.*

*The proposed grilling location is too close to combustible mater-
ial, including dead trees, dry brush, and, I assume, a Timber-
branded napkin caddy.*

*Finally, as you are aware, the company applying for the permit
is currently on a temporary probationary status in regards to fire
safety compliance due to previous "incidents". (See mugshot
attached.)*

*So while I admire your commitment to the "ignore all safety
protocols for a good burger" approach, I respectfully deny your
permit before I start explaining to bereaved families why their
homes burned down because someone needed a flame-grilled mushroom and Swiss.*

With sincerest regard (for fire safety),

Judd Kincaid

Chief, Legacy Fire Department

I shot it off without stopping to think about it too hard, which
was probably a mistake. But the day ahead was slammed, and I
was out of patience with Alex Marian.

After replying to several more emails, making a few follow-up
calls, and checking in with the crew on shift, I headed out to SERA
to help with one of their wildfire response exercises.

Slingshot Emergency Rescue Academy was a widely known
and respected educational school for wilderness emergency
response. They taught first responders in wilderness emergency
medicine, wildfire response—including smokejumping, search
and rescue, swift-water rescue, and helo extraction.

Today's exercise was a wilderness pump and hose deployment
exercise, using portable pumps creekside, running progressive
hose lays uphill, and maintaining necessary water flow.

By the time I returned to the station, I was drenched in sweat, filthy with creek mud, and starving. The drill had been delayed twice by pop-up storms, and we'd ended up finishing at dusk.

I walked into my office and closed the door before tossing down the fire-retardant Nomex shirt I'd already taken off, peeling off my cotton undershirt to join it in the pile, kicking off the woodland fireboots, and reaching for the button on my Nomex trousers. My goal was to get into my private shower and stand under the cold spray until my stomach's complaints were louder than the pounding headache I had from overheating.

"Um, I feel like maybe I should alert you to my presence. But, by all means, continue the show."

I jerked up and stepped back, tripping over the pile of dirty clothes and boots until I fell against the closed door and landed on my ass. "Fuck!"

Alex Marian stood by a tall filing cabinet, half-hidden in the shadows created by the sunset shooting warm, slanted beams across the floor. From this angle, I could see his muscular calves and thighs exposed by twill shorts, his shoulders and cut biceps bare, thanks to a plain navy tank top, and his long, slender feet in brown leather flip-flops.

I forced my eyes up to his face, where I saw twinkling eyes but also a rosy blush on his cheeks.

"Why the fuck are you hiding in here?" I snapped, hoping my anger would be enough to keep my dick in line. My attempt to stand back up gracefully was less than elegant, and I felt new aches and pains joining the ones from the grueling exercise in the woods.

"I'm not hiding," he said. "I came to see you, and one of the guys told me I could wait in here since you were due back any minute."

I made a mental note to kill my entire crew. "Normal people

wait in one of those chairs," I said, nodding to the two chairs in front of my desk. I moved to the bathroom, unwilling to let Alex Marian's inability to understand the word "no" keep me from my shower.

Alex's voice followed me. "I was too upset to sit still. I need you to reconsider about the Slingshot Showdown."

"No."

I closed the bathroom door before he could argue with me, and then I turned on the water before shucking off my boxer briefs and stepping into the shower. The cool water was the sweetest kind of relief, and I let out a groan as I felt it wash away the sweat and grime of the day. The fact that the frigid water also helped tame my dick was just a bonus.

"Hear me out," Alex said, his shadow appearing through the frosted glass of the shower door.

"No," I growled. "What the fuck are you doing following me into the bathroom?"

"Don't tell me you're modest because I won't believe you."

I reached for the bottle of shampoo on the shelf. "Why not?"

"Pfft. The kind of guy who gets naked in front of a local business owner—"

I barked out a laugh. I couldn't help it. "I did not get naked in front of a... Jesus fuck, what are you doing?"

His hand appeared over the shower door, empty and making a grabby motion. "Give me that shampoo. I can tell by the smell it's the same kind my cousin JJ uses. That shit will ruin your hair. Gross. Your hair is way too nice for that discount shit."

The compliment must have gone straight to my head because that was the only explanation for my handing him the bottle. "You've successfully stolen my shampoo. Now, go away."

I grabbed the bar of soap and began to scrub myself, hissing as the soap found little cuts and scrapes I hadn't noticed acquiring during the day. My burn scars covered unpredictable nerve endings that never seemed to be able to decide when they wanted to send numb signals or sensory signals.

"What happened to you?" he asked, sounding more serious, as if unable to keep up the provoking banter. "You kinda looked like shit when you arrived."

"I'm fine," I grunted.

I drank down as much water from the showerhead as I could, desperate to rehydrate and regulate my body temperature. Fire-damaged skin had sweat issues, which meant I was more sensitive to overheating than most people. I'd borne these scars for most of my life, so I knew how to manage them, but the heat sensitivity had made my life hell when I first got overseas, and I'd had one too many close calls with heat exhaustion in Philly when I was back stateside.

It was one of the many reasons I'd decided to move to Montana.

"Judd?"

I'd never heard my name in his voice before. Didn't even know he knew or remembered it, to be honest.

"Yeah?"

"Was it a fire?" He sounded unsteady and surprised, as if just now realizing I might have been responding to an actual fire.

"No. Not a fire."

"Then what happened?"

I finished rinsing off and cracked open the door to reach for a towel. Alex's hand bumped into mine as he handed the towel to me. I pulled the towel back inside the shower stall and began to dry off. "Wildfire drills up at SERA," I explained, finally wrapping the towel around my waist and opening the door.

Alex's cheeks were still adorably pink, and his hair was messy like he'd run his fingers through it. His eyes were wide with concern, and I got the feeling he was trying hard to keep from sneaking a peek at my body. For some reason, that disappointed me. I wouldn't have minded seeing his interest confirmed. I'd thought the pink cheeks were a sign, but maybe not.

"W-were you—I mean, was my cousin Tommy hurt?" he stammered, eyes flicking to the floor.

I could tell from the janky way his eyes were moving and the deepening red of his cheeks that he was asking about his cousin to cover up his discomfort about asking after me. Or maybe my body being on display was making him act funny.

Either way, it was goddamned adorable. And wholly unexpected from the sassy restaurant owner.

"Your cousin's fine. He's a great instructor. The students love him."

He nodded. "Good. But, um..." His eyes flicked up, landed on my chest, moved to my groin and down to my legs before moving back up to my face and flicking to the ground again. Thankfully, he didn't seem to spend much time noticing the burn scars on my arm or have the right angle to see the ones on the back of my thigh. "Were you hurt?"

I frowned and stepped closer to reach for his chin, raising it up so he was forced to meet my eyes. "I'm okay. I promise," I said softly. "No one was hurt."

His eyelids opened and closed rapidly, and his chest rose and lowered with shallow breaths. The familiar scent of wood-fired pizza and summer sun radiated into my personal space as he gathered his thoughts. "Good, that's good. Um, so, yeah. I, uh. Okay."

And then he stepped out of my bathroom and took off like a rubber band snapped across a classroom.

"What the hell just happened?" I muttered, staring after him and wondering why he hadn't stayed to ask me to reconsider the permit.

My dick tented the towel as I remembered the feel of the slight stubble on his chin, the larger-than-normal pupils eclipsing his irises as he blinked up at me, and the fullness of his lower lip as he scraped his teeth over it.

Alex Marian had a swooping divot over the inside of his left eyebrow that deepened when he was confused or unsure. Or angry. I hadn't remembered that from Amsterdam, or maybe it had been too dark in the hotel bar to notice.

I had the feeling that tonight, insecurity had deepened it, and I'd wanted to smooth it over with my thumb while reassuring him everything was okay.

Why had he been so worried about a standard firefighting field drill?

I blew out a breath and moved across my office to close the door he'd left ajar. Then I made my way to the tall filing cabinet and pulled out my spare clothes from the top drawer. Once dressed, I gave up on the idea of getting any more work done and headed out.

"G'night, Chief," Cody called over his shoulder from the kitchen sink as I passed him on my way out.

"'Night."

Instead of heading back to my rental house and the too-peaceful quiet of the surrounding trees, I headed to a local burger place called Frank's. The small place was fairly full with tourists spilling out onto the deck at the back. I stepped up to the counter and ordered a BLT burger with cheese, onion rings, and a beer before finding a spot at a long table filled with people.

"You're a hard man to find," a woman nearby said as she took the seat across from me. I recognized her from her social media, attractive, probably in her mid-thirties, with a thick blonde braid, straight bangs, and a few scattered freckles across a suntanned face.

"I'm at one of the most popular restaurants in town during the dinner rush," I said, shooting her a friendly smile. "Maybe you're just a terrible seeker."

Her laugh was easy and warm as she reached out a hand. "I'm Max's friend Katherine, but everyone calls me Kaidee. Nice to meet you."

I stood partway to take her hand so she didn't have to stretch across the table. "Oh shit, was that today?"

She waved me back down in my seat with a laugh. "No. I was supposed to arrive tomorrow night, but there was a storm headed through Yellowstone. I decided I'd prefer to be tucked up in your place than in a muddy tent puddle. Hope that's okay."

"Yeah, fine." I did my best to hide my exhaustion and disappointment with friendly conversation. It wasn't her fault I'd made subconscious plans to make love to my bed tonight. "Did you order yet? Want me to get you something? They have great burgers and razor-thin onion strings."

She held up a glass of beer. "Already ate and got myself a refill, but I'm happy to keep you company."

"Tell me about Yellowstone," I said.

Thankfully, she carried the conversation from there, even drawing interest from some of the people sitting near us. By the time my meal came, I'd made several new local friends and felt comfortable with my new houseguest.

The food helped wake me up, and the beer calmed my aching muscles, so that within an hour, I felt like a different person.

"Ah, so you can laugh. Max said the two of you used to laugh until you puked," Kaidee said, eyes twinkling over the amber beer in her glass.

"Max has never met a story he couldn't turn into a joke," I said, remembering the man who'd been my friend since we were placed in the same group foster home. I'd learned years later that cracking jokes like Max did was a common coping mechanism, but at the time, I'd simply thought fate had finally brought me someone good to lighten my load. "I've never laughed as hard as I do when the two of us get together."

She reached across the table to squeeze my scar-free arm. "He misses you, you know. Said you broke his heart when you moved away."

The hairs prickled on the back of my neck. For a split second, I thought it was some kind of childhood trauma response brought on by these memories, but movement out of the corner of my eye revealed Alex Marian coming to a sudden stop. His eyes seemed riveted to my table. Or maybe to the half-empty beer glass next to where Kaidee's hand still clasped my forearm. Or maybe I imagined it because he lurched forward toward the ordering counter as if he hadn't even noticed I was there.

"...go back to your place?" Kaidee asked.

My eyes had followed Alex, noticing the stiffening of his back and shoulders, but I quickly blinked back at Kaidee. "Sorry, what?"

"You look tired, Judd," she said with a kind smile. "I think we need to get you home and into bed."

I glanced back at Alex, wondering if I should say something to him, to ask why he'd left my office so quickly or why he hadn't fought me harder on the open-flame permit. Before I could decide, it was his turn to order, and someone nearby asked if my seat was available.

"Er, yeah. I'm headed out," I mumbled, standing to dispose of my dishes so he could take my place.

After the heat of the small, crowded restaurant, the cool night air was a relief. I sucked in a lungful of it and tried to relax my shoulders.

"You want to talk about it?" Kaidee asked.

At first, I wondered how she knew about my mixed-up feelings regarding Alex Marian, but then she added, "Must be a pretty big change living in such a small place after Philly."

I let go of my thoughts about Alex and gave Kaidee an amused side-eye. "Who's asking, you or Max?"

She shrugged, and it was the first time I noticed her body. She was fit and trim in a sleeveless cotton sundress that was cut low enough in the front for me to get a hint of her full breasts. The dress itself was shorter than I realized, showing off shapely legs and delicate feet with purple-painted toenails in strappy sandals.

Max was right. Kaidee was a beautiful woman. The kind who didn't use makeup or fancy clothes to impress.

The kind who would normally be just my type… if I weren't so bone-deep tired.

"Yeah, I guess it's a big change," I admitted. "But I like it. Today, we had a wildfire drill on the mountain, and it was a hundred times better than any training exercise I did in the city. Bright sunlight with zero humidity, mountain air with a cool breeze, and we even saw a cow moose and her calf in the distance. Can't find that in Philly."

"Sure can't. That sounds amazing."

I nodded. "It was, but I'm glorifying it a little. It also kicked my ass. I almost slipped into the river, got covered in mud, and used muscles carrying portable pumps that I'd forgotten I even had. I'm wrecked."

She laughed as we arrived at a Subaru that had a muddy bike strapped to the back. "This is me."

I nodded further down at my SUV. "I'm just there. Want to follow me?"

"Yeah, and I have you in my GPS, too." She touched my arm again. "Hey, listen. I know you weren't expecting me tonight, so I'll completely understand if you just want to show me a horizontal place to lay my sleeping bag before calling it a night."

I appreciated the out and took it. "I can do a little better than that. Come on."

When we got to my place, I showed her around the small cabin, helped her carry her things into the guest room, and then escaped into my own bedroom.

I expected to fall asleep the minute my head hit the pillow, and I did.

But dreams of Alex Marian teased me all night. I tried to touch him, but as soon as my fingertips brushed his warm skin, he either skittered away or disappeared.

In the morning, I awoke hard and aching. My stomach tightened with need as my breath sawed in and out of me as if I'd been fucking the man in my dream.

"Fuck," I hissed, reaching into my shorts to squeeze my dick. When had I last been this turned on by a dream? I felt like a teenager.

After blindly fishing the lube out of my bedside drawer, I shoved down my boxer briefs and slicked up my cock, shuttling it in and out of my fist while shamelessly imagining Alexander Marian face down on my desk, gripping the far edge with white-knuckled fingers while I railed his plump ass.

I came embarrassingly quickly. Thick jets of cum shot over my lower belly, clumping into the trail of hair below my belly button.

"*Fuck.*"

I closed my eyes and waited for my breathing to slow down.

Alex had spent more time yesterday asking after my well-being than trying to convince me to give him an open-flame permit.

And as I got up and started my day, I couldn't stop thinking about it.

So as soon as I got into the office, I shot off another email.

7

ALEX

DrunkenPoet: *Are you close with your family?*

IndexEcho: *No.*

I STARED at the laptop screen in disbelief.

> *Subject: Re: Timber's Application for Exemption Permit*
> *Mr. Marian,*
> *You may pick up your open flame permit for the Slingshot*
> *Showdown at the firehouse on two conditions:*
> *1. You will agree to an increased number of fire-safety inspec-*
> *tions for the next six months as I bring my crew up-to-speed on new*
> *inspection techniques. Legacy needs a volunteer training guinea pig*
> *and you're it, Marian.*
> *2. You will not set shit on fire that's not supposed to be set on*
> *fire. Period. This includes, but is not limited to, napkin holders*

(again), grasses or underbrush of any kind (even if privately-owned), any part of your bar (including the walnut countertop you keep crying about), fancy cocktails (no matter how Instagramma-ble), or my patience.

This is not a negotiation. Take it or leave it, Firebug.
Judd Kincaid
Chief, Legacy Fire Department

My heart thundered. "He's giving us the permit," I said to no one in particular. In reality, that wasn't what was causing my heart to stampede under my sternum.

Firebug.

It wasn't the first time he'd called me that. Somehow, it had seemed... almost affectionate. Like an endearment. But I knew that was ridiculous. The man saw me as an annoyance, a pest. And when I'd witnessed him leaning toward the beautiful blonde woman he was with last night, I'd gotten a firm answer to whether or not I might have sensed attraction from him.

He was straight.

I'd been asking around as casually as I could, and so far, no one had any evidence he was anything else. Of course, it wasn't fair of me to assume a default of het, but it also wouldn't be fair to allow myself to get my hopes up when so many sexy men were, in fact, into only women.

And why wouldn't he be? The woman he was with last night was great. Warm smile, easy laughter, outdoorsy and fit.

Maybe I even had her to thank for his one-eighty on the permit. Perhaps all it took to soften the man was a good night in the sack.

A little growl vibrated my throat. My sister was probably right. I'd find any reason to avoid dating someone actually attainable. It was leading me toward wanting unavailable men.

Because I was still obsessed with a ghost.

"Did you say something?" Karim asked as he poured a bucket of ice into the well behind the bar. "Because either you've been mumbling lately or I need my ears checked."

"Yeah, we got the permit to serve at the Slingshot Showdown. Tell Juni we'll need to call the Sysco guy and update our order."

He nodded and headed back to the kitchen while I opened the staffing schedule to try and cover both the Showdown and a busy Saturday here at the restaurant on late notice.

While I was grateful to have the permit, I wasn't about to run the risk of seeing Kincaid in person while retrieving it from the station house. I waited until the lunch crowd slowed before begging Deena to go.

"Bro, for real? I still have a six-top sitting on the patio," she said, sliding a receipt into the till drawer and stacking the empty leatherette folder on the stack above it.

"Fine, but after that, will you go? Please?"

She crossed her arms over her chest. "Promise you won't make me work the Showdown, and I'll do it."

I glared at her. We both knew she was my best server, and I'd never force her to do anything she didn't want to do, but we also knew she'd be my first choice to handle an event like the Showdown. "You'll do it anyway because you love me."

"Only because love hurts, Alex," she teased. "Fine. But if I'm working the Showdown, promise me Karim will be working the grill. He's the only one who can handle the crowds without murdering people."

It went unspoken that my head chef was a moody pain in the ass who didn't handle change well.

"Do you think I have a death wish?" I whispered. "Karim and I will do the cooking. You and Tyler can be customer-facing."

She grinned and fist-bumped me. "Perf. Should be done with the six-top in the next few minutes. I'll grab the permit."

I let out a breath as she bounced off to check on her last table again. If I could just stay away from the fire chief, maybe I could get past this ridiculous little crush on the guy.

Several hours later, Ella showed up for a drink after work with our cousin Hazel, who also happened to be her boss.

"Where's Avery?" I asked Hazel, setting down a glass of the Chianti she liked and a beer for my sister.

"Working late at the gallery. I told her I'd grab her pickle pizza on my way out."

I made a note to tell the kitchen, and then I pulled out a chair and joined them for a few minutes. "How are things going at work? Did the update roll out smoothly?"

My cousin's tech company was her baby. At least, it had been up till now. But she and her wife were expecting a human baby, which meant Untrace was getting ready to be demoted. Hazel and Ella, along with the rest of the company's employees, had been working hard on rolling out a big update this past spring, and it was finally over.

Hazel smiled. "For the most part. I'm just glad it's done. I have plans to take Avery down to the Red Lodge Inn tomorrow night for a nice dinner and overnight. She has a prenatal massage booked the next morning before we head back." She eyed me. "What about you? Doing anything besides work these days? Anything fun?"

I shook my head. "Newp. Nothing fun at all. In fact, I think the last fun thing I did was come over and help you finish painting and set up the crib."

"Alex, that was six weeks ago!"

Ella swallowed another sip of beer. "He thinks his job is fun," she said, like she was making fun of me. Like I was infantile.

"It *is* fun," I argued.

"What about dating?" Hazel asked.

I groaned. "Don't start. You sound like my father."

"Uncle Blue takes after Aunt Tilly," Hazel said with a grin.

Ella nodded. "Truer words."

Hazel met my eyes. "Your dad's not wrong, though. He, of all people, understands the difference having someone in your corner makes."

"I have plenty of people in my corner," I said, gesturing at the two of them.

"There's a cute guy at SERA named Monroe." Ella bounced her eyebrows. "He's a rescue pilot, and Tommy said he thought the guy was checking out your ass the night they all came to Timber."

My face heated unexpectedly. "Which one was Monroe? What does he look like?"

"Tall, wavy brown hair pulled back in a short ponytail, kind of like Uncle Jude."

Hazel crinkled her forehead. "Wait, I know him. Yeah. Super sweet guy. He bought one of Avery's paintings last year. He's been with Trace and SERA for a while. I'm surprised you haven't met him before."

Ella pinned me with a knowing look. "The Grape's been working so hard, he hasn't allowed himself to see anyone that way. I say that ends now. It's time you went on a date. Started meeting guys and having a life outside of work."

"I meet guys," I said, ignoring her use of my childhood nickname. "I meet plenty of guys."

Ella bit back a smile and nodded, pretending to be serious. "Right. What was the last guy's name?"

"J... John." I forced myself not to wince. "John... Jones...ie." I'd added on the last bit when I'd realized how generic-sounding my made-up name was.

Hazel's eyebrows shot up, and she huffed out a laugh. "Is that right? John Jonesie."

I nodded, committing to the bit. "That's right. He's in... sales."

Hazel sat forward and leaned her chin on her fist. "And where does John Jonesie live?"

"In, um... Montana."

Ella tilted her head. "Convenient. Since you also live in... Montana. What does he sell, exactly?"

I glanced around the restaurant, catching sight of the new napkin caddy and remembering Kincaid's comments about the fire. "Insurance."

Hazel picked up her phone and texted someone. I assumed she was texting her wife until she glanced up at me. "Don't worry, I asked Tilly for help setting you up. You know... in case things go pear-shaped with good ole John Jonesie."

A hush came over the table as her horrible, ugly betrayal settled between us. "You'd better be bluffing," I growled, imagining the shitstorm that would come from having our belligerent, nosy great-great-aunt foisted upon me and my nonexistent love life.

Hazel was the oldest of all of us grandkids, so she was pretty much the boss of everyone. Getting openly annoyed with her was walking a razor edge I'd never skated close to before.

"I'll make you a deal, Alex," she said, taking a final sip of her wine and standing up. "You let me set you up with Monroe, and I'll tell Tilly to stand down."

"Fine," I said, remembering the only two men I had any interest in were completely unavailable to me. And I definitely wanted to get touched by another man in this century. "I'll go on the date."

Both women beamed at me.

And then turned and high-fived each other.

Unfortunately, late the next afternoon, before Hazel had a chance to set me up, she and Avery were in a horrible car accident during a sudden thunderstorm. I was in the middle of reviewing payroll when I got a call from Ella.

"Hazel and Avery's vehicle flipped over," she wailed. "Avery's okay, but they can't get Hazel out."

Thankfully, she'd already called our cousin Tommy, an ER doc, and he was making his way from SERA out to the accident site.

"Where are you?" I asked, checking my pockets for my car keys and racing to the back in search of a raincoat. Blood roared through my ears as I imagined our strong, bossy cousin trapped and injured as the storm raged around her. "Do we know how bad her injuries are?"

We spent the rest of the evening communicating with Tommy, who was on the scene and carefully coordinating details between all the other family members, as we made our way to the ER in Billings to meet the ambulance.

Poor Avery was soaking wet and terrified, but Ella had thought to have me grab some clothes for her before leaving my place.

After they took Hazel back to surgery and Ella took Avery to the ladies' room to change, I stood alone and scared in the lobby, unsure how to proceed. My body shook with fatigue and fear, and I wondered what the hell my Uncle Pete and Aunt Ginger would do if anything happened to Hazel.

My whole family, including Hazel's twin, Chloe, was already on their way, or would be as soon as the weather cleared enough to allow the flight in.

"Hey."

My head snapped up at the familiar rumble. Chief Kincaid stood there in his uniform, hair wet around the edges, where a few streaks of gray stood out against the dark strands, and his nose pink from the cold, wet night.

"You okay?" he asked softly. "Someone said Hazel is your cousin?"

I nodded, unable to say anything.

Kincaid looked around as if seeking someone. "You here alone? I know your cousin Tommy's here somewhere."

"Talking to the doctors, I think. My, um... my sister is with Hazel's wife."

Kincaid's forehead creased for a second, and then he blew out a breath and pulled me tight against his chest, wrapping me up in a big bear hug. I was so surprised by the gesture, I froze for a beat before hugging him back and holding on as tightly as I could.

He smelled like rainwater and sweat, faded diesel fumes and noxious smoke, but underneath it all, there was the scent of something new and somehow comforting coming from the spot where my nose nestled at the base of his throat. The combination made me dizzy.

"She'll be okay," he said in a low voice. "Your cousin was amazing out there. Saved her life. We got to her as fast as we could, Alex. I promise. But the storm made it hard and—" He shuddered. "I'm sorry I couldn't get her out quicker."

I held him even tighter. "Thank you so much. I'm glad you were there."

His big hands moved up and down my spine before one moved up into my hair as he cupped the back of my head. He pulled back to look at me. "I have to go, but will you please promise me to call if you need a ride home? I don't want you on the road tired or upset."

"No, I'm fine. I'll be okay."

"Alex... please. Just promise me."

I looked up into his eyes, wondering how it was possible this man was two entirely different people. The ornery, by-the-book fire marshal and the kind and caring protector.

"I promise," I said.

Tension crackled between us. I wondered what the protocol was for saying goodbye after such a charged moment, but before I could figure it out, Ella and Avery came up. Avery looked a little silly in my sweats and hoodie, but at least she was dry and warm.

I quickly pulled out of the fire chief's arms as he stepped back. Kincaid nodded to my sister and Avery before letting them know Hazel was in good hands.

As I watched him walk back out into the stormy night, I wondered if he was heading to the site of another crash. Or maybe responding to fires caused by lightning. Either way, he was the one who needed to stay safe, not me.

And I hadn't even thought to ask him for any promises.

8

KINCAID

IndexEcho: *Work took twice as long today because someone broke security protocol.*

DrunkenPoet: *Was there a reason?*

IndexEcho: *Never a good reason to break the rules, Poet.*

WELL, that was fucked up. And a huge mistake. And fucking weird on top of everything else.

I had no business offering comfort to Alexander Marian.

Who was he to me? A fucking civilian whose restaurant I inspected. He wasn't a friend. Hell, he was hardly even an acquaintance.

And I'd hugged him in the middle of a family crisis. Why?

To be fair, he'd looked lost. Upset and alone. And my heart had gone out to him. For some reason, he was the kind of person who made you want to offer protection and comfort. Some people were like that, I guessed.

Who, Judd? Who in your life have you ever wanted to offer protection and comfort to?

I closed my eyes and hung my head, the rain still steady on the roof of my vehicle in the hospital parking lot. Fine. I'd once had a friend like that, back in the group foster home. I was seventeen, and she was sixteen. She'd lost her home when her mother had gone to jail for assault. Never mind that her mom had been defending her against high-school bullies behind the gym after she came out of band practice. I'd always assumed that was why I'd felt protective of her. She'd been small and nerdy, but also meek, which had made her an easy target.

I'd had a crush on her, too. Which made me wonder if comfort and protection were some kind of love language. Or, more likely, they were my own fucked-up way of trying to give someone what I wish someone had given me when I was younger.

Love and security.

"Stop this shit," I muttered to myself as I started the engine. There were hours of work left before my shift ended, and sitting in a Billings parking lot, wondering why I wanted to comfort the local fire hazard, wasn't helping.

THE FOLLOWING week was spent balancing time between work and showing Kaidee around Legacy. I enjoyed the distraction of hosting her since it forced me to check out some of the places that made Legacy so popular.

"We have to stop in town to pick up some sandwiches before heading to the trailhead," she said, zipping up her backpack before slinging a strap over her shoulder. "I called in an order from a place I read about online."

I was itching to get out of town and stretch my legs. Half the workweek had been spent on interagency Zoom calls keeping everyone up to speed on the current wildfire conditions and preparedness plans. I'd spent way more time talking about the wilderness than enjoying it, and it was time for that to change.

"Appreciate you doing that," I said before closing the top to my water bottle and grabbing the keys to the truck. "Where're we stopping?"

She followed me out to the vehicle with her nose in her phone, scrolling through the details of the order. "Place called Timber. It's on Founders Row, I think. Is that Legacy's Main Street?"

I felt a foolish little twist of excitement in my gut. "Yeah."

She glanced at me as she pulled on her seat belt. "What? You don't like it?"

"No, I do. It's great food. Good wine. Mostly pizza, though."

"And Italian sandwiches," she corrected. "The reviews on this place are amazing. And it has an interesting history. Well, the building does, anyway."

As I drove toward Founders Row, Kaidee told me about the historic roadhouse, which I'd already heard had been a down-low meet-up spot for gay guys over the years. More recently, it had become openly gay-friendly, even before being sold to Alex Marian to become a more modern wine bar and pizza restaurant.

"My brother's gay," she said offhandedly as we pulled up and saw the Pride flag waving lazily from one of Timber's flower planters out front. "Wonder if he's heard of this place."

I glanced over at her in time to see her cheeks flush. "I didn't mean it like that," she added. "He's also a rock climber who's spent a lot of time in the Rockies. He'd like Legacy. I know he's climbed Three Daughters down in Majestic."

I nodded as I threw the vehicle into Park and got out. "Buddy of mine from my time in Iraq has done some mountain biking around there," I said. "Says it's gorgeous. And great trails."

Kaidee threaded her arm through mine. "Does it make you want to try it? I know they have bike rentals in town. I'd love to go out with you sometime."

Since she'd been here, Kaidee had been just the right amount of friendly and flirty without making me feel compelled to either ask her out or tell her I wasn't interested. Which had allowed me to continue walking this stupid line of not having to decide how I felt about her one way or the other. She was a nice woman whose company I enjoyed. And that was all I had the mental or physical energy for at the moment.

"Let's start with foot trails first," I said with a smile.

We stepped from the bright sun into the dimmer interior. Thankfully, the person who greeted us was a bubbly young woman, not the owner. "How many? Two?"

Kaidee grinned at her. "Just picking up a to-go order."

The woman led Kaidee over to the bar area, but as I began to follow, I heard a muffled yelp from the hallway that led to the restrooms. I headed in that direction to see what the sound was when I saw a precarious tower of cardboard boxes stacked beneath a wooden chair, with a young man balanced on top, stretching to reach a burned-out light fixture.

"Jesus Christ," I barked, causing the kid to wobble danger-ously. "You want a broken neck?"

I lunged forward and grabbed the chair, steadying it, while the young man—who couldn't have been older than twenty—scram-bled to regain his balance. He was slight, with dark hair and wide, frightened eyes that reminded me of a startled deer.

"Get down from there. Now." I kept my voice firm but not harsh. The kid looked scared enough already.

"I—I was just trying to fix the light," he stammered, carefully climbing down. "The boxes were fine. I was being careful—"

"Like hell you were." I kicked at the stack of boxes, which immediately toppled over with a crash. "You see that? That's what would have happened with you on top of them if I hadn't shown up. You ever heard of a ladder?"

"What's going on?" Alex's voice came from behind me, sharp with concern. He rushed past me to the young man, placing protective hands on his shoulders. "Tavo, are you okay? What happened?"

Tavo. I wondered if this was the person Alex had lied to protect the night of the first fire incident. The person who'd somehow managed to spray sanitizer near an open flame, since it had been clear to everyone that Alex alone couldn't have caused the fire.

"He's fine, Chief. Leave him alone. He's just helping out." Alex positioned himself between me and Tavo in a way that made my annoyance flare hotter.

Kaidee appeared behind us, drawn by the commotion. "Oh my, is everyone alright?" She looked between the scattered boxes and the trembling young man with genuine concern. "Are you hurt, honey?"

Alex's entire body went rigid. "He's fine," he muttered, the words clipped and defensive.

I studied the interaction, noting how Alex's protective instincts had kicked into overdrive, how the kid—Tavo—kept glancing nervously between Alex and me like he was waiting for permission to speak. Everything about their dynamic screamed that Alex was hiding something significant.

"You can't have untrained staff performing maintenance," I said, keeping my voice level despite my growing irritation. "Especially not with whatever the fuck this was. This is exactly the kind of reckless safety violation that—"

"He's not staff," Alex interrupted. "I just... stepped away for a minute to—"

"To what? Let a kid risk his neck because you couldn't be bothered to buy a proper ladder?" I gestured at the fallen boxes.

Kaidee laughed, a bright sound that cut through the tension. "He's just a kid, Judd," she said, shooting me an amused look. "I'm sure you did a foolish thing a time or two at his age. In fact, didn't you and Max throw ropes into the struts of a bridge one time to—"

"Not the same thing," I clipped quickly before she could launch into a story about my shitty teenage years in front of someone like Alex Marian.

Kaidee's attempt to lighten the tension should have been charming. Instead, something sharp and uncomfortable twisted in my chest as I watched Alex's face darken.

"We have a ladder," Alex said quietly but firmly, his sunshine demeanor notably absent. "And Tavo isn't foolish. He was trying to help."

"Like he did the night of the fire?" I suggested, raising my eyebrows.

The words hung in the air like smoke. Tavo went pale, Alex's jaw clenched, and Kaidee looked between us with growing confusion.

"This has nothing to do with the fire incident," Alex said carefully.

"You sure about that? You lied about the circumstances of that fire, and now I'm finding out there are people 'helping out' around here you've failed to disclose." I stepped closer, and Alex unconsciously moved to shield Tavo further. "What else are you hiding, Marian?"

"Nothing," Alex said, but his voice lacked conviction. "And I told you, Tavo doesn't work for me. He's... a guest."

"A guest who comes behind the bar and into the back hallway to help himself to supplies?"

Alex firmed his jaw and narrowed his eyes. "I do not have to waste another minute dealing with you and your ridiculous over-reactions. I have a restaurant to run." His eyes flicked over to Kaidee, and suddenly, the fakest smile I'd ever seen widened his mouth. "And apparently, you have plans with this lovely woman. So... enjoy your day."

Kaidee touched my arm gently. "He's right. Let's—"

"No." I shook her off, focused entirely on Alex's evasive answers and defensive posture. The revelation that there'd been someone else playing fast and loose with fire safety in his bar. Someone who wasn't covered under his liability insurance. If Tavo wasn't an employee, then who was he? "You're hiding something."

His nostrils flared. "Is there a rule about who's allowed to change a lightbulb in a restaurant, for fuck's sake? And what does it have to do with fire safety?"

"The stack of boxes alone is a fire hazard, and you know it! I want a full staff roster on my desk by tomorrow morning," I continued. "And documentation for any maintenance or repair work done in the past six months. If I find out you've been cutting corners or hiding employees to avoid proper safety training—"

"For fuck's sake, Judd!" Alex exploded.

His use of my first name stopped me in my tracks. There was an intimacy in it that immediately brought to mind that charged moment in my office. I blinked and tried to clear it from my head.

Tavo whispered something in Spanish and started edging away, but Alex caught his arm.

"It's okay." Alex spoke to him softly, then looked back at me with a mixture of defiance and desperation. "Look, Chief, can we just... can we talk about this privately?"

I felt Kaidee's questioning gaze on the side of my face and realized how this looked—me browbeating a local business owner over what appeared to be a minor safety issue. But every instinct I had screamed that Alex Marian was hiding something big, something that could put people like this kid at risk.

"So you can give me more of your lies?"

Alex's face flushed, but before he could respond, a short, angry woman in a chef's coat appeared from the kitchen.

"Everything okay out here?" she asked, taking in the scattered boxes, Tavo's pale face, and the tension crackling between Alex and me. "I heard shouting."

"Everything's fine, Juni," Alex said quickly. "Chief Kincaid was just... inspecting our light fixtures."

The chef's eyebrows lowered as her eyes narrowed. "He wants to check something, he can check how impossible it is to cook with a fire extinguisher up my—"

"Bupbup!" Alex chirped. "Thank you, Juni. Why don't you show Tavo out through the kitchen? Appreciate the help, Tavo, but I have it under control."

"Clearly," I muttered under my breath. I turned to Tavo, who was sneaking off toward the kitchen. "Hey, kid, one last question. What's your last name?"

The young man's eyes went wide with panic, and Alex stepped forward again.

"You don't need to answer that," Alex said, his voice low and dangerous. For some reason, it went straight to my groin, which was incredibly inappropriate and distracting.

"Actually, he does. He was the one causing the safety concern today," I snapped. "And you're hiding his identity, which makes both of you look guilty."

Kaidee shifted uncomfortably beside me. "Judd, maybe—"

"I live here," Tavo said quietly, his voice barely above a whisper. "Upstairs. With Alex."

The admission dropped like a stone into still water. I felt my assumptions reshuffling, my anger shifting into something more complex and confused.

"You live here?" I repeated.

Alex's shoulders stiffened, and his chin came out. "That's right. In fact, we... we're... together. So you see, not an employee."

Tavo blinked, and Juni's eyebrows shot up in surprise before a neutral mask fell over her features.

"The two of you," I said, wanting, for once, for him to lie to me.

He hesitated just a moment too long before saying, "Tavo and I live together."

I studied Alex's face, looking for deception but finding only exhaustion and worry. Whatever was going on here was more complicated than I'd assumed.

Alex glanced at Tavo, who nodded. "It's true."

They were both lying. And for some reason, I was so relieved I wanted to laugh.

There was definitely something here I wasn't seeing, some context I was missing, but it wasn't about Alex Marian dating jailbait. Before I could press further, Kaidee spoke up.

"Our sandwiches are ready," she said gently, clearly trying to defuse the situation. "Maybe we should hit the trail before the day is half-over."

"Yeah." I ran a hand through my hair, suddenly aware of how public this confrontation had become. "Okay."

But as we walked back toward the front of the restaurant, I couldn't shake the feeling that I'd just seen something important about Alex Marian.

Something that didn't fit with my image of him as an entitled member of Legacy's beloved Marian family. And that bothered me more than I wanted to admit.

"Your order," the hostess said brightly, handing Kaidee a paper bag. "Have a great hike!"

"Thanks," Kaidee replied, but her smile was strained.

As we walked back to the truck, she was unusually quiet. It wasn't until we were driving toward the trailhead that she finally spoke.

"That was intense," she said carefully.

"It's my job."

"Is it, though? I mean, the safety stuff, sure. But that felt... personal."

I kept my eyes on the road. "I don't know what you mean."

"Judd." Her voice was gentle but firm. "I may not know you well, but that was more emotion than I've seen out of you in a week of living with you. What's really going on with you and the restaurant guy?"

I was quiet for a long moment, trying to sort through my own motivations. Why had I pushed so hard? Why did Alex Marian's evasions and half-truths bother me so much?

"He's reckless," I said finally. "And he thinks he can charm his way out of consequences."

"Maybe. Or maybe he's just trying to protect someone who can't protect themselves."

I glanced at her, surprised by the insight, that she'd been able to put into words what we'd seen.

"That kid—Tavo—he looked terrified. Not of the boxes or the broken light, but of you. Of being noticed." She shifted in her seat to face me. "Sometimes there are good reasons why people don't want to be noticed by authority figures."

Her words settled uneasily in my chest. I thought about Tavo's panicked expression when I'd asked for his last name, the way Alex had immediately moved to shield him.

"Maybe," I admitted grudgingly.

We drove the rest of the way in silence, but I couldn't stop thinking about the way Alex had positioned himself between me and Tavo or the fierce protectiveness in his voice. It reminded me of something, though I couldn't quite place what.

It wasn't until we were halfway up the trail, Kaidee chattering about the wildflowers and the view, that it hit me.

It reminded me of *DrunkenPoet*. Of the way he'd written about protecting people, about doing what was right, even when it wasn't entirely legal.

He'd told me a story of someone in his extended family undergoing harsh conversion therapy years ago when a guardian angel swooped in and saved him, taking him away from his abusive father and bringing him to a shelter for LGBTQ kids. Years later, the victim and his rescuer met again and fell in love. But the act of "saving" one man from his abuse had been illegal. It was obvious kidnapping, even though none of the legal alternatives would have worked.

Sometimes the right thing isn't the same as the legal thing, he'd typed. *Sometimes you have to choose between following rules and protecting people.*

I'd disagreed with him then, argued that rules existed for good reasons. But he'd patiently pushed back against my black-and-white thinking, gently urging me to see the gray areas.

Not everyone has the luxury of trusting the system, Index. Sometimes the system fails the people who need it most.

DrunkenPoet didn't know I was one of those kids who'd been in the system. One of the people he was advocating for.

I made a noise in my throat. The same pain that always accompanied memories of *DrunkenPoet* tightened in my chest.

"You okay?" Kaidee asked before slipping her hand into mine.

I squeezed and let go before realizing that might have been her move. "Yeah. Just... thinking."

She let out a little huff of laughter and stopped walking, so I stopped and turned back to her.

"Okay, I'm just going to say what I think and damn the consequences," she said.

The look on my face must have shown my confusion because she let out a sigh. "I've been trying to send you signals all week that I'd be up for more than just being your houseguest, but you haven't seemed to notice. I know you're into women because Max told me you've dated women before—"

"I'm bi," I said without thinking, because it was true, and I'd been asked enough times in the past that I was used to it.

"Yeah, well, maybe that explains what happened at that restaurant," she said with a glint of amusement in her eyes. "Maybe that's the real reason you haven't been picking up on my signals. That guy gets under your skin. Ever consider there could be a non-fire-safety reason why?"

I made a scoffing noise because her suggestion was ridiculous.

Of course I'd considered it.

I'd considered the hell out of it every night for the past week and every morning in the shower with my hand wrapped around my cock.

"Can you imagine me going out with someone so careless?" I muttered. "I'd be the laughingstock of my profession."

Kaidee reached out and put her hand on my chest, patting it with reassurance and also conviction. "You don't seem like the kind of guy who gives a shit what other people think, Judd. And maybe he's not as careless as you think."

I scoffed. "You didn't see him practically light himself on fire with a sparkler."

"He's cute," she said. "And if he was protecting that kid the way it seemed, he's thoughtful and kind also."

I took her hand again so I could get us both moving forward

down the trail. "Can I say what I think and damn the consequences, too?"

Her laugh was warm and light in the afternoon breeze. "Please do."

"I'm definitely attracted to Alex. There's just something about him that has its hooks in me. I can't decide if it's because he's reckless or because he's hot."

"Or because he's not interested," she teased.

I thought back to the day in my office when his eyes had bugged out of his head as I'd stepped out of the shower. I'd felt his gaze like a caress.

The sexual attraction went both ways. That much had been clear. I just wasn't sure if Alex had any interest in doing something about it.

And I wasn't sure if I did either.

"Maybe so. But..." I hesitated, wondering if I was ready to confess the rest of what was in my head to a near stranger.

Kaidee let go of my hand and wrapped her arm through mine to get closer. "I'm a good friend, Judd. Talk to me. It's okay that this isn't going to be more than that, but I like you. And I'd love to be your friend."

I put my hand over the one on my arm. "I had an online relationship a few years ago. It was intense and happened when I was overseas for work."

"Go on. What happened?"

The trail wound through a grove of lodgepole pines, their straight trunks filtering the afternoon sunlight into shifting patches of gold on the forest floor. To our left, the mountainside dropped away toward the valley where Legacy sat tucked between rolling hills, the town's rooftops barely visible through the trees. A mountain creek trickled somewhere nearby, its sound growing fainter as we climbed higher into the foothills of Slingshot Mountain. The air was thin and clean, with that particular Montana clarity that made every detail—from the lichen on the bark to the distant snowcapped peak—stand out in sharp relief.

"I fell in love with him. A complete anonymous stranger. We chatted over a period of a year before I was in a very bad accident."

She glanced up at me. "Max told me you were injured in a fire. I assumed it was on a job."

I shook my head. "The accident overseas wasn't a fire," I said. I knew Kaidee had seen the burn scars on my arm, but I didn't offer an explanation. Recounting one tragic accident was enough for a single afternoon. "There was a mortar strike at the air base where I was doing contract work. The building I was in partially collapsed. I was knocked unconscious, among other injuries, and evacuated to Ramstein in Germany for treatment. They ended up keeping me under sedation for a while. When I finally started coming out of it, I had memory and brain fog issues from the blast and head injury, I was in pain and all kinds of therapy, and I didn't have access to a cell phone or the internet."

"So he had no idea," she whispered, understanding and empathy in her voice. "Poor guy. And, shit, poor *you*."

I nodded. "It took me four months just to get back on the message board, let alone fully recover. By then, his account was gone. Completely closed. I had no way of contacting him."

"Damn. You didn't know where he lived? Where he worked?"

I gave a single headshake. When I'd told Max about *Drunken-Poet*, he'd asked those questions and more. *But how do you know he's even real, Judd? How do you know he's who he said he was?*

He hadn't understood that our anonymity had been part of the draw at first.

I wasn't supposed to give out personal information while I was working overseas in the first place. But hiding behind our usernames, *DrunkenPoet* and I had told each other things that were hard to talk about with others. His love of poetry. My desire to have a family. Our favorite places—Montana for him, in my own place for me. Our daydreams and worries and triumphs. I'd felt known and understood in a way I never had before.

Later, I think holding back that information felt kind of like a game. One that made us look forward to the day we'd meet in person like we were kids looking forward to Christmas, with the promise of a happy surprise to keep us going through the last few months of my contract.

And in retrospect, it had been criminally fucking stupid.

When I'd gotten out of the hospital in Germany to find *DrunkenPoet*'s account deleted, I'd have given anything to go back in time and get his phone number, his address. Hell, even just his name.

But it had been too late.

"The only real identifying details I'd picked up from our year of chatting came down to these few clues: his family owns a farm in California that he works for, he graduated college a couple years before we met, which means he's probably in his late twenties, and he's close with his family but doesn't want to be a farmer like they are."

Kaidee thought about it for a few minutes as we separated our arms and continued making our way up the trail. "So you still have feelings for him. And that's why you're not sure if you can move on with anyone, Alex or not, right?"

I nodded.

"Judd... how long has it been since the accident?"

"Four years, one month, and twelve days."

9

———

ALEX

DrunkenPoet: *Hypothetically, if someone accidentally started a very small fire while using a glue gun, what's the best way to put it out without calling 911?*

IndexEcho: *Hypothetically, stop lighting shit on fire. Maybe stop using the gun. What did glue ever do to you anyway?*

———

IT HAD BEEN two weeks since being on the receiving end of Judd Kincaid's overly strict safety-consciousness.

Two weeks of feeling the embarrassment of claiming a relationship with a twenty-year-old kid.

Two weeks of waiting to get served some kind of official paperwork declaring me a lying liar who lied on a fire incident report... whatever the hell that would mean. Was there such a thing as fire court?

But nothing happened. No paperwork, no random inspection, and no to-go orders called in by Judd's perfect girlfriend.

And that was completely fine. Good, even. Because I was busy.

My cousin Hazel was recovering from her accident well, but it had brought half my extended family to town in the process. When I wasn't dealing with the tourist season at Timber, I was at my grandparents' lodge, visiting with my parents, aunts, uncles, cousins, and every other person they'd seemingly attracted from various and sundry encounters over the years. Fortunately, the lodge was completely full with family and visitors, which meant I had an excuse to leave every day or night and return to my apartment over the restaurant.

When I wasn't busy with work or family, I was trying to make sure Tavo stayed under the radar—both the fire chief's *and* the skeevy judge's. Thankfully, this seemed to be going okay. When I'd gone upstairs to apologize to Tavo after the confrontation with Judd, I'd caught him telling Ella about it in such a way that the two of them were crying with laughter. On the one hand, it had been good to see Ella laughing after how upset she'd been about Hazel's accident, and a relief to see that Tavo hadn't been too frightened by the incident. On the other, it hadn't been *that* funny.

And ever since then, Ella had taken to calling me Tavo's Sugar Daddy, which I did not appreciate.

But after two weeks, I had to admit the truth to myself.

Not seeing Judd Kincaid was exhausting.

I didn't see him at the Slingshot Showdown. I didn't see him at the SERA firefighters' charity bonfire. And I didn't see him any of the four hundred times I accidentally drove past the station house.

I was tired of not seeing him.

So... I may have set a teensy-tiny, itty-bitty fire and called in an anonymous tip.

"What the fuck are you doing?" Judd roared, slamming the

door to his vehicle after squealing into my back lot. "Drop the fucking box!"

I looked up from the open cardboard box I was holding carefully. Inside was a celebratory cake with way too many candles on it, but I knew from his angle it looked like whatever was in the box was on fire.

"Why?" I asked, putting on my most innocent face.

"Alex, set the box down carefully and step away." He moved to his back seat to grab an extinguisher, but before he could pull the latch on it and point it at me, I sucked in a breath.

Made a wish.

And blew out the candles.

"For what it's worth, my wish was for you to write me a ticket for illegal birthday candle usage."

He stepped toward me slowly as if dreading what was in the box. When he got close enough to see the *Happy Birthday, Alex!* written on it, he paled.

"Is today your birthday?"

I may have been a schemer, but I was not a liar. Well... not much of one, anyway. "Yes. And my family is waiting at the lodge to surprise me, but I wasn't in the mood for the whole production." Which was all true. Marian surprise parties were more exhausting than not seeing certain fire chiefs.

"So, you..."

"Picked up a cake at Beartooth Market and decided to celebrate on my own. Except, well... my friend Kincaid wouldn't like me having open flames inside the building, so..."

He looked horrified. "So you're out by the dumpster, celebrating your birthday alone?"

I almost felt bad. But then I remembered him trying to write Tavo up for changing a damned lightbulb while I was busy filling out compliance paperwork, while also trying to help Juni fulfill a large catering order. "I guess. It's okay, though. I can go inside now that the candles are out."

"I think you should go to your party!" he said, sounding the slightest bit panicked.

I stepped closer and inspected his facial expression. "Be honest. Did you get an invitation? Is that why you're trying to get me to go?"

He shook his head, and for some reason, the movement drew my attention down to the tight fit of his navy tee over muscular shoulders, a broad chest, and a slightly and *deliciously* padded abdomen.

"Promise."

I blinked up. "Promise what?"

"I didn't get invited to anything tonight, Marian or otherwise."

"Ah. Going home to your lady friend, then?"

I bit back a wince. Did I have to sound like an annoying brat? It was none of my business. "I'm sorry," I quickly added. "She's very nice. I'm glad you're with her."

Kincaid tilted his head at me and then smiled widely. "Are you?"

I pressed my lips together and remembered calling myself a not-liar only a moment ago. "No. Definitely not."

"And why's that?"

He still looked entirely too smug. "Well, because you have a very nice body under all of that rule-followy..." I waved a hand at him and nearly dropped the cake. "Whatever. And I wouldn't mind... um, never mind."

He took the cake from my hands and held the entire box under one arm like it was nothing. I shook out my arms after holding it so long. "Rule-followy whatever?"

"You're very smarmy," I said with a sniff. "Probably for the best that you're straight."

"Probably."

I couldn't help but deflate a little at the confirmation. So much for my birthday wish. "Well, why don't you take her the cake, then? I'm not really in the mood to celebrate."

He stepped a little closer. He smelled like woodsmoke and citrus. "I would, except she went up to Glacier."

"Ah."

"And then she's headed home to Colorado," he continued, stepping even closer. He lifted a devastating eyebrow at me. "Which is fine with me since we're not together."

Kincaid leaned down until our noses were practically touching. His voice lowered to molten honey. "And Alex?"

"Huh," I breathed, intoxicated by his nearness.

"I'm not straight."

I reached out a hand to grab the front of his shirt to keep from toppling into him as I leaned the rest of the way forward and shot my shot.

His lips were dry and soft, full and warm. I let out a little noise of apology but also not. Because I wasn't really sorry.

Maybe I should have been, but I wanted to kiss him so fucking badly. And I wanted to be kissed. And four years was too long to spend in love with a memory.

Kincaid's big hand clasped the back of my head and held me there while his lips took complete control of the kiss. It was strong and decisive like he was, and I realized then that I'd never kissed anyone like this. Someone who took complete control, was clearly stronger than I was. And who enflamed every fucking part of me from the jump.

When he pulled back, his eyes were dark and intense. "Fucking flammable."

"What?" I breathed, feeling dizzy and untethered.

"Happy birthday, Marian," he said as he backed away. "And

next time you call in an anonymous tip, maybe remember the station house has caller ID."

I blinked at him.

"Go see your family, Alex. They love you. And not everyone has that."

I stared after him, face flaming, until he was long gone.

And then I went to see my family.

10

KINCAID

DrunkenPoet: *Ever have one of those moments where you're abso-lutely sure you've met someone before, but they act like they've never seen you in their life?*

IndexEcho: *Story of my life overseas. Everyone thinks all Americans look the same. Why?*

AFTER KISSING the fuck out of Alex Marian, I quickly realized it was a mistake. Not because there wasn't a spark there—that spark could have lit up the entire state of Montana—but because this man had already proven fickle once before.

He'd bailed on me in Amsterdam when someone better came along, and I had no intention of putting myself in that situation again. Despite how much I wanted him.

Not only that, but he was also currently under active permit suspension, which meant cavorting with him could be seen as inappropriate in my job. I had no intention of letting a one-night stand fuck with my career.

And it was clear Alex Marian wasn't interested in more than a quick conquest anyway. He was playing with me, and I didn't appreciate it.

The reasons to avoid him vastly outweighed the reasons to fuck him. And I needed to remember that.

I lasted one week, and then I decided two could play at his game.

"Please tell Mr. Marian I'm here for an inspection," I told the hostess.

When Alex came out of the kitchen, his cheeks were already flushed dark pink. I wasn't sure whether it was due to recalling the kiss or anger at yet another inspection.

In my defense, he was due for a random inspection, but to be fair, it didn't have to be done by me. That was just a bonus to needle the guy.

"What do you want?" he asked. "Because we're expecting a very large party for a special lunch event."

"I'm here to follow up on the vent hood as well as check a few issues that will remain unnamed until after my inspection." I raised an eyebrow in challenge. You didn't get to have a list of what I was inspecting before a random inspection. That was the whole point.

He flapped a hand at the kitchen. "Fine. Then just get on with it, will you? We have work to do."

I wasn't proud that I took three times longer than necessary, but I couldn't help my curiosity about the kid I'd met the last time I'd been at Timber. So I asked a few seemingly casual questions of Alex's staff as I took my time inspecting clear exits, seasonal decor, and the pesky vent hood nozzle.

Alex must have trained them well on the art of stonewalling, though. Because they were all friendly, and no one was willing to say anything about Tavo other than "he's a great guy."

"I didn't catch his last name," I tried with a sous chef and server at different times. Both times, they shrugged and pursed their lips. "Can't remember. It's hyphenated, I think," said the sous chef. And, "No clue," said the server.

The visit was a bust. Maybe if Alex hadn't gotten a large delivery of beer while I was there, he would've spent more time challenging me or, at the very least, glowering at me. But as it was, he passed the inspection, and I had to get on with my workday.

"See you next time," I said on my way out the door.

"Asshole," Alex muttered under his breath.

I turned back to him with as charming a smile as possible and reminded him he'd volunteered for these inspections. "Also, I forgot to ask how the Slingshot Showdown went? Was it any good for business?"

The answer had already been obvious. Everyone in town talked about how great the Timber food truck had been and how they'd run out of burgers because the turnout had broken event records.

"In fact, it was. Thanks for asking. I earned just enough to pay for the new sprinkler system you recommended in my residence upstairs."

I couldn't tell if he was joking or not. "I never recommended a sprinkler system for your residence. Hell, I didn't even know where you lived."

Alex pursed his lips in a mock thinking expression. "Really? I could have sworn I heard you say this whole pile needs built-in sprinklers to keep it from murdering half the town."

Now it was my turn to flush beet red. "It was my personal commentary. Not a professional recommendation. Although you can't go wrong with additional fire suppression in an old timber building like this."

Honestly, I was happy to hear he'd have such a system. If he wasn't being sarcastic. There was one way to find out.

"Who's doing the work?"

He frowned. "Vic Norman, why?"

I thought of the no-nonsense woman I'd met at a local training event in May. "Good. I like her."

He rolled his eyes. "Oh, good. I wouldn't want to use someone who wasn't Kincaid-approved."

"Glad to know you're falling in line," I said before walking away.

I could feel the heat of his glare on my back as I went.

THE REST of August was pretty much the same. When we saw each other, there was both an undercurrent of annoyance and undeniable attraction. But when Labor Day weekend rolled around, there was also flirtation and an unexpected confession.

I blamed the alcohol.

Well, that and the fact that Alex's cousin Tommy and his new boyfriend, Foster Blake, were inadvertently providing a hot peep show with lots of touches and kisses that made my fingers itch and my mouth water.

The SERA crew had invited me out to one of their big bonfire nights, and Timber was there supplying tasting flights of their new autumn beer selection along with tables full of pizzas, sandwiches, and large trays of pasta. Everyone was happily buzzed, and there was quite a lot of flirting going on. Just as I'd promised Max there would be, when he'd interrogated me on my personal life over Zoom earlier in the day.

"Promise me you'll at least find someone to fuck tonight," he'd said with a laugh. "Jesus, Judd. You sound uptight as hell. You used to be fun. What the fuck happened?"

I'd wanted to tell him the explosion had happened. And that it had happened because of lax standards on the air base. And that being in charge of the safety of this town was a responsibility I took seriously.

But I couldn't deny he was right. There was more to life than my job, and I needed to blow off steam.

"You're the fire chief, right?" a tall, attractive man asked as he transferred his beer cup from one hand to the other in order to shake my hand. "Name's Monroe Travers. I'm one of the instructors here."

"Nice to meet you. Judd Kincaid." I returned his friendly smile. "What do you teach?"

As he began to tell me about rescue aviation and helicopter evacuation, I paid close attention. Not only was I interested in aviation, since I was specialty trained in ARFF, but I also couldn't deny the man was sexy.

"If you have your Airport Master Firefighter designation, what are you doing here? Wouldn't you rather be working in aviation?"

I shook my head just as my ears picked out the sound of Alex's laughter nearby. "I wanted to get away from big cities. And the best aviation jobs are at the big airports." It wasn't the whole truth, but it was true enough.

We talked about ARFF for a little while longer. It turned out, his brother was a commercial airline pilot. Eventually, the subject changed.

"You an outdoorsman?" he asked, smiling enough to pop a dimple at me. "I'd be happy to show you some of the great trails around here, if you're into hiking."

Before I could answer him, I caught sight of Alex Marian

escorting a much older woman to a seat by the fire. Her arm was in his, and his hand covered hers. He leaned in and grinned at her, saying something that made her cackle.

"Sorry, I... yeah. I'd like that," I said. "Thanks."

"That's Alex Marian," Monroe said, catching me staring. "And his great-great-aunt Tilly. She's a wildcat with a barbed tongue, that one. Approach with caution." His chuckle was warm and easy.

"There seem to be a million Marians around here," I commented.

"No shit. They're everywhere. Seem to have bought up the whole town, not that I'm complaining."

"How do you mean?"

He shrugged. The golden light from the fire caught a few strands of hair that had come loose from his casual ponytail. "They helped Trace start SERA. Donated the land and invested seed money. They're rich as fuck. You know Jude Marian, who was a country singer like a million years ago?"

"Shit," I said, as I put two and two together. "That's his family?"

Monroe nodded. "Yeah, and I think they were rich before that. Jude's parents bought the old lodge and all this land. Gave parcels to each of the kids and grandkids. Alex's dad married some rich guy who owned a vineyard. Another one of them started a software company here. She's cool, though. Hazel Marian. She and her wife, Avery, do a lot of charity shit in town. It's been good for Legacy, you know? 'Cause they're all dripping in money."

It was the reminder I needed that Alex Marian wasn't struggling financially the way he implied. He didn't need to stand out in the summer sun and sell burgers to pay for fire safety upgrades on his historic building.

His attempt to get sympathy by pretending to be a regular guy was disappointing. And, yeah, maybe I shouldn't trust the gossip of a random guy at a party, but then again, what twenty-something could afford to buy his own restaurant?

None of it mattered, but the fact that I couldn't get it out of my head did.

"Tell me more about *you*, Monroe," I said, deciding to forget Alex Marian and have a good time, as Max had encouraged me to. Monroe seemed closer to my own age. "Where are you from, originally?"

It turned out, he'd been a Marine aviator who'd spent time flying casualty evacuations at Al Asad, so we had plenty to talk about. As the night wore on, I began to relax and enjoy myself. I was even contemplating inviting Monroe back to my place for the night when Alex walked up.

"Hey, can I talk to you for a minute?"

One look at him up close in the firelight, and all my plans for a quick fuck with Monroe went out the window. With that image in my head, there was no way I was getting hard for anyone else tonight. "About what?"

Monroe turned his flirty grin on Alex. "Hey, I've heard a lot about you, but we haven't actually met yet. I'm Monroe Travers."

Alex turned on the afterburners of his megawatt smile. His face was flushed and his eyes almost glassy. How much alcohol had he consumed? "Hey. My sister told me about you. I'm Alex. I hear you're amazing on the stick. Rescued my cousin Tommy when he was stuck up on the pass."

What the actual fuck? Was he flirting? With my hookup?

Too much alcohol.

"You needed to talk to me?" I reminded him.

Alex's smile calmed a bit. "Yeah. If Monroe doesn't mind me stealing you for a minute."

"As long as you bring him back," Monroe said with a wink.

"And you're welcome to stick around and hang with us. The more, the merrier, I say."

Alex's smile came back at full wattage. "Sounds like more than I can handle, but thanks."

His words surprised me. They were incongruous with the flirty playboy I'd seen in Amsterdam. Or maybe they weren't. Maybe he was a one-man guy but just wanted the best man available. Whatever that meant.

We stepped away from the light and warmth of the bonfire into the dark, cool night.

"What do you need?" I asked.

There was no longer a trace of his smile, only his wide eyes, still a little glassy but also glancing at me with curiosity. "When were you in Amsterdam?"

The question took me by surprise. "You know when because you were there, too. Three years ago."

"Yeah, see, that's what I keep coming back to. Because I was in Amsterdam *eight* years ago, and I haven't been back since."

I studied his face. He definitely didn't look like he was lying. Alex Marian wasn't a good liar.

He shifted on his feet and crossed his arms in front of his chest in a defensive posture. It made his arm muscles pop. "Will you tell me why you think we met and why you're mad at me for not remembering?"

I blinked at him. "We did meet. I picked you up in the bar and asked you to come back to my room. You agreed. And when I came out of the men's room, you were leaving with another man."

Alex's eyes widened as I told the tale. "But it wasn't me. I promise. Three years ago, I was here. Scoping out property and starting renovations."

"I know it was you because I looked down at the receipt on the bar, and the last name on the signature was Marian," I told him, frustration bubbling through my voice.

He jerked back. "But that can't be! I... shit. Oh, fucking fuck. Hold on." He held up his finger and pulled his phone out of his back pocket with his other hand, scrolling until he found what he wanted and then pressing a button.

"Pick up, asshole," Alex mumbled. After a moment, he snapped into the phone, "You'd better check this voicemail and call me the fuck back. Tell me you were in Amsterdam three years ago and why the fuck you would have blown off the world's hottest man." Then he repeated for good measure, "You asshole."

He ended the call and scrolled through his phone for another moment as if looking for something else.

I felt a glimmer of hope I'd gotten it wrong. "Are you a twin?"

Alex shook his head. "No, but I have a cousin in South Carolina who looks a lot like me. His name is Jett Marian. Here." He shoved the phone in front of me.

I stared at the picture of five guys at the beach who all appeared to be in their late teens and early twenties. Only two of them looked related, and sure enough, they looked nearly identical.

Except I could tell right away which one was Alex.

"Fuck," I said, staring at the photo.

"Jett is..." He blew out a breath. "Let's just say he likes to sleep around. He's a lover of love. Well, maybe it's more accurate to say he's a lover of sex. I'm not sure if there's a psychological component to it or if he's just sowing oats, but we're nothing alike. Don't get me wrong. I love him. Mostly. He's great fun, and he makes a killer teammate for beach volleyball, but when it comes to guys... Let's just say we're complete opposites."

I glanced from the photo to his face as I handed the phone back. "How do you mean?"

Alex scraped his lip with his teeth as if unsure how or whether to answer. Finally, he weaved a little on his feet and said, "Jett's had all the sex. I've had none. So, you see? Opposites. And that's how you know it wasn't me in Amsterdam."

Even in the dim light, I could see the red on his cheeks. He was flustered and embarrassed at making the confession, which was crazy. If only he knew how much it had turned me the fuck on.

But it also reminded me of just how much younger he was.

"S-so, anyway," he murmured. "Just wanted to clear that up. You can go back to Monroe now."

He turned away, toward the SERA parking lot.

"Wait," I growled. "You're not driving."

He shook his head. "Was thinking I'd sleep it off in the SERA instructor lounge and then drive home whenever I wake up. If I ask someone in my family to run me home, I'll never hear the end of it."

"I'll drive you," I said. "You can catch a ride out here tomorrow to pick up your car."

Alex's eyes pinned mine as if looking for a catch. "Why?"

"Because I owe you an apology for being an ass when we first met."

He stuck his chin up, and it was so fucking adorable I wanted to laugh. "So give me one."

"One what?" I said, just to provoke him.

He stepped forward and poked me in the sternum with an index finger. "Apology, asshole."

I grabbed his hand and used it to pull him toward the parking lot, where my vehicle was. "You like calling people that, don't you?"

"Only when they deserve it." As we walked, he looked down at our joined hands. "Your hand is warm."

"You cold?"

He shrugged. "A little. I meant to grab a fleece, but it was so warm this afternoon, I fell prey to the Montana weather trick."

I laughed. "What's that?"

"Back home, if it's eighty during the day, there's no chance it gets down to forty at night. Montana... not so. It's a trick."

When we arrived at my truck, I opened the passenger door and let him in. He glanced at me with a funny look on his face. "You didn't need to do that. I'm not a child, you know."

"Yeah, because adults have to remind people of that fact."

I walked around the truck and got into the driver's side before turning to look at him.

"I'm sorry," I said, trying to meet his eyes.

He shrugged. "I get it. You're old, so you make age jokes."

I barked out a laugh that made him jump and his eyes go wide.

"I wasn't apologizing for the joke. And I'm not old. I'm forty, for fuck's sake."

The edge of his lips curled up. "And you think that's young? Cute. No, no, it is. It's adorable."

I reached out and took his chin between my thumb and forefinger. "I'm sorry I blamed you for something your cousin did. That wasn't fair. Instead of assuming it was you, I should have asked." I couldn't help but add, "But young people make mistakes, so you should forgive me."

He burst out laughing, and the sight made my pulse quicken. "You know who mixes up people? Old guys, that's who."

I leaned back between the seats to grab a Legacy FD fleece and heard Alex suck in a breath. Suddenly, I realized how close our faces were.

But I also smelled the beer on his breath and remembered he wasn't sober. And he was a virgin. *Fuck.*

"Here," I said softly, handing him the fleece. "Put this on."

He shivered and did as I said with a murmured thanks.

I put the truck into Drive and pulled out of the lot. Silence sat heavy and full between us for a few minutes. The highway was dark and still, and the night air whistled through the small open gap in my window.

Alex tilted his head back and closed his eyes. I thought he was going to drift off, but then he spoke. "If you'd invited me back to your room in Amsterdam... or anywhere else... I would have gone. There's no man on Earth who could've changed my mind."

It took all of my self-control to resist his implication. To drive the man back to his place and pull away.

But I did it. Because even if Alex hadn't been the Marian who blew me off in Amsterdam, he was still too young, too inexperienced, and too under the influence.

It made way more sense for me to head back to SERA and seek out Monroe for a night of fun. But I didn't do that either. Instead, I went home and got in the shower to wash off the smoke smell.

And jack myself off to the memory of Alex Marian saying he would have given himself to me without question.

11

ALEX

IndexEcho: *Sorry I was MIA for a couple of days. Food poisoning.*

DrunkenPoet: *Should I send you photos of my meatloaf?*

IndexEcho: *If only that was a euphemism for something much better.*

I'D DONE everything in my power to send Chief Kincaid the message that I was into him. I'd even cleared up the misunderstanding about a previous meeting. And still... rejection.

Not gonna lie, it stung like a bitch. But I was a grown man, and I could take it.

But I was sick and tired of being rejected. And yes, I realized I wasn't actively rejected by *IndexEcho*. Chances were high that he was killed. Regardless, it was time to move on. Watching Monroe flirt with Kincaid reminded me that I would've appreciated being on the receiving end of that attention, and my sister had even tried to make that happen for me earlier in the summer.

"Can I find a hookup in Billings, or do I have to use an app?" I asked my cousin Lennon while helping him load feed into his truck at Palmer's Feed and Seed on the edge of town.

Lennon glanced up at me like a deer in headlights. "How would I know?"

I rolled my eyes. "Listen. You can play recluse monk to the rest of the family, but I know you hook up. What I don't know is how or where."

He grunted and went back to the stack of feedbags on the pallet. "In summer, it's easy since the tourists are here. In winter... it depends. You either find someone local like Nate Lewis, who's usually up for a quick fuck with no strings, or you head to Billings, Bozeman, or Missoula. I usually need something from Costco anyway, so I kill two birds."

I squinted at him. "That's your idea of a Costco run? Bulk laundry detergent and a quick beej?"

He shrugged. "Honestly, if you want to stay in Legacy, there's usually someone up for it at SERA. I just don't like to fuck around with Trace's guys too much in case people start talking."

"And since you need ten pounds of almonds and a three-pack of mustard, might as well, right?"

The edge of his lip quirked up a little in his version of a wide smile. "Convenience comes in many forms, Alex. Don't knock it."

I watched him load the truck with his broad shoulders and big arms under a wash-faded cotton tee with a barely visible "Legacy Beef" logo on the back. My cousin was a catch. Fit and good-looking, an all-American rancher. Son of a famous country music star —though that part he kept as close to the vest as possible. It was one of the reasons he'd moved to Montana. To hide out on his ranch and work.

"Why don't you date?" I asked.

He shrugged. "Don't have the time."

"Bullshit. You're a multimillionaire. You could hire people to take some of that load off you in a minute. Tell me the real reason."

He didn't take his eyes off the bags of feed as he started a new stack in the bed of the pickup. "One too many people more interested in who my papa is than who I am."

"Fair," I said on a sigh. "I'm sorry for that. It's bullshit."

He shrugged again, but I could tell it was more serious than he let on. His older brother, Wolfe, didn't date either, but we were all convinced it was for a different reason. Wolfe had been obsessed with his dad's best friend, Trace, who also happened to be here in Legacy, for as long as anyone could remember.

"So back to hookups," I said. "Can I find someone without the apps?"

Another shrug. "If you go to Billings and try to do it old-school, just remember what Uncle Beau says. You get what you get, and you don't pitch a fit." Then he looked over at me and winked. "Or stay local. It's still tourist season enough. Just try and find someone who's only in town for the night so if it sucks, you don't have to see the guy the next day at Timber."

I groaned. "I hadn't thought of that. Fuck. I think I'll try Billings."

"Why don't you let Ella fix you up? There's a guy at work she's always talking about. She knows a lot of the guys at SERA, too."

"No, thanks. I don't need my sister in my sexual business."

Of course, Morris Watt walked by right as I said that. His bushy eyebrows lifted and dropped. "Mornin', Mr. Watt," I called, trying not to act guilty.

As soon as he got into his old truck and lumbered out of the lot, Lennon chuckled softly. "You act like you're not allowed to have sex. You're a grown-ass man, Alex. And you can't seriously tell me you haven't had sex in the three years you've lived here."

Okay, so maybe I was more of a liar than I thought.

"No, pfft. Of course not. I just... You know. Various other... like... that time we went back to California for Christmas. Or, um, when we have... tourist visitors or whatever. You know? So." Now it was my turn to shrug. Like it was no big deal. Like I was some kind of playboy.

Like I was Jett Marian.

Lennon nodded. "'S no different. Just find someone and make it happen. No big."

Except... it was big. It was definitely big.

Two weeks later, I came across an excuse to travel up to Billings. A band I liked was playing live music at the Palomino, so I booked a hotel room close by and dressed as slutty as gay Montana could handle in a town known for its huge-ass refinery.

There were plenty of guys looking for connections, but I was way too nervous and definitely too sober when I first walked in. My plan was to catch a little buzz, listen to some music, and then get my flirt on in hopes of finding someone who wanted to kiss and grope a little in the bathroom or out back. Wasn't sure I was exactly up for bringing anyone back to my hotel room, but I also knew that the chances of me not coming the minute another man glanced at my dick were slim to none.

"Hey, cutie, what can I getcha?" a bartender asked when it was my turn to order a drink. He was younger than I was, with two long braids twisted into buns on top of his head like panda ears. "We're running two for one on Bud Light, or I've got a great local IPA...?"

"Vodka cranberry, please," I said, flashing him a smile. "Thanks."

He nodded and got to work as I turned to take in the scene. It was a decent crowd for a bar in Billings, but it was definitely not like going to a bar in San Francisco or Davis. Many of the people in the casino area looked like they might have come from a long day at the refinery, and others looked like they'd been holding down their vinyl stool since the building had been erected early in the previous century.

But there were quite a few guys giving me a quick up-down, so I flashed my smile early and often.

"You okay, there, buddy?" the bartender asked, setting a refill down in front of me.

"Yeah, why?"

"You just seem... Never mind."

The guy next to me leaned over and chuckled. "Little awkward. Boy, you wanna suck a dick, just lick your lips at someone. They'll get the hint. Believe me."

I... didn't want to suck some random stranger's dick in a gay bar in Billings. "What if I just want to make out on the dance floor a little?" I joked back.

The bartender and the guy next to me roared with laughter. "That's a good one. Maybe the band knows Elvis's 'Love Me Tender,' and you can even slow dance with your sweetheart."

Okay, I was in over my head. The whole thing left a bad taste in my mouth, but at least I wasn't desperate enough to have an even worse bad taste in my mouth.

Thankfully, the band was on fire, and I was able to relax and enjoy it once I stopped assessing everyone who came through the door as a potential hookup. How Lennon had ever found anyone here for a quick connection was beyond me.

Maybe I was being too picky or too snobby. Hell, I was definitely too scared, and I was using everything else as an excuse. It didn't really matter in the end because the flirty bartender ended up being good company, and enough people started dancing that I was able to join and let loose a little.

Unfortunately, no one non-intimidating seemed interested. Plenty of guys tried to get me out back, but none of them seemed to want a little kissing and heavy petting.

Maybe the barfly was right. I was a little old lady whose idea of getting to first base was way too antiquated for a gay bar in Billings.

Before getting back on the road the next day, I went ahead and swung by Costco to get a few things I couldn't get in Legacy. My plan was to pick up a bulk container of nuts for Lennon as a joke and shop the big-screen televisions, even though mine was already plenty big. But as soon as I opened my car door, I almost took out the man getting out of his truck beside me.

"Oh shit," I blurted. "Sorr..." My voice trailed off as I realized it was Judd Kincaid.

His eyebrows lifted. "Alex? What're you doing here?"

My face heated. "Um. Nuts? And stuff."

He hesitated as if unsure how to take that. I didn't blame him. So I added more. "Also, I was here in town to see a band play last night. At a bar. Palomino."

"Ah. Was it good?"

I nodded. "Yeah. I had a good time. Drank and danced a little. You know."

How long had it been since I'd felt this awkward?

"Good," he said. "That... sounds good. Glad you had a chance to relax."

Suddenly, I had a horrible thought. "Wait. Are you in Billings for a Costco run or a... *a Costco run*?"

Kincaid looked at me for a beat. "I... don't understand. I'm here to get food. For the station house."

And now I was on fire. "Of course! Well, I'd better go in. My plan was to get back in time to be at Timber for the dinner shift."

He nodded. "Sure. Same. Er, well, I need to be back in time to make dinner for the crew. I promised to bring rotisserie chicken and a big cake."

We started making our way toward the entrance, still speaking as awkwardly as if we were two fourteen-year-olds introduced by our parents and told to "make friends."

When we got to the giant trolleys, I grabbed one and glanced up at him in question, as if asking if the plan was to go our separate ways or shop together. He nodded and followed along, as if that somehow gave me a clear answer.

"Tell me about the band," he said after we showed our membership cards to the greeter. "I gotta say, I'm surprised you drove all the way up here to listen to music. Why not offer to have the band play at Timber instead?"

"Uh, because bands like to be paid for their work?" I said with a small laugh. "And since I'm still paying back my startup and renovation loans, there's not a lot of extra money for fancy shit like live music."

He looked surprised. "Oh, I thought... well, it doesn't matter what I thought."

It did to me. It mattered a whole lot what he thought. "You can't just leave that hanging there. Tell me."

Judd threaded fingers through his hair. It was unusual to see him less than confident. "Sorry. I just heard you came from money. It wasn't fair of me to make assumptions."

I felt the familiar mix of embarrassment and self-consciousness creep up, and I struggled to shut them down. "You aren't wrong. But I didn't accept my family's help when opening Timber. It was a source of many fights, actually. My parents weren't happy about it."

That was an understatement. When my uncle Jude tried to release my trust fund early, I refused that, too.

"Why didn't you accept their help?"

It seemed a personal conversation to be having next to the Tupperware sets and mini Keurigs, but I decided to go ahead since the chances of anyone around us knowing who I was were slim.

"Lots of reasons. First, I guess because I wanted to prove to myself and to them that I could succeed on my own. A lot of restaurants fail in the first few years, and I knew that pressure would light a fire under my ass." I shot him a sideways glance. "Not literally."

He snorted.

"And then also because... my dads own a vineyard, and they wanted me to take over. So when I left Napa to do something different, something for me, I felt guilty. I didn't want to ask them to help finance my abandonment, so to speak."

Kincaid stopped and turned to face me with an odd expression. "Really? I had a friend in a similar situation. How did your parents take it?"

"They tried to be supportive—and don't get me wrong, they have been—but I could see my dads' disappointment. The vineyard's been in our family for a long time, and neither of my sisters is interested in running it either. There's a cousin who's working there now who might end up getting the bug, but I don't know."

"You still feel guilty." Kincaid's hands looked huge, grabbing bags of apples and palming whole melons.

I shrugged as I reached for a large container of grapes. "My feelings on the topic are... complicated. Oh, hey, look, fire extinguishers! My local fire chief probably wants me to buy five hundred of these. Zip-tie them to every available surface just in case."

"He sounds like someone who cares about the safety of the people around him," he said with a firm nod.

"He sounds like a stickler for the rules."

"Rules save lives, Marian. Don't forget that."

We moved from the produce to the milk as Kincaid continued loading up the cart. "I didn't mean to pry about your family," he said after a few minutes of silence.

"It's not that. I just... don't know what to say. I do feel guilty. They don't want me to feel guilty. But you can't just tell yourself how to feel or not feel. And I'm learning I don't let things go very easily," I confessed.

I felt his stare on the side of my face as I leaned in to get a giant block of American cheese slices I didn't need.

"What else can't you let go of?" His voice was deep and steady, like the man he seemed to be. Judd Kincaid carried a kind of commanding authority I couldn't deny. It made me want to do exactly as he said. No matter what he said.

"You," I said, laying it out there. "I can't stop trying to figure you out. One minute, you seem interested, and the next, you're not. I wish I didn't give a shit, but there it is."

Kincaid was silent for a long moment. Then he blew out a breath and said, "My feelings on the topic are... complicated."

The way he threw my own words back at me almost made me smile. But I wasn't interested in complicated. And I sure as shit wasn't up for another rejection after last night.

"No problem! I'm not looking for complicated, so don't worry about it."

He lifted an eyebrow. "What are you looking for, exactly?"

"Someone to kiss," I said like a school marm with a secret stash of Harlequin romances under her twin bed.

The edge of his lip quirked up, and his eyes brightened with curiosity and amusement. "To kiss?"

I nodded. "And believe it or not, that's hard to find in this town. Everyone just wanted me to suck..." I glanced around guiltily. "Stuff," I finished lamely.

His smile disappeared. "I thought you hadn't done that before."

"I haven't. Which is why I wasn't interested. But the guy I actually want to kiss blew me off. And not in the way you're thinking."

"Who?"

I rolled my eyes and reached for a big box of dog biscuits. My cousin Tommy's boyfriend had the most amazing hound dog. Chickie would probably love me forever if I brought her ten pounds of excess calories.

"If you're asking me that question, Chief, you definitely haven't been paying attention."

"Wait. What did you mean when you asked if I was doing a *Costco run*? Is that code for something?"

I flapped a hand in the air. "You're too old to get it. Don't worry about it."

He grunted.

"I'm thinking of letting Ella set me up with a guy she knows from work. She was going to set me up with Monroe, but I guess you beat me to the punch there."

"Hey. I didn't do anything with Monroe. Remember? I drove *you* home that night, not him."

"Yes, Chief," I murmured. "I remember." In fact, I had his fleece in my car. Thank god he hadn't caught me in it.

He threw a giant vat of olive oil into the cart before reaching for the spaghetti sauce. "It's complicated because I'm older than you are."

"Ah, yes. You're in your fifties, yes?"

"Shut the hell up. You know I'm forty."

"I only know it because you were trying to tell me how not-old you were," I reminded him.

"And you're part of a current permit suspension," he continued.

I nodded. "Practically a hardened criminal. Bad for your reputation. I get it." I pointed to the cart. "You probably want the spaghetti noodles to go with all that sauce."

He grunted again and grabbed for the noodle boxes. "And I…" He closed his mouth, clenched his jaw, and admitted, "I still have feelings for my ex."

This was news to me. "You have an ex?" What was I saying? Of course he had an ex. The man was forty years old. "Who? Why'd you break up? What happened?"

He didn't answer the questions I peppered at him. Instead, he said, "So maybe that explains a few things, okay?"

Not okay. I wanted all of the details. "Was it Kaidee?"

"No. I already told you we're just friends."

"Was it a woman?"

His eyes were stormy, not with annoyance but *sadness*, his jaw still clenched so tight I felt a moment of genuine concern for his molars. "I'm not talking about it with you."

I reached for his arm and stopped his forward motion. He blew out a breath of frustration like he was expecting me to ask more questions. Instead, I simply said, "I'm sorry."

"Me too. Anyway, now you know why the mixed signals."

We started walking together again down the next aisle. "Have you hooked up since your breakup? You said you tried to pick up my cousin. Was that before or after? Before, right?"

He shook his head.

"After?" I asked in surprise. "Your breakup was a long time ago."

"Yes, I've been with other people since. But only for sex."

I couldn't believe we were having this conversation in Costco, next to an industrial-sized box of granola bars. "Then why... why can't we..." I couldn't get the question out because it would put me right in the crosshairs for another rejection.

"You're looking for more than that. You've been saving yourself for someone special, and I'm not him." Kincaid's long legs stalked down the aisle, pushing the cart so hard it nearly took out a display of early bird Halloween candy before he yanked it back on track.

This was so fucking frustrating.

I rushed to catch up with him. "It's not like that. I was a late bloomer, okay? And then I was busy getting multiple degrees while also working full-time. It wasn't that I didn't want to screw around; I just didn't have the time. And then..."

Kincaid lifted an eyebrow without slowing down. "And then?"

I blew out a breath and dodged around some clearance patio furniture. "And then I was into someone. Someone I did wait for. But he... disappeared, so."

I deliberately avoided telling him the man had died since the snack foods aisle didn't pair well with awkward and morbid declarations.

"So here you are?"

"Here I am. Ready. Beyond ready. I just..." I glanced around to make sure no one was listening. "I didn't exactly want to give it up to a random guy in a bar bathroom, you know?"

He slowed, finally, as we reached the toiletry aisle. "I'm glad you didn't. That shit can be dangerous."

"You should take me on," I blurted. "Show me the ropes. Like a teacher."

As I spoke, Kincaid's eyebrows shot up. "Like a teacher?" he asked in disbelief. "A... sex teacher?"

I thought about the best way to play this. "Well, not everyone's cut out for teaching, and you did say you were kind of old…"

His eyes narrowed. "Don't reverse-psychology me."

I shrugged. "Maybe it's for the best. You seem very dom-toppy, and I'm more of a bottom. At least, I think. You probably wouldn't be the best teacher in my case. I've read that bossy tops can be insensitive or oblivious. Not the most patient. And I don't want to be rushed or pressured."

"I would never rush or pressure you," he ground out, in a voice low and fierce as if forcing himself to stay calm and not throw me across the toothpaste aisle.

I shrugged. "We'll never know. I'll have to find someone else. Would Monroe be patient, do you think?"

Instead of waiting for his response, I turned around to search for lube.

12

———————

KINCAID

IndexEcho: *If you had to save one sentimental thing from a burning building, what would it be?*

DrunkenPoet: *I have a wine key that's been in my family for generations. It means a lot to my dad and his uncle before him. Over the years it's come to represent family and home.*

———————

EVERYONE KNEW a Costco run made you pick up things you didn't need.

Never in a million years did I think it would be a mouthy virgin who would tempt me the most. But this wasn't my first trip to Costco, and I knew better.

"Fine. See what Monroe can teach you," I said, retaining my patience by the thinnest filament. "He seems like a nice guy."

Alex tried hard to hide his annoyance, but the tips of his ears stayed hot. "Sounds like a plan. If that doesn't work, I'll head back here to the Palomino and give it another shot. Maybe I just wasn't drunk enough."

Even though I knew he was only talking like that to provoke me, it worked.

I was provoked.

Hardcore provoked.

"Maybe," I said, trying to keep hold of my temper.

"Anyway, I'm going to stock up on condoms and lube just in case Monroe is into it. Or maybe the guy Ella works with." He shrugged. "I'll have to ask her if she has pics of the work guy."

Instead of responding, I focused on throwing a giant bottle of bodywash into the cart for the station house shower and grabbing a bulk pack of toothbrushes and mini toothpastes. For the amount of attention I was paying, I was lucky I didn't accidentally wind up with hearing aids and diapers by mistake.

Alex Marian was a grown man. He was plenty old enough to be fucking around with whoever he wanted. I had done some risky shit myself in the past, so I sure as shit wasn't in a position to judge.

Even if it was massively stupid.

We made our way toward the checkout counters, only slowing down enough for Alex to make a big production about whether or not he needed the multipack of smoke detectors on special near the front.

"Can never have too many when you're prone to setting shit on fire," I stated.

His playful grin turned into a glare. I separated my things from his and checked out, finding a giant box to put everything in. When he was done, we moved out of the store toward our vehicles.

"Guess I'll see you back in Legacy," he said after loading his things in the back of the car.

I closed the tailgate on the truck and turned to him. The

teasing bravado had disappeared, leaving him looking a little sullen.

Even though I knew better, I stepped forward. Call it Costco-induced insanity, but I didn't want this man to go home without getting the kiss he both wanted and deserved.

So I reached behind his head and pulled him in.

It was supposed to be quick—enough of a kiss to check the box on his wish list but not enough to get our picture on the internet for Montanans Behaving Badly. But within seconds of having his mouth under mine, I forgot all about any of that. The only thing in my head was the need for more.

The little noise of surprise he'd made when I grabbed him. The whimper of surrender when I deepened the kiss. The tight clench of his hand in the front of my shirt.

Alex was the spark, and I was tinder doused in kerosene.

Unfortunately, I saw our cart start rolling away out of the corner of my eye, and I had to lunge after it to keep it from careening into an older couple.

"Sir, ma'am," I said with a nod. "Sorry 'bout that."

The woman's eyes lit up. "Hank once accidentally fell into the Yellowstone River while kissing me, didn't you, dear?"

His grumble was unintelligible, but his hand tightened in his wife's grip, and the hint of a smile appeared as they continued into the store.

When I turned back, Alex was still standing where I'd left him, staring at me.

I tilted my head at him and grinned. "Close your mouth, Fire-bug. It's still yellow jacket season."

"You... kissed me." He blinked, and damn if he didn't look fucking edible. "After all your bullshit about Monroe."

I stepped back into his personal space. "Seemed a little unfair for you to come all this way for a... *Costco run*... and go home empty-handed."

Alex's breathing quickened. "You do know Costco is known for selling things in bulk, right? You can't get just one of anything."

I leaned in and brushed my nose against his, then got even closer and dragged it along the apple of his cheek. "You have too much of a good thing at once, and you wind up spoiled, Marian," I murmured before kissing him on his earlobe. "Be safe."

And then I got into my truck and learned just how hard it was to drive with a rock-hard cock down I-90. The damned thing didn't go down until I made the turn off to Highway 212.

Thankfully, when I got back to the station house, Javier Sujo was making fart noises and being a giant fucking clown, so I quickly lost whatever interest in men I had left.

Until, of course, I got home later that night and... once again... fell asleep sated and relaxed after jacking myself off to the memory of touching Alex Marian.

Unfortunately, I was awakened only an hour later by a wildfire alert.

The shriek of the pager yanked me out of sleep like a cattle prod. For a moment, I didn't know where I was—my rental cabin, the woods pressing in, the fan still whirring against the late-summer heat. Then the dispatcher's voice came through, clipped and calm:

"Legacy Fire, respond to a reported wildland fire. Smoke showing, southeast ridge of Slingshot Mountain, near mile marker fourteen on Olivado Loop. Ten plus acres, heavy brush. Initial attack requested."

Fuck.

I was on my feet before she'd finished. Pants, boots, Nomex shirt. Radio clipped to my belt, flashlight jammed in my pocket. I was already moving for the truck by the time the second tone went out for county mutual aid.

Wildland start. Not a structure, not a dumpster, not a bar-top flare-up from some adorable asshole playing with Bacardi. This was the real thing. A live fire chewing its way through bone-dry fuel in the middle of a high-wind watch. The kind of call that made your stomach knot before you even laid eyes on the smoke column.

My job wasn't supposed to be crawling around in the brush anymore. Chief meant command, coordination, paperwork, politics. But in a town like Legacy, the fire chief didn't stay behind a desk when the mountain lit up. Until DNRC or the Forest Service rolled up, the fire was mine.

I keyed my mic as I threw the truck into gear. "Legacy Incident Command en route. Show me taking command until relieved."

Static, then the response. "Copy, Chief. Legacy IC established."

I got on the radio to my crew and barked commands. Headlights carved the road in front of me, trees flashing by as the scent of smoke found its way through the vents. My pulse kicked harder. Even small fires here could turn into something ugly in minutes.

I thought about the crew—McMasters and Pope suiting up back at the station, Sujo dragging the brush truck out of the bay half-dressed. Good firefighters. But young and eager to prove themselves. They'd throw themselves directly into the flames if they thought it would put out the fire, and that meant I damn well better keep my head clear.

Up ahead, an orange glow pulsed against the dark ridgeline. The sight made my throat go tight.

I'd been on plenty of ugly calls in Philly—warehouse infernos, tenements with stairwells like chimneys, nights that stank of smoke for a week after. But I'd never been the one holding the line. The guy whose decisions meant the difference between contained and goddamned catastrophe.

There were already a few volunteers on scene when I rolled up, doing their damnedest with a couple of shovels, a backpack pump, and the skid unit off someone's ranch truck. Not nearly enough equipment, but plenty of heart. They'd managed to slow the head of the fire, keep it from racing up the slope, but it was still chewing through cheatgrass hungrily.

I threw on the rest of my gear, grabbed my radio, and slid into incident command. First step was size up: quarter acre, wind pushing it north, fuel mostly grass and scrub. Manageable if we got on it hard, a disaster if we didn't.

My crew came in fast—brush truck, lights bouncing off the pines. Relief hit as I recognized the crew was already in top form. McMasters pulling line, Pope spinning up the pump, Sujo wrangling the volunteers.

"Anchor on the black, work the flank, watch your spacing," I called, pointing them into place. They moved without hesitation, trusting me to keep the bigger picture in mind while they kept the nozzles and Pulaskis moving.

Several SERA firefighters showed up to help, along with a Forest Service crew, and we fought it together—foot by foot, hour by hour. Dig, spray, mop, repeat. The glow shrank. The smoke thinned. Every time I thought the bastard was out, another hot spot flared, and we were back at it, stomping embers, soaking roots.

By the time dawn painted the ridge pale gray, the fire was finally boxed in. It wasn't heroic or pretty. Just a long, bone-deep grind until the flames had nowhere left to go.

It was long and hot, relentless but manageable. And when it was done, I felt exhausted but satisfied. I could tell my crew felt the same way.

"We hit it hard, held the line, and nobody got hurt. That's the job, and you did it damn well. Get home, get cleaned up. Legacy's safer today because of you."

Sujo's smile dimmed as he gestured to his eyebrow. "Chief, you're bleeding."

Pope moved to the truck to grab the first aid kit, but I waved her off. "Just got in the way of a branch, it's fine. I'll shower and clean it up at home."

Brody Mayes, the lead fire instructor at SERA who I'd met shortly after arriving in Legacy, shot me a wide grin. "Would never know this was one of your first ICs at a Montana wildland fire. Good job, Chief."

I rolled my eyes at him and grinned. "I'm just happy we weren't taking live fire at the same time."

The former Marine laughed and fist-bumped me before heading back to the SERA truck with the two students he'd brought.

I left everyone else to finish loading up the trucks and made my way home to my quiet rental house, noting the property could use a bit more of a fire break. While I loved living in the trees, I didn't want them close enough to light the cabin on fire.

After showering off the worst of the dirt, sweat, and blood, rehydrating and making sure my core body temperature had returned to normal, I tugged on a pair of pajama pants and slid between the cool sheets.

Hours later, someone banged loudly enough on my front door to wake me from a dead sleep. I grumbled my way to the door and threw it open, ready to bark my strong opinions at whichever one of my crew had decided to show up here.

But I didn't get the words out before I realized that someone was Alex Marian. And he was holding another cardboard box.

Thankfully, this one didn't seem to be on fire.

13

———

ALEX

IndexEcho: *I had a dream about you last night. Nothing inappropriate, just... us talking in person. Your voice was different than I imagined.*

DrunkenPoet: *Better or worse different?*

IndexEcho: *Soooo much better. I wanted to listen to it all night.*

———

WHEN I WOKE up and heard about the fire, I didn't think much of it. Unfortunately, brush fires were common around here in summer, and we'd had plenty of them. But then I'd overheard that the Legacy FD had been called in for the initial response and had stayed all night to contain it.

"Chief Kincaid was a beast," Kinsey Pope had told Sadie at the Pinecone when I'd stopped in for coffee and a muffin. She'd looked exhausted and proud, her hair still wet from a shower and her eyes bright with excitement. "Man's a good leader who gets right in there side by side with the crew. And he's strong as hell, hauling timber and equipment."

Sadie had winked at her. "Sounds like someone has a crush."

Kinsey had shaken her head and grinned. "Little hero worship, maybe. But no crush. Besides, I think he has a girlfriend."

I'd felt a little smug satisfaction knowing he didn't, but I hadn't been about to spill Kincaid's beans all over town. "Hey, Sadie, can I get the breakfast special to go along with two coffees and an extra cinnamon roll?"

And now, here I was, stupidly standing on the fire chief's front porch with breakfast in my hands when all the man probably wanted was some peace and quiet to catch up on sleep.

Well, fuck that. I was here, and his eggs were getting cold.

I banged my fist on the door again, and this time, I was rewarded. Except instead of seeing an angry Kincaid, I saw a bleeding Kincaid.

"What the hell happened to you?" I asked, shoving past him so I could put the box of food and coffees down. "No one said you were hurt."

"Because I'm not." His voice was sleep-graveled and rough. "What are you doing here?"

I pointed to the box while moving to the bathroom I could see across the open kitchen and living area. "You have a first aid kit in here?"

He poked through the box, pulling out one of the coffees. "Ah, I'm less annoyed now," he grumbled before taking a sip and groaning in pleasure.

I found Band-Aids and ointment in the cabinet below the sink and moved back out to the kitchen, where he was propped against the counter, cradling the coffee cup.

"You just here to rifle through my shit?" he asked, lifting an eyebrow.

He looked downright edible. Shirtless and wearing nothing but a faded pair of cotton pajama pants slung dangerously low on his hips. My brain skidded to a halt.

I took him all in. The broad chest peppered with crinkly hair that made my fingers itch. The patchwork of raised scars on his forearm I felt the strangest urge to kiss. The slightly padded belly I wanted to drag my lips down. The hint of pubic hair above the drawstring of his pajama pants.

I may have let out a gurgle.

"That right?" he asked, amusement clear in his voice.

I blinked at him. "You have blood crust on your face."

"Baby, you weren't lookin' at my face," he drawled before taking another sip of coffee.

Maybe I hadn't been, but I was now. His dark eyes danced, and his grin was wicked. I cleared my throat. "Sit. Let me clean you up and see what's going on. How'd you hit your head?"

He moved over to the kitchen table, but not before grabbing the to-go container with his breakfast platter in it. "It's only a scratch from a branch. I cleaned it last night in the shower."

I wetted a paper towel in the sink and then moved close to stand between his legs. When he tried to fork a bite of eggs around me, I swatted his hand away. "Stay still."

Kincaid dropped the fork and moved his hands to the backs of my thighs. That's when I realized my dick was very visible from his position. And it was misbehaving.

"Staying still," he murmured. Except he wasn't. Because his hands slowly moved up the backs of my thighs toward the crease of my ass.

Oxygen wasn't as plentiful at Kincaid's house as it was at mine, but I did my best to wash off the crusty remnants of dried blood before putting ointment on the nasty cut and bandaging it carefully.

Throughout the entire process, I felt his dark eyes on me and his warm hands on my legs.

"Er, thanks for... the fire," I began stupidly. "I mean... fighting the fire. Putting it out."

"It's my job."

"No, I know. But from what I heard, it was near the back of Lennon's ranch. It could have been really bad if you guys hadn't gotten it under control."

He moved his hands up, skimming them over my ass until they were curled around my hips. "You're welcome."

I stared at the clean bandage and the place where one of my hands was still brushing his hair back from his forehead. His hair was messy and wild, sticking up on one side. There was a pillow-case crease on his cheek.

"Sorry I woke you," I breathed, not moving an inch. If I moved, he'd take his hands off me.

"I'm not." He moved forward to rest his forehead on my chest. "Because Sadie makes the best hash browns ever."

I moved my hands into his hair, holding him against my chest for a beat. "The eggs are probably gross by now. But there's bacon. And I picked up a cinnamon roll in case you wanted something sweet."

Kincaid pulled back and met my eyes. "I do want something sweet."

Okay. I was in way over my head. "Well, um. It's... it's in that box, so let me go grab..." I moved out of his reach and escaped to the kitchen counter to grab the rest of the food I'd brought. The sound of his low chuckle followed me.

Kincaid dug into the breakfast I'd brought him and finished up the coffee while I took nervous sips of mine in the chair next to his.

"Are you going back to sleep?" I asked, then answered before he could. "Probably not with all that caffeine, sorry."

He shook his head. "I need to head to the station. And I appreciate you bringing me breakfast and coffee."

I felt suddenly awkward. Why had I come here? It wasn't to thank him. For fuck's sake, he was right. Fighting fires was his job. Was I going to thank him after every fire?

"I was worried," I admitted in a soft voice. My finger traced the whorls and lines of the wood grain in his kitchen table.

He moved his chair a little closer and put his hand on the side of my neck, moving my face with his thumb until I had to look at him. "Why?"

I pressed my lips together, trying to determine whether to confide in him or not. "I had a friend who was killed. He was a firefighter, too. I..." I blew out a breath. "I don't want to lose another friend." I stood and began gathering the breakfast trash. "Anyway, glad you enjoyed the food. I'd better head to work, too."

Kincaid reached for my wrist and then pulled me until I was straddling awkwardly over his lap. "Sit."

As soon as I let my weight settle, I felt the press of his hard cock under my ass. His eyes watched me. "I'm sorry about your friend."

I nodded and felt a little bit like crying. *IndexEcho* had been a good man. A kind soul. And I missed him dearly.

But I couldn't deny being nearly as overwhelmed by *this* man as I'd been by my online boyfriend. "Thanks."

"I want you, Alex," he said in a low voice. "But I meant what I said. I'm not looking for a relationship."

"Me neither," I said quickly, lying better than I ever had in my life. "Not at all. I just want some experience. Physical. Sexual, I mean." My cheeks ignited. "Obviously, that's what I mean."

He bit back a smile and rolled his hips so I could feel his cock was still hard beneath me. "Okay, so we're going to lay out some ground rules."

My eyes began blinking maniacally. Was this actually happening? "Yeah, 'course. Me too. Ground rules."

"First, we're going to take it slow. And you're going to tell me to stop when I do something that makes you feel uncomfortable."

I nodded. "That's not going to happen. What's next?"

"Second, our jobs come first. If one of us has to work, that's it. No questions asked. We both care a lot about our careers, and I need you to know where my priorities are. Okay?"

There was me, the bobblehead again. "Of course. Same. Timber means everything to me."

"This also means that my inspections of Timber continue per our agreement. You can still be annoyed as hell, but that doesn't change anything. My job is more important to me than you are, Marian. And I don't plan on putting myself at risk of being seen as influenceable if anyone catches wind of us fucking around. If anything, I want them to think us hooking up made me more of a hard-ass. Do you understand?"

Now, this one made me pause. "Are you going to be worse than you already are?" I asked incredulously. "Because you're hot, but not that hot."

He grabbed my face and pulled me in, crushing our mouths together in a hard kiss. Once again, I was powerless under the sheer intensity of his commanding presence. He owned that kiss. And me.

When he finally pulled back, I sucked in a heaving breath. "Yeah, okay."

Kincaid's bottom teeth pinched his upper lip to keep from laughing. "Good."

He leaned in and kissed me again, only this time, he started with my lips and moved across my cheek and down one side of my neck until his stubbled chin moved the collar of my shirt down. His warm tongue tipped into the little divot at the base of my throat.

"Last rule," he murmured against my skin.

"Yeah." My voice was breathy and strange.

"No Monroe." His voice was firm and the message clear. "If you're kissing me, you're not kissing anyone else. Do you understand?"

A bubble of incredulous laughter escaped. "There's not a long line of people waiting."

"Bullshit."

I shrugged. "No sense in arguing because I agree. But that rule goes both ways, Chief."

"Noted."

I reached out and flicked his bare nipple. "Say you agree."

"Ow," he said with a laugh, covering the injury. "You're a cruel negotiator."

I moved my hands to his shoulders and up into the back of his thick hair. "Oh, is this a negotiation? These are *negotiable* terms?"

His eyes were bright, and his cheeks were flushed. He looked downright edible. "Definitely not."

"Mm." I moved my hands around to cup his cheeks before meeting his eyes. "So when do my lessons start, Professor?"

"You haven't agreed to the rules yet."

"Yes I did!"

"Tell me it's just me until it's over. I'm really not good at sharing, Firebug."

His large hands moved up my back under my shirt, and my skin prickled with millions of goose bumps. "Yeah. Okay. Yeah."

The edge of his lips quirked up on one side. "I have to go into the station. And then I need a regular night's sleep. Come back tomorrow night. We can start then."

Somehow, there were enough vestiges of rational thought left in my brain to remember, "Tomorrow's Monday night. We're doing a big pizza-and-beer-flights thing for the football game. It's going to be too busy for me to—"

He cut me off. "Enough said. Work comes first. What about Tuesday night?"

I nodded with relief. I could make it to Tuesday night. No problem.

Except when Tuesday night rolled around, Kincaid was caught on the mountain on a training exercise. And then Wednesday night, I had a family thing.

It started to feel like by the time we both had another night free, I'd be the oldest virgin in the modern era.

And then the texts and stolen moments began.

14

———

KINCAID

———

I DIDN'T WANT to think about Alex Marian as often as I did, but he was damned near impossible to forget. So after two weeks of not being able to find a night alone, I broke.

I pulled into Timber's back lot and parked in the darkest corner. It was late, and I could hear music and crowd noise coming through the open kitchen door. It didn't seem like Timber's Friday night crowd was thinning anytime soon.

As soon as Alex appeared, I didn't waste any time. I yanked him behind the giant dumpster enclosure and kissed the fuck out of him.

We kissed like we were both starving, but all too soon, he was called away.

"Boss? You out here?" someone shouted.

Alex pulled back with a dazed expression on his face and whispered, "What?"

I used my thumb to wipe his bottom lip. "Call back that you'll be there in a minute," I said with a soft laugh.

"Be there in a minute!" he shouted, and then he leaned in to kiss me again, his eyelids still only half-open.

We would have lost track of time again if the radio hadn't squawked in my truck.

"Fuck, gotta go," I said, pushing him gently away while already counting down the minutes until I could see him again.

Two days later, he was the one who started it.

FIREBUG

I have to drive past your place on the way to deliver a catering order. You home?

Have to leave here in twenty. Make it quick.

He sped down my driveway twelve minutes later, and we spent another ten with our hands up each other's shirts and our mouths locked together.

"Fuck!" Alex barked, shoving me away. "This is the worst! I fucking hate this."

I stared at him for a beat, trying not to take it personally when

I realized he was talking about the stolen moments of time. Not the kiss.

"Give me a night and I'll block it off. I'll get someone to cover me, no matter what," I said without thinking. While work definitely came first, I didn't need to work *every* night. Or so I told myself.

Alex's hair was wild from where I'd had my hands in it. "You mean it?"

I blew out a breath. "Yeah. Tell me when."

Three nights later, I heard the crunch of gravel outside and hastily finished wiping down the counters. Not that I gave a shit what Alex Marian thought about my housekeeping skills. I simply liked a clean kitchen. Or so I insisted on telling myself.

When I opened the door, I couldn't help but stare. The weather had gotten colder, and Alex stood there in a heather-green sweater and faded jeans. Somehow, the green brought out the reddish tones in his hair and made his lips look rosy.

"Get in here." I yanked him in and immediately began kissing him, forgetting at first that we didn't need to rush. By the time I remembered, Alex's hands were on my ass, and I'd be damned if I was gonna do anything to stop him.

"Kiss lessons, check," he said against my mouth. "Ready to level up, Professor."

His hand moved to the front of my jeans, where my cock was already plenty leveled up. As soon as he pressed his palm against my length, I groaned into his mouth. "You're picking up skills like a pro," I teased.

"Fake it till you make it."

Alex's fingers moved along my length, testing the size and shape of my erection through the fabric until I was sure there was probably a wet spot on both my boxer briefs and my jeans.

"Hand jobs. Good place to start," I said breathlessly. "Open my jeans. Take me out."

He chuckled at my instructions. "Gee, thanks, Prof. Wouldn't have been able to figure out the steps."

"Five points off for mouthing the teacher."

The word choice landed between us and set us both off laughing. Alex grinned at me. "I was hoping that would be bonus points, not deducted ones."

"Mouthing *off*," I corrected. "I'm not working with a full set of brain cells right now."

When Alex looked down at the fly of my jeans, I caught a whiff of his shampoo, that same sweet and tart combo that had drawn my attention early on. Cherries, maybe. I ran my fingers through his hair to get more of it.

As soon as his warm hand clasped my dick, I sucked in a breath. "Jesus." I wasn't going to last. This was going to be laughable. How long had it been for me? At least since before I'd moved here.

Alex's free hand shoved my jeans and underwear down until I was bare enough for him to stare at me while he began stroking me. "Just like that," I murmured.

Honestly, he wasn't doing anything miraculous. It was simply the fact that it was him, *his* hand was warm and solid on my dick, that had me riding the edge.

Alex used his other hand to cup my balls, testing them in his palm before rolling and tugging them gently. "This okay?"

I gripped his jaw and pulled him in for a hard kiss. "Yes, dammit. Fuck."

The little noise he made as I put my tongue in his mouth made my cock weep. His thumb swiped over the tip and spread the slick precum over the cap.

"Wanna taste it," he said in a voice that sounded unsure.

"Baby, I'm about to blow right now just from your hand on me. If you—"

He dropped to his knees and licked across the head of my cock. It took all of my self-control not to come in his face. "Fuck! Alex. Fuck. You don't... oh fucking Christ. That... just like that."

"This okay?" he asked, pulling back after licking and sucking experimentally. I could tell he was asking truly, but I also knew he was well aware of how good he was making me feel.

I nodded frantically. "Whatever you want to do is okay. Whatever feels good."

One hand held on to my sac while the other held the base of my shaft. His mouth covered me again, and he took me deep enough to gag.

The sight of Alex Marian gagging on my cock was all it took. "Move," I warned, nudging him off.

He fell back on his heels as I tried to keep my release from hitting him. It was messy and fumbling, but my orgasm shot through me like liquid fire, racing through my nerves and lighting sparklers in my vision.

As soon as I finished, Alex moved my cum-filled hand away and leaned forward to take my cock into his mouth gently, licking and sucking as if recording everything in his memories.

He pulled off and stood up, leaning in to kiss me again. The salty taste of my release was on his tongue, and I explored it with my own. His hands moved around me to cup my ass.

"Wait here," I said, pulling back. "I need to clean up, then I want to make you feel as good as you just made me feel."

"Oh," he said, eyes wide. "No, that's... it's fine, I already, um..." His cheeks reddened, and his ears turned scarlet.

"Alexander Marian, did you get off just from sucking my cock?" I asked, relishing his discomfort. He was so damned adorable. Inexperienced and fresh.

Young.

"You should take it as a compliment," he said, wiggling his hips uncomfortably.

I nodded my head toward my bathroom. "Come on, you can clean up back here."

On the way to the bathroom, I considered how to play this. Theoretically, this was physical only. A chance for Alex to get a little sexual experience with someone trustworthy. And since we'd both already had an orgasm, that meant tonight's official reason for getting together was complete.

But... shit, we'd both gone out of our way to make time for this, and I kind of didn't want it to be over already.

It seemed Alex was having similar thoughts.

"I could cook you something," he said as I handed him a pair of clean joggers. "To be honest, I'm kind of starving. Today was crazy at work, and I barely had a chance to think, much less eat."

"What if all I have in the fridge is a carton of eggs and a left-over leaf of kale?"

He shrugged. "I'll make an omelette."

"What if it's an apple and a heel of old bread?"

His grin quirked up. "Apple crumble if you have sugar and cinnamon. If not, we might need to order in."

I led him to the kitchen. "You're in luck. I went shopping yesterday, so there's more than that in there. What are you in the mood for?"

Alex nudged me out of the way. "I offered to cook. Stand down, Chief."

I watched him move easily in my kitchen. "Don't set shit on fire," I grumbled. "That would be hell for my reputation."

His laugh was easy and sexy as fuck. It made my stomach clench with the desire to strip him down and continue our "lessons," preferably over the kitchen table or back of the sofa.

Instead, I sat on my hands and let him cook for me.

"Tell me about your life before Legacy," he said. "All I know is you're from Philly."

I nodded, wondering how much to tell him. Was this just a casual conversation, or was he interested in more than that?

"My parents died when I was young," I said, using language that was benign enough to keep from making things awkward. "So I ended up in the system." I watched Alex carefully in expectation of the face-dropping "aww" that most people did, but he schooled his face with the small exception of a divot of concern between his eyebrows.

I continued. "Mostly, I stayed at this group foster home I actually liked. But a couple of times, I was sent to live with foster parents. In one case, the lady I was placed with tried really hard to convince me I was part of her family. Which would have been good if I'd liked her or been happy there. But I didn't, and I wasn't. She has a son my age who was and still is a giant pain in my ass."

Alex looked up from dicing chicken breasts on a cutting board. "So what happened?"

"I graduated high school and joined the state fire academy in Lewiston. After I became a firefighter, I moved all over with my job. Eventually, I moved back to Philly for an assistant fire marshal role there. Somehow, she found out about it and started asking me for favors. Did I want to rent a room from her? Could I get her son a job? Stuff like that. Eventually, it escalated. Among other things, she added the guilt factor. 'You owe us,' and 'It's the least you can do after everything I did for you.' Needless to say, I wasn't interested in any of that."

"Shit, Judd. Did you call the cops? Get an order of protection or anything?"

I shook my head. "Nah. It didn't really reach the threshold for anything like that. Nothing threatening or harassing. Only annoying as fuck."

"But it was enough to make you move away?"

"That and a few other things. I was restless. The guy I told you about, my ex—"

"The one that got away?" he teased, gesturing for me to hand him the onion on the counter next to me.

I moved the onion over to him and got out another cutting board. "Yeah. I was, ah, having trouble moving on. I kind of threw myself into the hookup scene, which made it worse, in a way."

"How do you mean?"

I thought of *DrunkenPoet*, of his inherent sweetness and empathy. Of the way he asked about me and worried about me. Going back online after the accident to see dozens of messages from him escalating in panic and desperation.

AND THEN NOTHING. I could still see the old messages, but the username was gone. Instead, it indicated the messages had been written by a deleted user. His account had been closed and he was gone. Unreachable.

"There's a world of difference between being with someone to get off and being with someone you care about," I said.

It wasn't until I noticed his slightly flared nostrils and reddened cheeks that I realized how insensitive my words were. I opened my mouth to say something, but there was nothing to say. I couldn't tell him things were different with him, that I cared about him more than a casual fuck. Because I didn't want to.

I didn't want to care for Alex Marian at all. And I didn't want to send mixed messages.

"I get it," Alex said at length, and something in his tone—a hint of longing I recognized all too well—made me think he actually did understand.

As Alex got out a frying pan, I found myself thinking about *his* "one that got away." The guy he said had disappeared on him before they'd had a chance to do much together.

The fact that I almost wanted to find the guy and knock some sense into him suggested I wasn't doing nearly as well at not-caring about Alex as I wanted to believe.

I stayed quiet, and we made awkward small talk for the rest of the time it took him to make a simple chicken and rice dish.

"This is fucking incredible," I said in surprise after taking the first bite.

"Don't sound so shocked," he said with a laugh. "My uncle's a chef. I worked at his restaurant and learned from the best. I've been thinking I *might* even open my own restaurant one day." He winked, but I could tell he was a little hurt. *Again.*

"Sorry, that's not what I meant. It's not pizza. And I guess I think of you as a restaurant owner, not a chef."

He straightened the paper napkin in his lap before piercing me with a stare. "It's possible to be both things. You know, like fire chief and fire marshal."

"I apologized," I said, reaching over to squeeze his arm. "And I'll apologize again. I'm sorry."

Alex blew out a breath. "No, it's my fault for overreacting. I'm sensitive about it." He waved a hand. "Family shit."

I realized then that Alex hadn't changed the way he spoke to me about family after learning I'd had a shit one and then none at all. It was uncommon for people to be so comfortable with it. I almost asked him if he'd known someone in the system, but I held back.

Until I remembered Tavo.

"Tell me more about Tavo," I said.

And it was the exact wrong thing. Alex's body stiffened, and his eyes widened. "Why?"

"He in the system?"

Alex sat still for a beat like he was considering how to answer. And then he stood up and cleared his plate to the kitchen, rinsing it in the sink and setting it in the small dishwasher, where he'd already put the dishes he'd used making dinner. "Sorry, I have to head out. Thanks for the, uh, lesson."

I stood up and approached him carefully. "Alex, whatever I said—"

He turned a smile on me that would have been radiant if it hadn't been so damned fake. "Don't worry about it. I really do have to go. Besides, we're done here, right? Physical transaction. No emotions. And I told you I'm good with that."

He leaned in to drop a quick kiss on my cheek in the most platonic way possible. As if we were acquaintances and nothing more. Which, I guessed, was probably true...

Since that's what I'd done my damnedest to make clear to him.

"Yeah, uh. Okay," I said. "Thanks for dinner. It was amazing."

Within moments, he was gone. And I found myself staring at the empty doorway and the empty driveway beyond.

It was for the best, really. Because being with him had reminded me painfully of the man I'd lost. The one I still desperately wanted to find.

An hour later, when I couldn't get thoughts of either man out of my head, I dialed my friend Max.

"You remember how you said I owed you one, but we both know you owed me one instead?" I said after the pleasantries.

"He saves me one time from getting beaten up for borrowing Anthony Varrasso's headphones without his permission when I was fourteen," Max grumbled, complaining good-naturedly as usual. Which was fine since he would do just about anything for me, and I'd do just about anything for him, too.

I heard background noises like he was out with friends, but he hadn't hesitated to take my call, and even now, his voice turned serious as he asked, "What do you need, Judd?"

Ordinarily, I might have told him it was no big deal and to call me back later, but my mind was whirling. So instead of giving him an out, I continued. "You said you had a friend who was a private detective, right?"

"Few of them, actually. One was a detective on the force and retired early to go into the private sector. Then there's the woman he hired on. Frannie. She's a hoot and smart as shit. Also hot as fuck in bed. Oh, and remember that guy Buck we went to school with? He's with a security firm that does background checks and shit. Not hot in bed, though. What are you looking for?"

I hesitated. How far was I willing to go to find someone who didn't seem to want to be found?

Max knew what I was thinking without me saying a word. "This is about the forum guy, isn't it? Are you finally gonna take my advice and try and run him down?"

I blew out a breath. "I don't know. Might be nice to get closure."

That wasn't really true, and Max and I both knew it. What I really wanted was to find him.

"Alright, I'll send you the name of an investigator. But Judd..."

I steeled myself for the lecture about falling for a guy I'd met on the internet. He'd already given it to me once or twelve times before when I returned to Philly from Germany after the mortar attack that had cost me four months of my life... and my relation-ship with *DrunkenPoet*.

"You deserve better than someone who gave up on you that easily. You've been all over those forums for years now, making yourself as visible as possible. If he wanted to find you, it wouldn't be hard."

"It wasn't like that," I gritted out. "I told you already. We didn't have a defined relationship or any kind of understanding. I would never have expected him to wait four months for word from me. Wouldn't you have given up on someone after four months of no word?"

"If I didn't care about the guy? Sure. But I wouldn't have gone out of my way to avoid those forums for years, J."

Max's words weren't intentionally cruel. He was trying to help me move on in his no-bullshit way. But I knew *DrunkenPoet* hadn't moved on because he hadn't cared about me enough. I suspected he'd moved on because he *had*.

And that wasn't something I was willing to walk away from easily.

"Send me the name of the investigator," I said. "And go back to your friends."

"Okay, but now you really do owe me one, right?" he teased.

"Yes, Max. I owe you one."

I ended the call with a smile on my face. I may not have had a biological brother, but I was convinced Max Franco was even better than a real brother would have ever been.

And with his help, maybe I would finally find my *Drunken-Poet*... or put his memory to rest for good so I could move on.

15

ALEX

DrunkenPoet: *What if we meet and we don't click in person? What if this is all just fantasy?*

IndexEcho: *Then we'll have had something beautiful for however long it lasted. But I don't think that's going to happen.*

BELIEVE IT OR NOT, Kincaid's callous reminder that our arrangement was just physical and didn't mean anything to him was welcome. If there was no chance at feelings—and he'd told me straight up there weren't—then I needed to stop getting all gooey, let's-make-dinner-for-the-guy over Judd Kincaid.

I made my way back to the apartment and found Tavo playing *Grand Theft Auto* on PlayStation. Seeing him laughing and enjoying himself made me feel better about my abrupt departure from Kincaid's house. I'd vowed to protect Tavo, and that included well-meaning inquiries from the fire chief, even if they were just polite small talk.

And I hoped to hell it *had* only been a well-meaning inquiry because if Kincaid had used our closeness this evening to sniff around for information on Tavo for any other reason, I would lose my fucking mind.

"Hey, did you eat?" I asked as I set my keys and wallet on the table next to the door.

Tavo glanced at me over his shoulder before focusing back on the screen. "Yeah, Hot Pockets in the freezer. Some left if you want."

I stared at the back of his head. "You live above a restaurant with fresh pizza and calzones, and you microwaved that shit? Are you... I can't decide whether to throw you out right now or simply murder you in your sleep."

He laughed. "No offense, Alex, but your prices aren't as great as Beartooth Market's BOGO deals."

I moved to the fridge to pull out a pitcher of lemonade and pour myself a glass. "I've told you you can have whatever you want from Timber. Just tell them to put it on my tab."

"And I told you thank you, but I'm only going to take you up on it from time to time. Not every day. Besides, I have money. I can pay for my own food and shit."

I let it go. He was young, but he was still an adult. And he had a right to his pride, even if I did want to ease his burdens.

When he finished his current game and got up to stretch, I told him about the new barback I'd hired. "Cute kid named Drew," I said, wondering if Tavo would have any interest in meeting the guy. "He's new to Legacy. He and his mom moved here to take over his grandmother's craft shop. You know Dot's Doodads across the square on Windwalker? That's Drew's grandma."

"Yeah. Dot's place is great if you have the patience to dig

through stuff. Her grandson came here to help her, but he's working for you instead?"

"Just nights when the craft store's closed. But since he doesn't know anyone and he's around your age, I'd like you to meet him."

Tavo shrugged. "Sure."

"He does leather work. Belts and straps. Bridles and stuff. I thought I'd introduce him to Lennon, too, if he's looking for anything like that."

"Wonder if he knows about the farmer's market. Could try and sell his stuff there."

I eyed him. "Maybe you could drop by Dot's tomorrow. Introduce yourself and tell him about the market."

"Yeah, okay," he said, nodding. It was one of the things I liked about Tavo. His situation with the shitty judge hadn't destroyed his general confidence and willingness to meet people. I was sure it had done a number on his ability to trust potential romantic partners, but at least he was still able to make friends and live a fairly normal life here in Legacy.

After offering him a glass of lemonade, I sat down at the table and asked him how his day had gone.

"Mr. Peterson paid me to clean his woodshop. I ended up helping him haul some junk to the dump, too. He said I could come back to wash his truck tomorrow, and then his neighbor—Sanders, I think his name is—wants me to come to his place and help him move some furniture around. They're paying me twenty bucks an hour, so I'll take as much of that as they're willing to give."

While I hated that he couldn't have more as long as he was trying to lie low from the judge, I was impressed he'd gone out of his way to find paying work. Not that Tavo's work ethic had ever been in doubt. Even when he was at Marian House, he'd made a point to contribute with hard work.

"Good. But block off a weekday soon so we can take Lennon up on his offer for fly fishing. You can't spend time in Montana and not learn how to fish."

After talking for a little while longer, I headed to the bathroom and stripped down to take a shower before bed. The hot water cascaded down my body, relaxing muscles that had been tense since leaving Kincaid's place.

There's a world of difference between being with someone to get off and being with someone you care about.

I closed my eyes and let the water pound on my shoulders and back. If Kincaid was right, then what the hell was it like being with someone you cared about? Because our encounter had been fucking incredible. The memory of it made me hard again, which wasn't difficult these days. Lately, all I had to do was think of Judd Kincaid in his grumpy fire marshal mode, and my dick was on board.

I ached with the need to get close to someone, to have a true partner. Someone who cared about me and whom I could confide in. The pressure to succeed at Timber was immense, not because my family pressured me directly, but because I was very aware they were all watching. And I didn't want to let them down.

I came from a family full of beautiful, successful people. And it was nearly impossible not to compare myself to everyone else.

But I also came from a family full of beautiful, successful *relationships*. And it was nearly impossible not to want that for myself.

Once I was showered and dressed in a pair of sweats, I slid into bed and video-dialed my dads.

As soon as Papa's face came on the screen, I felt a familiar twinge of family and love. "My baby," he said, eyes crinkling with a smile. "You're damned near impossible to get a hold of these days. How are you?"

He was sitting at the desk in their bedroom with the dim but warm light of the bedside tables on and the usually neatly made bed a rumpled pile of sheets and blankets. In the background, I heard Dad shout, "Blue, dammit, this wet towel is disgusting! You're a pig."

Papa glanced over his shoulder. "Then based on what you did to me a little while ago, I'd say you're playing fast and loose with bestiality. Get in here, Tristan. Our beloved youngest child is on the phone."

"Gross," I said. "Can you please save me from the sex talk?"

I saw Dad walk into the room, dressed in an old UC Davis T-shirt and pajama pants with border collies on them. Papa had given him those pajama pants the Christmas after my childhood dog, Piper, had died, and it had made the entire family sob. A few minutes later, when Papa had brought out the new puppy, Papa had sheepishly admitted his plan hadn't been thought through very well.

Now, Lottie was curled up in the corner of their room on her cushy bed, only waiting for my parents to get into their bed before she'd inevitably jump up and wedge herself between them.

Dad leaned over Papa's shoulder after dropping a casual kiss on his ear. "Hey, sweetheart. You're a sight for sore eyes. How's the restaurant? Ella says you've been slammed at work."

I spent a little time catching them up on everything going on. They asked about Tavo, so I updated them on how well he was doing, too. Finally, I could tell Papa had something to say.

"Spit it out, Pop," I urged.

"How's your love life?"

Dad closed his eyes and sighed. "Blue, we talked about this."

Papa waved his hand at Dad. "Hush. I'm talking to my son."

Instead of being annoyed at Papa, Dad simply smiled and rolled his eyes before kissing the man again. On the cheek this time. Papa reached up and caressed Dad's face. "You're trying to distract me."

"Is it working?" Dad asked, turning to wink at me.

"Not yet. But maybe after I've finished my interrogation." He patted Dad's cheek and turned back to me. "Answer the question."

Between the two of them, Papa was known for being the nosy one. The Marians were a nosy people. Well, to be fair, it was mostly my great-great-aunt, and then all of my aunts and uncles. I would think it was a generation-skipping trait if my sisters hadn't been just like our great-great-aunt Tilly. Nosy as fuck.

"I hooked up with a guy tonight, as a matter of fact," I admitted. "But it's not serious. He's not relationship material."

Papa's eyes widened comically.

Dad moved around to kneel next to him at the desk, and this time, it was Dad who said, "Tell us everything. Who's the guy?"

"Is he hot?" Papa added with a mischievous grin. Dad elbowed him.

"He's hot," I admitted. "But grumpy sometimes. Also an asshole sometimes. But yeah. Hot."

Dad narrowed his eyes. "Don't date an asshole, Alex. You deserve better than that."

Papa nodded but didn't pile on.

"He's not that kind of asshole. He's more of a stickler for rules, that kind of thing."

Papa gasped. "You slept with the fire chief!"

My face flooded with heat, which was probably answer enough. "I didn't *sleep* with him, Jesus."

"He's a hundred and fifty years old!" Papa said.

Dad shook his head. "Blue, take a breath and remember where you're getting your information. Our oldest child takes after you."

"What does that mean?" Papa asked.

"She's a gasper," Dad said, raising his eyebrows to make his point. "And prone to exaggeration."

Papa gasped again. "He's the chief of... of fire, or whatever. Those guys have to be over forty, if not fifty!"

"He's forty," I said. "And I'm twenty-seven. It's hardly the kind of age gap people write salacious articles about. Besides, I told you we're not dating."

"No," Papa said. "He's only taking advantage of you for his nefarious purposes."

"I would *like* for someone to take advantage of me for nefarious purposes!" I said, if only to get him back for referring to his own sex life with my dad. "Don't make me regret telling you."

They both stopped and looked a little chagrinned. "Fair," Dad said. "But I thought that guy was your sworn enemy."

"He is," I admitted. Then I shrugged. "But he's also sexy as fuck."

Papa nodded knowingly. "Attracted to the bad boy. I can see it."

I laughed, and it felt good. "He's not a bad boy. He's honestly just doing his job. And I agreed to all the inspections. I just..."

"What, sweetheart?" Dad asked.

"I'd like to find someone to go out with. Ever since I left, I've been putting so much time and effort into getting Timber up and running. Now it's more steady, and I have a little bit of room to breathe. It'd be nice to find someone to spend time with outside of work."

The two of them exchanged a knowing glance. "It's about time," Papa said. "You should let Ella set you up. She said there's a very nice guy at work she's been dying to introduce you to, and Hazel agrees he's a good one. She apparently recruited him out of Silicon Valley."

I thought about Judd, about watching him fall apart with my mouth wrapped around his cock, about the way he'd gently threaded his fingers through my hair and locked eyes with me. About the way he'd grabbed me the minute I'd walked in his front door and kissed me for ages, until I was the one who took it a step further.

If he was only into me for a physical transaction, why did he go out of his way to meet me several times just for kissing? The man could have any number of people over for a quick fuck at the drop of a hat. Why me? Why be willing to take it slowly?

What if he cared about me for more than a physical transaction but was denying himself a relationship for some other reason?

I let out a laugh. Who the fuck was I kidding? These were the pathetic thoughts you had when you had feelings that weren't reciprocated. These were the hoops you jumped through, wishing and hoping someone was into you when they'd made it very clear they weren't.

"Yeah, okay. I'll tell her she can set me up. That sounds like a good idea."

When I got off the phone, I texted Ella. Then I fell asleep wondering if I needed to inform Kincaid that I was planning on going out with someone.

If you're kissing me, you're not kissing anyone else.

His rule had been clear. But who was to say my date would end in a kiss? It probably wouldn't. Which meant maybe I could get away without telling the chief.

And maybe it would have gone down exactly like that… if Judd hadn't shown up for another random fucking inspection right when I was supposed to leave for my date.

16

KINCAID

I WAS HAVING MIXED-UP emotions about whether to reopen my search for *DrunkenPoet* or allow myself to fall into a vat of temptation named Alex Marian.

Neither one was probably good for my mental health, but I couldn't stop myself from wanting both.

My feelings for Alex were proving to be more than I expected, but before I could even consider pursuing someone I might catch real feelings for, I knew I needed closure about *DrunkenPoet*. Even if he didn't want to hear from me, even if he'd moved on... hell, even if we'd both grown and changed and didn't fit anymore, I wanted to explain what happened. Surely he'd cared enough about me, once upon a time, that he'd want that, too.

But I hadn't pulled the trigger on calling Max's private investigator friend. And I was keeping my distance from Alex, too.

Sort of.

I couldn't stop thinking about him, of course. But I'd managed to go four whole days without texting or seeing him...

And then an inspection reminder popped up on my calendar for Timber.

We were sitting around the big station house kitchen table, having an impromptu schedule debrief over lunch on Friday, when Lieutenant Pope said, "I can take the Timber follow-up, Chief. I've got to head over to Sullivan Hardware anyway to pick up a few U-bolts for the storage room shelving thing."

Letting Kinsey take the Timber inspection would have been the smart choice, but I just couldn't bring myself to do it. "No, I'll take this one. But while you're at Sullivan's, ask Maddox if he still wants to sponsor an ad in the fire safety leaflet for next year's camping season. Hayden Thomasson is typing it all up for us and having it printed after the holidays. We'll be able to send out the bundles by February."

We continued the meeting, discussing everything on next week's schedule, plus addressing new concerns, until a call came in for a possible gas leak out on the edge of town. Sujo and McMasters took the truck out to respond to the call, and Pope headed to the hardware store.

I spent some time with two of our rookies, going over some training before Sujo and McMasters returned. Then it was time to head out. Timber wasn't the only inspection I had in town this afternoon. I also needed to stop by the Pinecone for Sadie's semi-annual inspection. My plan was to grab dinner to go from whichever place I visited last.

Which was, of course, a lie. Because if Alex Marian was at Timber and not too annoyed by yet another one of the inspections he'd agreed to, my strong preference would be to eat at Timber. Preferably with his company.

Four days had been too fucking long.

So I decided to head to the Pinecone first and knock that out. Thankfully, I hit it at just the right time between the hectic lunch hours and the dinner shift. It was my first time inspecting Sadie's cafe, so I had to familiarize myself with the place as I went through the inspection checklist. Everyone was very friendly and accommodating, and there were only a few minor things she needed to fix.

"A friend pointed out a good deal on a value pack of fire extin-guishers at Costco up in Billings when I was there recently. Those would do just fine for the cash register stand, and you can take the other one to your house to store in your kitchen. Or Sullivan Hard-ware has singles. Theirs are just smaller. Maddox can probably order you the bigger ones."

"Oh, I didn't think of Costco. Thanks. You want to stay for an early dinner?" she offered. "Fresh meatloaf tonight, and it's getting chilly out there."

I shook my head. "Heading to Timber next. I'll grab a pizza to take home. Thanks, though."

As I turned to finish tucking my tools and tablet away into my bag, I heard one of Sadie's servers lean over to gossip with her. "Speaking of Timber, I heard Alex Marian's going out with Will Wascomb tonight. He's so cute! I had no idea he was into guys. Maybe that explains why Sydney couldn't get him to look at her twice."

The two of them kept chatting while I made my way out to the truck.

Will Wascomb? Not only was Alex violating our agreement, but he was doing it with the preppy pissant who'd left a folder on top of his mug-warming plate and started a fire in his office? *Christ.*

When I got to Timber, my jaw ached from clenching it. It wouldn't be professional to mix personal feelings with work, so I shoved down my annoyance at Alex and focused on the job.

The now-familiar woman at the host stand welcomed me with a big smile. "Table for one?"

I held up my tool bag, which also had my tablet sticking out of the top. "Afraid not. An inspection. Is Alex around?"

Her smile dropped. "Oh, I... let me see. I know he has plans later. I'll just go check in the back."

She came back from the kitchen a moment later. "He said go ahead and do whatever you need to do."

I blinked at her. Alex wasn't going to come give me hell about the inspection? Or ride my ass to make sure I didn't dare look into anything not on the list?

Was he feeling well? I almost wanted to ask, but I held back. "Great, thanks."

I moved back to the kitchen, where his ornery chef gave me the evil eye. I was not Juni Song's favorite person. From what I understood, most of her anger came from the placement of one of the fire extinguishers that she took as a personal affront.

"I don't set fires," she muttered every time I came back there. As if the mandatory safety regulations had been my personal choice of how to annoy the fuck out of her.

I didn't bother responding; I simply got to work.

From time to time, I could hear Alex speaking in his office either on the phone or to one of his employees, but it wasn't until I heard his warm laughter with a tinge of flirtatiousness in it that I snapped.

But instead of saying something intrusive or being a jealous prick, I simply waited until he was off the phone, entered his tiny office, closed the door behind me, and moved to his desk to kiss the ever-loving fuck out of him.

His little whimpers of shock and then surrender went straight to my balls. I knew this was dangerous. Before coming in here, I'd sworn not to mix business with pleasure. But something about this man lit a short fuse in me, and if I hadn't kissed him, I would have railed at him in anger.

When I pulled back, seeing that Alex's lips were now red and damp with my own saliva, I felt a kind of satisfaction that was ten times more powerful than if I'd yelled at him.

He cleared his throat and tried to regain his composure. "What exactly are you here to inspect, Chief? My tonsils?"

"Was that our last kiss, Marian?"

Alex blinked at me in confusion. "What do you mean?"

"You and the Wascomb kid. Your choice. It's totally up to you. Just let me know."

My gut twisted as I waited for a response. While I was acting like I didn't care, I definitely did.

"H-how did you hear about that?"

I sat back with my ass propped on the edge of his desk and crossed my arms, facing him. "You live in a town of eight thousand people, and at least seven thousand of them have big mouths."

He groaned and ran his hand across his mouth. "Fuck. I don't... I don't know. I just..." He glanced up at me. "You seemed..."

I waited, but he simply shrugged and didn't finish the sentence.

I thought of *DrunkenPoet*, the reason I wasn't taking Alex out on a real date tonight.

None of it sat right with me. Not the idea of moving on with Alex before I'd gotten closure, and not the idea of Alex moving on from *me* because I refused to let go of a dream that might have died four years ago.

But it wasn't fair to keep Alex from having a good time with someone else simply because my head was a mess.

"Just don't kiss him, Marian," I said. "Tell him you wanna take it slow. Leave your options open."

His eyes followed me as I straightened up and reached for my bag. "You passed the inspection. Tonsils and fire safety, both. Well done."

And then I left and spent the drive back to the station kicking myself for being jealous about a man I wasn't willing to date for real.

After quickly returning to the station house and reinstating Timber's special effects permit as a result of the inspection, I went home and emailed the private investigator I'd reached out to for a consult and told him to proceed. If *DrunkenPoet* was gone forever, I needed to know so I could move on.

Before Alex Marian moved on, himself. With someone else.

17

ALEX

DrunkenPoet: *Sometimes I imagine your hand at the back of my neck.*

IndexEcho: *Holding you down or pulling you closer?*

DrunkenPoet: *Either? Both.*

I ASKED Will Wascomb if we could go to the high school football game as our date. There were several reasons for this, not the least of which was that I felt like maybe that would be the least likely scenario where we'd end up making out at the end.

But also, my friend Maddox's little sister was being presented on the homecoming court, which meant a bunch of us Marians had agreed to go cheer for her. Several years ago, when Maya and Maddox's parents had passed away in an accident, my cousin Rosie had been Maya's emotional support person. They'd become close when Rosie had done some babysitting for Maya, but now they were more like family. Which meant Maya was an honorary Marian and would get the largest cheer squad in Legacy.

And I would have an excuse not to have to sit directly across from my date and exchange awkward small talk. My hope was to get past the awkward small-talk phase while watching Legacy High's team crush the Columbus Cougars.

"You a big football fan?" Will asked, handing me a coffee and a hot dog before taking the seat next to me on the bleachers. I'd brought a thick wool throw to cushion the seat and also keep the metal from freezing our asses off.

"No. Definitely not," I admitted before launching into the explanation of why we were there. "So I appreciate you agreeing to come with me. What about you? Are you a fan?"

He shook his head. "Oh, god no. Hate football. Mostly because my brother played, and he and his friends were complete jerks to me and my friends. We were more of the beach volleyball type. I grew up in Santa Cruz, and my friends and I played all the time."

"You're kidding! I'm from Napa. And I played beach volleyball also, but not at home. I played with my cousins whenever I visited them in South Carolina."

We talked about California and volleyball, exchanging several war stories while the Lumberjacks ran for thirty yards, threw a ten-yard pass, and finally made it into the end zone.

Will turned out to know quite a lot of the locals, considering he'd lived there less than six months. Every time someone stopped to say hello, I couldn't help but look around in case our local fire chief had decided to come.

But of course, he wasn't there. Most likely, he was enjoying a night off, cleaning his dryer's lint trap and triple-checking the functionality of his smoke detectors.

"What about you?" Will asked with a playful grin. "Any other hobbies besides beach volleyball with cousins?"

"I like poetry," I confessed. "If I hadn't been studying wine and business in college, I would have taken more poetry classes."

"Like writing it?"

"Oh, no. God, no. I suck at writing it. I love reading it, though. My family makes fun of me for it." I didn't add the part about them making fun of me because I was usually drunk when I began spouting it. Otherwise, it was more of a silent, solo hobby.

"That's not very nice of them. Do you get along with your family?"

I heard my sister snort from somewhere behind me.

"Not really. They're awful people. Ugly, too. And mean. Especially Ella."

Will's mouth opened in surprise, so I thumbed over my shoulder and mouthed, "Sibling spy."

He glanced behind us and smirked. "Ah. I have three of those. You're lucky you only have two."

As I began to explain that my sister Mattie was getting married next month, I realized this was nice. Easy. Will was a good guy, just like Ella and Hazel had said. And we seemed to have plenty in common.

While he sat there telling me about his brother the commercial real estate agent, his sister the mechanic, and his sister the wedding planner, I even thought about how well he'd get along with the rest of my family.

At no point did I consider what he was like in bed...

At least, until he tried to kiss me after the game in the dark parking lot, and I jerked back.

"Oh," he said, stepping away. "I'm sorry. I didn't mean to..."

I reached for his hand. "No, it's not your fault. I just... I'm... I'm sorry. Can we... take it a little slow?"

Ugh, how virginal did I sound right now? And it wasn't even because I really wanted to take it slow. I just... didn't want to fuck up what I had going with Kincaid.

Will's expression was one of kindness and understanding, not judgment. "Of course we can. I'd really like to see you again, and I definitely don't want to make you uncomfortable."

"Thanks." I stepped forward and hugged him briefly, pulling back and shooting him a smile of appreciation.

"Text me tomorrow?" he asked, his smile turning flirty again.

"Definitely."

I hopped in my car and headed home. Halfway home, my phone buzzed with a text, but I assumed it was either a thanks from Will or a nosy inquiry from Ella. Either way, there was no rush to check it. Which was why I ended up in the back lot of Timber before I realized Kincaid had been the one texting me.

LORD HIGH SHERIFF OF FIRE SAFETY

I'm home for the night if you need any coaching.

My stomach tightened with hot need. *Fuck.*

ETA ASAP

I took a few minutes to race upstairs and shower thoroughly, throwing on clean clothes that didn't smell like hot dogs and popcorn.

During the drive to Kincaid's place, all I could do was chastise myself for leading Will on. I was a selfish human being because if I had to choose between Will Wascomb and Judd Kincaid when deciding who to lose my virginity to...

There was seriously no fucking choice whatsoever. Even Jesus would choose Judd Kincaid. I was pretty sure, at least.

When I got to his house, I was already half-hard. I hadn't spared a single thought about why the man had texted me for sex on a Friday night when he knew I was going out with someone else. Nor had I considered how desperate and rude it made me look that I was taking him up on it.

No. All of my thoughts had been more along the lines of *holy shit. Oh, fuck yeah.* And a lot of mental images of our local fire chief naked and hard. Which had essentially cut off all other thoughts for good.

The door was unlocked, so I let myself in and caught him pouring wine into two glasses at the kitchen counter.

"Serving wine to a vintner," I teased. "Brave choice."

Kincaid was wearing old jeans and a white long-sleeve T-shirt that said "South Philly Smoke Eaters" in red print on the back.

"Beartooth Market hardly has the biggest selection."

I stepped forward and took the offered glass. "You know I can get whatever you need. It never occurred to me you liked wine."

He held up the bottle of white. "Josh and I go way back."

The wine was a Josh Cellars Sauvignon Blanc from a particularly great year. "You did good, actually. I'm impressed."

He shrugged. "I didn't used to be a wine drinker, but I evolved."

The bottle was half-empty. I was curious about whether he'd opened it tonight and already downed half of it or kept it in his fridge for a glass every now and then.

"How was the game?" Kincaid asked, corking the bottle and leaning over to put it in the fridge. My eyes went straight to his ass in those jeans.

"We won. It wasn't a trouncing, but it wasn't a nail-biter either. Pretty sure it was Tavo's first in-person game, and I think he's a convert." I grinned. "I saw him enjoying himself with his friends."

Kincaid frowned. "Speaking of Tavo, I don't suppose you're ready to tell me—"

"Ah ah. We weren't actually speaking of Tavo, and we won't be speaking about him," I said with finality. "We were talking about the game. Cord McMasters was crowned homecoming king. I'm sure you'll hear about it at the station."

He reached for his wineglass. "Cody has a brother named Cord?"

"Nephew," I said. "Cody is the youngest of, like, six. Cord is one of ten nieces and nephews, but he's definitely Cody's favorite. He'll be bragging about him for weeks now. I'd put money on it."

"He a football player?" Kincaid began. Then he quickly shook his head. "You know what, I don't give a shit about football. Tell me about Will." He closed his eyes and took a deep breath before opening them and piercing me with a stare. "Actually, I don't give a shit about him either. Take your clothes off."

My heart thundered, and my breathing shallowed. "Yeah?"

"Yeah." He tilted his head toward his bedroom. "In there. Let's go."

I loved the gruff quality of his voice, the way he didn't make the words pretty or soft for me. I was here for sex, and there was no need to pretend otherwise.

And I wanted it so fucking badly.

I took a large gulp of wine as I moved toward the bedroom. When I entered his space, I quickly set the glass down and kicked off my shoes. There was already a wet spot on the front of my clean underwear, and I knew he'd be able to see it unless I was quick about taking off my pants.

"Stop."

I glanced up. Kincaid was leaning lazily against the edge of his doorframe with the wineglass against his lips.

"You wanted lessons, Marian. And tonight's lesson is about making it last."

I bit back a groan. "I think tonight's lesson should be about quickies."

His rumbled laugh made me grin. "That right? You feeling some kind of way right now?"

I ran a hand over the cock strangled in my own jeans and nodded. Kincaid's eyes darkened.

"Seduction is like building a fire, Alex," he began. "Start with the kindling."

While I was a virgin, I wasn't an idiot.

"Hm. Like this?" I asked, pulling up my shirt slowly, swaying my hips languidly, and turning in a circle.

When my back was to him, I pulled my shirt the rest of the way off and blew out a breath to let the waistband of my jeans fall lower on my hips.

"Mm." His voice took on a delicious grumble. "That'll do just fine."

I pressed my hand to the center of my chest and continued spinning, dragging my fingers down my stomach slow enough to make my nipples harden. Kincaid's eyes were riveted.

Instead of opening my jeans, I tucked my fingertips inside and closed my eyes, feeling the gentle tease of my own fingers against the head of my aching cock.

"That's cruel," Kincaid said, a smile clear in his voice.

"It's not cruel. It's tinder."

"Light the match, Firebug."

I flicked open my jeans and drew down the zipper slowly, using my other hand to pull the fabric open so he could see the guilty wet spot on the cotton of my shorts.

"Oh fuck yes," he breathed. "Show me more, Marian."

I put my thumbs into the waistband of my jeans and wiggled

my hips, lowering the jeans down to mid-thigh so he could see how hard I already was.

My stomach dipped and looped with nerves. I'd never done any of this with another person. I hadn't even gotten naked around other guys for things like sports or sleepovers or whatever. My dads were militant about teaching us that our bodies were our own growing up, and somehow, that translated into my being an intensely private person when it came to modesty.

But I was discovering that putting that hungry look on Judd Kincaid's face was worth any discomfort.

I turned around again and bent forward a little, shaking my ass again as I pushed my jeans down to the floor. Suddenly, warm hands were on my hips.

"Just like that. Stay bent over and let me look at you."

Oxygen sawed in and out of my lungs, and my cock continued leaking. Judd moved one of his hands to draw soft fingertips down my spine and into the top of my crack, pushing the elastic band of my underwear down a little. "Look at you," he breathed. "So fucking sexy. You have no idea how much I want to get inside you right now."

He moved closer until his erection pressed against my ass, slipping immediately into the cleft between my ass cheeks and thrusting gently up and down.

I let out a noise.

Judd leaned over me until his hot breath seared the back of my neck. "You want my cock, Firebug?" The words were low, but they were strong enough to make my skin prickle and my balls tighten.

I turned my face toward his and felt his stubble scrape my ear and cheek. "Please."

His hand came up to clasp my face and hold it where he wanted it while his lips devoured mine. We kissed long enough for him to maneuver me until I was sprawled back on his bed underneath him in nothing but my underwear while he was still fully clothed.

He rutted against me, his jeans-covered bulge making my toes curl as it rode up and down my shaft. I snuck my fingers into the back of his pants and felt the warm skin of his ass.

It took me forever to realize I could take his clothes off as easily as I'd done my own. Quickly, I grabbed his shirt and tore it off him. Then I reached between us and unfastened his jeans. He shimmied them off without pulling his mouth from mine and then reached for the band of my boxer briefs.

"You okay with this, Alex?" he murmured against my lips.

"Yes." No sense in wasting words. I wanted him so much I ached with it. And it wasn't just an orgasm or quick release I wanted. It was the entire experience. Hands on bare skin. Lips trailing from one spot to the next. Murmured encouragement or reassurance.

The full attention of this sexy man for as long as I could get it.

He tugged my underwear off and tossed it aside before pulling his own off. And then we were both fully naked, his larger body lying on top of mine. As soon as his bare cock pressed against mine, I let out a deep groan and arched up into it.

"Fuck, that feels amazing."

He quickly moved down until his lips were on one of my nipples, licking and sucking while his thumb fiddled with the other. After he was satisfied, he moved down to my stomach, running his stubbled chin down my hip to the crevice between my groin and hip.

"You're so fucking sexy," he murmured. "I want to taste that fucking cock."

And then he did. His hot, wet mouth swallowed my tip, his tongue dragging underneath it where something fucking amazing was.

"Oh god, fuck," I cried, reaching for the back of his head just to hold on to something. "Judd, fuck. Please more."

He smiled around my cock and began to lick and circle my shaft with his tongue before bobbing down over my entire cock. I felt it hit the back of his throat, but he didn't even gag.

I curled up, bending my knees and clenching my abs until I was practically hugging his entire head just to keep him there. My dick was rock-hard, and my balls were under his chin until he moved down to pull them into his hot mouth one at a time.

I stared at the sight of my cock, wet with Judd Kincaid's saliva, while his messy hair was between my thighs.

I am going to die a happy man.

Gone were the thoughts from earlier about wanting to slow things down, drag them out. Now all I wanted was the orgasm my body was screaming toward.

His large hand wrapped around my wet cock and jacked me. I fell back onto the bed with a groan and closed my eyes. The image of him was branded on the back of my eyelids.

I heard a wet, slurping sound, and then his mouth was back on my cock, and his fingertip circled my hole.

My body tensed, so he pulled off. "No?"

"Yes. Please, just... I'm not used to it. But I want..." I was too embarrassed to say the rest.

"You want my fingers inside you, Alex?"

I nodded, cheeks fully on fire.

Instead of using spit, he moved to the bedside table and grabbed a bottle of lube.

And then he tamped down the fire and started with kindling again.

Like a motherfucking pyromaniac who wanted to watch me burn.

18

KINCAID

IndexEcho: *I can't imagine you ever not being in my life.*

DrunkenPoet: *Then don't.*

I WASN'T proud of inserting myself into Alex's date night with Will fucking Wascomb. But I also wasn't sorry for it.

With Alex Marian naked and gasping beneath me, I was exactly where I wanted to be. Where I needed to be. He was so fucking responsive, so eager, that I cringed every time I considered him giving this to anyone but me.

"Hands to yourself," I growled when he reached for his cock.

His chest heaved up and down with labored breaths as he tried his best to stave off his orgasm.

"You're doing amazing," I murmured before taking his cock back in my mouth. I moved my lube-slick fingers to his hole and teased him a minute before pressing my middle finger in a little bit. He squeezed around me instinctively, so I doubled down on his cock to distract him.

Saliva rolled down his sac to his ass, making everything wet and sloppy. He smelled so fucking good, and now he was covered in my spit, my touch, my scent.

I slid my finger deeper. His high-pitched cry of pleasure made my own cock even harder than it was. It was taking all my self-control not to lunge up, slick myself, and thrust into his tight little virgin hole. I wanted him with a desperation I wasn't sure I'd ever felt. This moment was hot as fuck, and his reactions were ramping me up until my skin was hot and flushed and my balls were heavy.

Just a little bit more of a reach inside him and...

"Ah! There! Oh, fuck, oh fuck!"

The salty tang of his release flooded my mouth as I continued stroking his gland and swallowing his cum.

When I pulled off him, I glanced down to where his hole was still stretched around my thick finger. As I pulled out slowly and watched it contract, I imagined my cum leaking out of it, too.

I quickly lurched up and reached for my cock, swiping some of the lube on it so I could stroke it quickly over the sight of Alex's spent cock and his balls still dripping from my attention. Within moments, my release was streaked across his stomach and cock, adding to the mess.

My entire body shook with the aftershocks of my orgasm. Why was everything magnified with this guy?

I reached down and swirled my fingers through the cum on his lower belly. "Don't do this with him."

The words were out before I could stop them.

Alex sat up and reached for my face, pulling me in for a long, searching kiss. When he finally pulled back and met my eyes, he said, "I don't think it's possible to do *that* with him."

I wasn't sure what he meant, but it seemed like he was agreeing, so I left it alone.

"C'mon. I'll wash you off."

I stepped off the bed and pulled him up, keeping my hand around his until I had the shower on. I pulled him close while the water warmed up. "Good lesson or bad lesson?" I asked between more kisses.

"Mm. Incredible lesson. You're the kind of professor who makes a guy consider changing majors just to get more time with him."

I laughed and pulled him into the shower behind me before moving him under the warmth of the spray and wrapping my arms around him from behind. We stood together like that, with the water rushing around and between us, until I finally remembered I didn't have unlimited hot water.

"I've never done this," Alex admitted as I reached for the soap and began to wash him off. "Gotta say, I'm a fan. Ten out of ten, would naked co-shower again."

"There's a survey in your texts. If you don't mind filling it out, you can earn a discount off your next one," I said, moving him toward the wall and kicking his feet apart.

I soaped up the sweet cleft between his ass cheeks, taking my time and fingering his hole a little more. The quick intake of his breath was plenty of a reward, but seeing his cock fill again gave me all kinds of ideas.

"Ahh, youth," I teased, moving my soapy hand around to his front and plastering myself to his back while I stroked him.

"Okay, fine," he gasped. "Fifteen out of ten, but that's my final answer."

It didn't take long to get another orgasm out of him, and by the time the water ran cold, he was already shaking from exhaustion.

I dried him off and nudged him into my bed to warm up under the covers. "Let me grab something for you to drink."

When I came back with a couple of bottles of Gatorade, he was half-asleep under my duvet. "Hope you didn't want me to leave because that's not humanly possible," he murmured.

"It's okay. You're welcome to doze as much as you need. But drink some of this first."

It was silly, really, but part of me wanted to take care of him. And seeing Alex in my bed made me feel all kinds of things. He looked good there. And I could imagine sliding in beside him and wrapping myself around him for the night.

"You're staring," he said, the edge of his lips quirking up. "Is it the clown hair?"

I nodded and grinned. "It's giving 1980s hair band."

He reached up and patted it down, which did nothing to change the fact that it was sticking up everywhere in adorable flips and dips.

I shook my head. "Lost cause, I'm afraid. You'll have to slink out of here before sunrise just to keep from being chased out of town."

Instead of laughing or flipping me off, he dropped his smile and sat up. "Okay, but for real. Can we... *not* tell people about this?"

I was taken aback by the question. Not because I wanted to tell anyone I was sleeping with one of the restaurant owners on my inspection docket but because I hadn't expected *him* to be the one asking for secrecy.

"Uh, there a reason, or...?" I asked.

I moved closer and sat down before threading my fingers in his messy hair. The faint scent of my own shampoo wafting off Alexander Marian did things to me. Caveman things.

"Yeah, my family. I don't... they can't..." He blew out a frustrated breath. "They'll make something out of this. You and me. They'll turn it into a dating thing, when we both know that's not the case."

Alex met my eyes. "I know this is just physical. Just for experience. But can it also be just for me? I really don't want to have to explain to my sister that I—"

I leaned in and kissed him, hard. "Just you and me," I agreed before kissing him again. I held him where I wanted him with a grip of his thick hair.

Why couldn't I take my hands off this guy? What made him so different?

We kissed for a long time before he melted back against my pillows. "Killin' me."

Within a few moments, he was asleep. I looked over at the old digital alarm clock on my bedside table. Two twenty-three in the morning. We'd been fucking around for hours.

The full moon shone through the window enough to set milky stripes along his pale skin.

Don't go out with Will Wascomb again.

If I thought it hard enough, maybe the message would somehow pass from me to him.

I got up to close the curtains and lock the front door. Before I came back to bed, I stopped at my laptop, which was still open on the kitchen table.

The investigator I'd hired had gotten back to me with a boilerplate explanation about how it would "take time" to narrow the search down to "quality leads" but that he already had a few "irons in the fire" and we were "off to a great start."

I hesitated before hitting Reply.

Hey Tim,
Thanks for the email, but I've changed my mind about the

investigation. I was looking for closure, like I explained to you during our video call, but I think... I think I'm going to let it go. Please let me know how much I owe you for the work you've already done, and I apologize if I've wasted your time.

Thanks again,

Judd Kincaid

I hit Send and felt a weight lift off my shoulders. Max was right. *DrunkenPoet* had had a chance to find me for a while now, and I was easy to find. The fact that he hadn't come looking clearly meant he didn't want to. And I didn't want to choose a ghost over a real, live, flesh-and-blood man who made me laugh, who made me think, who made me *feel...* and who was literally in my bed waiting for me.

I closed the laptop and moved quickly toward the bedroom. Then I slid in beside Alex to hold him while he slept.

19

ALEX

IndexEcho: *If you could do anything, what would it be?*

DrunkenPoet: *There's an old building near my sister's place. I dream about turning it into something amazing.*

SLEEPING with Judd Kincaid was my delicious, forbidden secret. And I was giddy with it.

I'd slept over at his place three separate times in as many weeks. In fact, the entire month of October seemed to be Kincaid-themed. Or maybe sex-themed.

Did it matter? Was there a difference?

Giving Will the polite brush-off had been hard, only because he was such a sweet guy. I didn't want to burn that bridge, considering the thing with Kincaid was clearly only temporary, but at the same time, I wasn't willing to give up sex with Judd to start dating Will.

There was no question whatsoever. I'd take sleeping with the fire chief over dating the boy next door any day of the week.

Unfortunately, Judd and I were both still slammed with work, which meant once-a-week hookups were about the best we could do, especially if we didn't want anyone finding out about what we were doing.

And I definitely did not.

"Will said you blew him off," Ella snapped at me over breakfast at the Pinecone one morning. "Tell me why."

"No." I took another bite of bacon. It was crisp, salty, and perfect in every way.

She opened her mouth, turned to Tommy and his boyfriend, Foster, and then stared back at me. "You have to."

"Do not," I said.

Tommy leaned toward me. "Right, but like... just out of curiosity, what's wrong with the guy?"

Foster nodded as if it was obvious that something had to be.

"Nothing. He's great."

The three of them waited for me to say more. I took another bite of French toast instead.

Ella cradled her coffee mug and stared into it as if summoning courage from its depths before looking back up at me. "You have to tell me because of the sibling code."

I tapped my chin with my index finger. "I declare myself in contempt of the sibling code and sentence myself to... gosh, was it five weeks of isolation from family? That seems harsh, but okay."

Tommy muttered under his breath, "Mattie's wedding," to remind me I was shit out of luck on getting five weeks' reprieve.

"Fuck," I said, reaching for a sip of coffee. "Oh well, two weeks will have to suffice."

Ella smacked my arm. "Be serious. Poor Will is devastated."

I mock-frowned at her. "Is he? Because I saw his jeep in

Monroe's driveway a week ago. Didn't seem like the kind of thing someone would do during a mourning phase, but I could be wrong."

I was secretly glad Kincaid's driveway was at the end of a dead-end road and hidden by pine trees.

Foster grinned. "There are worse ways to mourn."

Tommy elbowed him.

"What, baby? Read a sad story and I'll show you." Foster chuckled as Tommy tried to elbow him again. He failed because Foster grabbed him and kissed him instead, pulling back and smacking his lips. "Mmm, coffee with my favorite flavoring on it. Marian flavor."

Ella and I shuddered and groaned. "Make Foster do your five weeks," Ella said, flicking her hand in his face. "Gross."

Foster shot me a look after his laughter died down. "I figure you've got something going with someone else and that's why you shot Will down."

Ella's face lit up in delight before falling in pity. "Oh honey... is this about *IndexEcho*? Are you having a hard time moving on? Still? I think it's time for you to call your therapist again."

I opened my mouth to say no, that I was completely over *Index*, when I realized it wasn't true. Even though I knew he was gone, I still cared about him deeply and worried I'd never have the same kind of emotional and intellectual connection with someone else.

"Maybe so," I said. Because I didn't want her trying to set me up with someone else as long as I was still sleeping with Kincaid. And I didn't want any remaining vestige of my hang-up on *Index* to mess with my ability to enter into a new relationship... preferably with the grumpy fire chief, if I could ever get him to consider me as more than a hookup.

The following night, after being greeted at Kincaid's door by a wet fire chief wrapped in only a towel, I fell on my knees in gratitude and expressed it orally and thoroughly.

An hour later, after he'd returned the favor and bundled me up in a blanket on his sofa while he devoured the pizza I'd brought him, I told him about the conversation at the cafe.

"I told my sister I was still hung up on an old flame," I admitted. "And that's why I turned down another date with Will."

He peered at me from the other end of the sofa, where he was holding a paper plate and pizza slice above where my feet were making a home on his lap. "And are you? Still hung up on the guy from your past?"

I hesitated. "Sort of? I fell for him, hard. It's silly because we didn't know each other that well, but... we had an amazing connection."

"What happened to him?"

It was strange talking to Judd about something personal. It seemed like I was breaking the rules, only... I wasn't quite sure whose rules.

"He was the firefighter who died," I whispered. "The one I told you about."

Judd's head swiveled to me in surprise. "Shit, Alex. I'm sorry. I didn't realize the two of you were together."

I didn't correct him because I felt like if I admitted we hadn't actually been together, he'd think my grief at losing the man was an overreaction.

"I'm trying very hard to be over him," I admitted. "But it's not as easy as it sounds. And I... I guess what I'm really not over is this fear that it could happen again. That I might fall for someone, and just when things are going amazing..." I broke off with a headshake.

I'd never admitted that out loud before, not even in my own brain, and part of me couldn't believe I'd just admitted it now. To *him*. I laughed softly. "Boy, I am a barrel of laughs tonight, huh? Anyway—" I tried to shift my feet, to put a little distance between us.

Judd laid a hand on my ankle, holding me in place. His expression was surprisingly empathetic. "I know exactly how you feel. It's similar when you've been ghosted by someone you cared for deeply."

"The ex," I said knowingly. "Do you... do you want to talk about it?"

"Maybe later. Right now, I want to ask how the fuck you're still a virgin when you were dating a firefighter. We're not known for being timid misses." He winked and took a final bite of pizza before leaning forward to toss his plate on top of the pizza box. Then he sat back and reached for my foot to begin rubbing it.

"Oh, I... well..." I felt my cheeks get hot the way they always did when we spoke of my lack of experience. I didn't want to admit I'd never met my "lost firefighter" in person, so I hedged. "I guess I wasn't ready. I was young, too. It was a while ago. In my early twenties."

He nodded. "Losing someone so young is hard. I can see why you didn't date for a long time after."

"That... and moving to Legacy to start Timber."

"Yeah, tell me more about that. I know it's a historic building and you spent time renovating before opening."

I launched into one of my favorite topics: the LGBTQ history of the Timber building. We ended up talking for a long time until I happened to mention Mattie's upcoming wedding.

"You don't sound excited for her," Kincaid said. "Is the guy a dud?"

"No, god no. We like him a lot. I just... I haven't left Timber for that long before, and I know it's going to be hard."

Kincaid lifted an eyebrow. "You a little controlling, Marian? Is that it?"

"Says the guy who commanded me to choke on his cock an hour ago," I said, nudging him in the gut with my toes.

His laughter made all of my shoulder muscles loosen, and I found myself relaxing even further into his sofa.

"Hey, some of the most controlling people like to give it up in bed. It can be freeing." His eyebrows bounced. "Want me to free you, Firebug?"

He ran his hand up the leg of my pants, his warm palm massaging my calf enough to make my cock perk up.

"Honestly, I want to very badly, but I'm about two blinks away from becoming one with your sofa," I murmured. "My dick says *yes, please*, while my eyes say *g'night*. So I should probably go now before I fall asleep at the wheel."

"You're not going anywhere this late while you're sleepy. Let's go."

He pushed my feet off his lap and stood, reaching for my hand and pulling me up beside him. Then he half-carried me to bed.

Once we were snuggled together in the cold sheets, I thought of something. Kincaid had always low-key panicked about me driving at night.

"Did your parents die in a car accident?" I asked in a soft voice.

He paused for a moment. "No. House fire."

I felt a wave of prickly numbness wash over me, leaving me dizzy. "Judd." What else was there to say? "*Judd.*" This time, it came out high-pitched and emotional.

His arms tightened around me. "It was a long time ago, Alex."

I shifted up so I could bury my face in his neck. "I'm so fucking sorry," I said, feeling and hearing the thickness in my throat. "Were you..." I couldn't even say the words.

"In the house? Yeah. Obviously, I got out. They didn't." He

touched the scars on his arm, and I realized they weren't from his job. It was the other way around. He had the job because he'd been through something terrible. Unimaginable.

"No," I breathed. "Oh, god. Baby, no. I'm so fucking sorry," I said again. Tears came unbidden, and I let them fall. It was kind of silly and certainly unexpected, but all I could picture was a scared boy all alone in a fire and then all alone in the world. If only my family had known, they would have taken him in. They would have moved heaven and earth to give him a home. A family.

Kincaid's hands moved up and down my back as if *I* were the one who needed consoling. "It's okay. I promise."

"It's not. It's not okay. It's so fucking unfair." My voice was ragged with frustration and tears. "And please stop comforting me when you're the one who experienced the loss. I just... I wish I could have been there to take it all away from you somehow."

He pressed a kiss into my hair, and when he spoke, I could hear the smile in his voice. "Shh. You would have been an egg. And eggs aren't much help in a fire."

I lifted my head and kissed him desperately, eager to give him all the care now that I couldn't have given him then. He let out a soft laugh and then a groan of pleasure. His hands moved along my back and down to my ass and back up into my hair. Like he couldn't get enough of me.

Like he was happy just kissing me.

I fell asleep that night feeling spent. But also knowing there was no way this was just physical anymore. Not for me.

And I suspected not for Judd Kincaid either.

Because I might be an almost-virgin, but even I knew hookups didn't hold you while you cried.

20

KINCAID

IndexEcho: *Just showered after four days away from fresh water. You can't imagine how disgusting I was.*

DrunkenPoet: *That sounds like an invitation. Hold on, imagining you in the shower now. BRB.*

ALEX MARIAN WAS A GOOD MAN. It had been two days since his late-night tears, and I still couldn't get over how upset he'd been when I'd told him about my parents. It had taken me a little while to get past my prejudice against Alex from the mistaken identity situation in Amsterdam, but this was the perfect example of how wrong I'd been about him.

Lieutenant Pope popped her head in my office. "There's a call for non-emergency fire response to a potential hazmat situation on Randolph and Gallatin."

I quirked my head at her. It was unusual for my crew to involve me in a call like that.

"The reason I'm informing you is because it involves a Timber employee. And since you seem particularly interested in keeping them in compliance... I thought you might want to know about it."

I immediately stood and grabbed my jacket. "Let's go."

When we arrived at the scene, a man I recognized as Karim Haddad was patiently scrolling his phone, while an older woman in Carhartt overalls and work boots shot him an evil eye from across the driveway. The small house behind them was divided into two apartments—one side neat and tidy, the other with a collection of half-rusted metal outdoor furniture and dead plants in front. The two-car garage was the same. One half was spotless, while the other was cluttered with a mishmash of storage totes and trash bags.

"What's going on?" I started with Karim since I didn't know the woman.

Karim tilted his head at his neighbor before sliding his phone into his back pocket and crossing his arms. "Sue seems to think I'm preparing to dispose of dead bodies."

Sue snapped, "It's a barrel of lye! What else does a man do with a barrel of lye, I ask you?" She stepped forward and held out her hand. "Thank you for coming, Chief. I'm Sue Garrison. Mr. Haddad and I share this garage, and I found multiple suspicious chemicals being stored there. Not just the lye. I'm concerned for my safety. I have two dogs, and the last thing I need is to wake up in the middle of the night dead!"

I saw Kinsey stifle a laugh out of the corner of my eye while Karim simply exhaled.

"Well, let's take a look, then, shall we?" I asked. "Show me what you're concerned about, and I'll figure out whether or not it's being stored properly. Karim, is that okay with you?"

Sue bustled forward. "He doesn't have to consent since I consent for both of us, and it's a single space."

"That's not exactly true," I said as Karim said, "Go ahead. There's nothing improperly stored, and I'd like her to have peace of mind, even though she's being a pain in the ass about it."

Sue huffed.

Just then, a car pulled up, and Alex got out. "What's going on here?"

I could tell right off the bat he was angry. "Alex—" But before I could ask what he was doing there, Karim's shoulders dropped.

"Thanks for coming. I'm sure it's fine, but I didn't want to be alone in case it wasn't," he said.

Alex moved closer and stood next to him, placing a hand on Karim's shoulder. "Of course. It's no problem. More problems with your neighbor?"

Sue's eyes narrowed. "Oh, so you've been complaining about me to other people? Sounds about right. Maybe I'm the one you're planning on using the lye on!"

I could tell Karim was considering agreeing out of frustration, but I didn't want the words out there. "Hey, everyone needs to take a breath and calm down. Karim, you and Alex can stand over there," I said, indicating one side of the driveway. "And Sue, if you don't mind standing over there, that would be great."

I met Lieutenant Pope's eyes and tilted my head toward one side of the garage so we could split the work.

Pope headed to the side that was the more obvious fire hazard. "Sir, right off, I can see empty cardboard boxes stored near a space heater."

Sue's eyes widened. "That's... that's not... those are mine! And those boxes are going to the dump next week. Look over there. Those barrels and cans." She pointed to the tidy side, where there was a clear workbench with various cans and barrels stored underneath. Each was clearly labeled.

I squatted to look through them. Sure enough, there was a giant barrel of lye. There were also chromatic oxides, argan oil, and essential oils such as clary sage and neroli.

I peered up at Karim. "You make soap?"

His face broke out into a huge grin. "Yeah. And I sell it at the farmer's market. Me and Tavo share a table. How'd you know?"

"It smells amazing in here," I said with a grin. "And I recognize the silicone molds on the shelf above your workbench."

Karim's body seemed to relax even more as he grinned back. "Legacy Lather dot com. I make a Himalayan cedarwood scent that you might like. Check it out."

Alex let out a huff of laughter. "I actually think he likes the white champaca," he murmured softly enough that only I could hear it.

Memories of sniffing up the column of his neck to the spot behind his ear that always smelled sweetest, of running my nose up the back of his leg as I dropped kisses everywhere, came flooding into my head.

I cleared my throat and tried to focus. "Okay, well... I should... Do you mind if I peek inside to make sure the contents match the label?"

Karim shook his head. As I began checking, I could hear Lieutenant Pope lecturing Sue on half-empty gas cans, rusted paint tins, and various other dangerous items on her side of the garage.

When all was said and done, I found no violations on Karim's side and wrote out several items in a written warning on Sue's side.

"I have to send a copy of this to the homeowner as well," I explained. Their landlord turned out to be Hazel Marian, who owned several rental properties around town. Instead of being there to watch over his cousin's property, Alex had come to provide support to his friend and employee.

Once again, Alex Marian proved himself to be one of the good ones. And it only made me fall harder for him.

"Thank you both for your cooperation," I said to Karim and Sue. "Hopefully, you'll sleep easier knowing you're plenty safe."

Karim scoffed but didn't say anything. I didn't blame him.

It was awkward leaving Alex without being able to say anything to him or acknowledge him as anything other than Karim's friend.

"Marian," I said gruffly, throwing him a nod.

"Chief." His eyes followed me as I trailed Pope back to the truck.

On the drive back to the station, Pope said, "I feel stupid. I knew Karim made soap, I just didn't put two and two together because I didn't know what was used in making it."

I shrugged. "Not sure Sue would have been okay with us taking those cans at face value anyway. He was generous to let us inspect without giving us a hard time."

Pope's voice softened. "He's a nice man. You should see his table at the market. He also has these lavender sleep masks that smell amazing. I didn't see their backyard, but I wonder if he grows his own lavender for them."

I glanced over at my second-in-command and noticed her slight blush. "Maybe I'll check it out. They doing it this weekend?"

She nodded. "It's the last one for the season, so it'll be big. And there will be a ton of pumpkins and gourds, things like that. Stu Old-Chief makes Bapa Wohanpi with timpsila, and Beth Bower sells pumpkin muffins. Both are not to be missed."

Which was how I found myself at the final farmer's market of the year, browsing Karim's soap selection, when the kid from

Alex's apartment—a subject that had been clearly off-limits the entire time we'd been hooking up—got into trouble.

"Hey, aren't you from San Francisco?" a man in a baseball cap asked Tavo, who was helping a woman organize her stock at the next table over.

I didn't think much of it until Tavo froze like a terrified animal faced with a predator.

"You are!" Baseball Cap continued. "I saw you at Pinch with Judge Miller last year sometime. I was waiting tables, and he handed me a hundred-dollar bill and told me to let him know if I saw you with anyone besides him in the back room." The man chuckled. "But you barely left his side except to dance. And it seemed like you were dancing just for him. You guys were cute."

Poor Tavo's face turned red, and he stammered. "N-no. That wasn't me. I've never even been to San Francisco."

He was a shit liar—possibly worse than Alex Marian himself —but his denial was enough for Baseball Cap to back off. "Sorry, dude. Didn't mean to upset you."

"I'm not upset," Tavo argued. "I'm just... not whoever you think I am."

Baseball Cap leaned in and lowered his voice. "If you're not out, that's totally my bad. I'm so fucking sorry, bro."

Tavo shook his head and indicated several of the flint and steel kits he was selling that were rainbow colored. "Not the problem. The problem is that I'm not that guy."

Alex must have sensed Tavo's discomfort from wherever he was because he started heading over. Meanwhile, I turned to the stranger.

"I couldn't help but overhear you, and it reminded me of something that happened to me. See that guy?" I pointed to Alex. "I could have sworn he was someone I met in Europe a few years ago, but it turned out it was just a guy who looked like him. Don't they say we all have a doppelgänger somewhere?"

I gave him an easy smile and waited until he huffed out a laugh. "Bro, I once met a guy on a ski slope who looked just like my cousin Abe. Like freaky-twin shit."

Tavo was able to relax enough to let out a weak chuckle. "Yeah. I've heard all kinds of stories like that."

The guy reached out a fist to bump. "Sorry, my guy. Tell me about these fire thingies you have."

As Tavo launched into an explanation of how to use the flint and steel kit, Alex moved up next to me. "Thank you," he murmured.

I glanced at him and noticed the stress in his expression. "You going to tell me what's going on?"

He shook his head. "No, but I'll at least tell you why I can't tell you." He glanced around. "Just not here."

I looked around and noticed a few people watching us. "See you around, Marian."

Once I made it back home, I texted him.

> Can I make you dinner tonight or do you have to work?

FIREBUG

> I probably can't leave till nine.

> I'll make dessert then.

FIREBUG

> Thank you again for helping Tavo. I owe you one.

I took a chance and fired back.

It seemed like forever before his reply came through.

As I spent the rest of the afternoon on boring shit like laundry and cleaning my bathroom, I couldn't help my anticipation.

Finally, after years of avoiding emotional entanglements, I had found someone I wanted to be tangled up with in the very best way.

21

———————

ALEX

DrunkenPoet: *I get the feeling you're bossy in bed.*

IndexEcho: *I get the feeling you're going to find out.*

———————

As I STARED down at Kincaid's text for the hundredth time, I still couldn't believe it.

A date. A real date.

He'd told me he was still hung up on an ex, some guy who'd ghosted him. So what the hell had caused him to change his mind?

Clearly, it wasn't the sex. I was a green newbie, awkward and fumbling. Gagging wasn't as sexy as porn made it seem, and I was a grade A gagger during oral sex.

Then there was the fact that I'd ejaculated the moment Judd put his fingers inside me. Again, green newbie shit. All I had to do was think about the fact he was fingering my ass and *thar she blows*. Gone.

I made my way out to the front of the restaurant to help our bartender catch up on drink orders. The night of the final farmer's market tended to bring a lot of visitors to Legacy, which meant Timber was busier than normal.

Unfortunately, people were asking for the Slingshot Flame, and I had to tell them it was temporarily off the menu. I made a mental note to bring it up to Kincaid. The least he could do was give me an update on the timeline for getting the permit back.

After I helped complete the drink orders, I moved back toward the kitchen to check the men's room in case it needed attention. In the back hallway, I saw Karim coming out of the men's room, smiling down at his phone screen. When he noticed me, he jumped.

"Sorry, boss. Had to take a leak."

"Since when do you need to explain a bathroom break?" I asked in surprise.

He shook his head and smiled. "I might have taken an extra minute to send some personal texts on Timber time. That's my guilt talking."

I rolled my eyes and thumbed over my shoulder toward the kitchen. "Christ. We're all human. Get back in there."

He shoved his phone into his back pocket and whistled his way to the kitchen.

Karim was acting like I felt these days. And I felt giddy with a new love interest. Was it possible he and Kinsey Pope—

"Your sister is looking for you," one of my servers said as she hustled past with a large pizza and a stack of plates.

I moved back out to the restaurant and looked around. There was no sign of Ella, so I pulled out my phone to text her. There was a wall of notifications from my other sister, and they all sounded a little like this.

MATTIE

Wedding postponed. Dress is fucked.

There were also texts from my dads.

PAPA

Mattie's dress doesn't fit. It's fine. It's not like hundreds of people will be looking at the bride or anything.

DAD

If you get any messages about the wedding dress, ignore them. Your father is a drama queen.

I moved out back into the crisp night and called Mattie.

"My life is over. I might as well go to the thrift store and grab any old white dress."

"Hey to you, too. I hear you're having a crisis, even though half your friends are literally seamstresses and tailors."

She moaned pathetically. "You shouldn't have to work on the bride's dress when you're a guest."

"They're not a guest for two more weeks. Ask Lisette to do you a favor. Doesn't she owe you one from that time you hooked her up with pointe shoes?"

"It's my job to hook her up with pointe shoes."

I wrapped my free arm around myself and rubbed my hand up and down my other arm. It was freezing out here. "You know what I mean. You got the specialty ones from... wherever. She basically thinks you're Jesus now. If you don't want to ask her to do the work, ask her for a recommendation, and we both know she'll beg to be the one to help you herself."

After talking her off the cliff, I ended the call and texted my dads.

> Crisis averted. I talked her into asking Lisette for help.

PAPA

> Oh right. She's friends with people who sew.

DAD

> Don't act like this is the first you're hearing this. I've been saying it all night. She's the *wardrobe* coordinator. Jesus fuck, Blue.

> See you next week. Love you.

PAPA

> My baby's coming home!

DAD

> Can't wait to see you.

As I slid the phone in my pocket and turned to go back inside, a red light swept across the back of the building. I spun around immediately... and found the fire chief was using his lights to flirt with me.

He pulled into the lot and rolled down the window. "It's too cold out here for you to be standing around soliciting people," he teased.

I put my hand on my hip and canted it out, striking a sultry pose in my black twill pants and Timber fleece. "I'm too expensive for you, boy."

He looked around to make sure the lot was empty before crooking his finger at me. I approached his open window and leaned in, enjoying the waft of Judd-scented heat.

"Come home with me," he said in a sultry rumble.

"How much you got, sailor?"

He moved his hand down between his legs and rubbed himself suggestively. "Just enough to make you let out that little sound that drives me up a wall."

I thought back to the restaurant and mentally checked in with the status of everyone's roles before I stepped out to make the call. The orders had died down, and my assistant manager already knew she was handling closing tonight.

Judd put his warm hand on mine where it clutched the rim of his door. "Get in the car, Marian," he said softly. "Please."

I moved around the truck quickly and got in. "What the chief wants, the chief gets," I said, reaching for my seat belt.

On the way to his house, I texted everyone I needed to at Timber, ignored a text from Ella asking me why I was suddenly Mattie's favorite sibling, and allowed the heat vents to thaw me out.

"Will you tell me about Tavo?" Kincaid finally asked.

The question was gentle. I didn't feel like he was prying for any nefarious reason, and after what he'd overheard at the farmer's market, he'd probably figured most of it out already. But I still owed it to Tavo to protect his identity. "How come you never believed me when I said the two of us were together?"

He reached over and took my hand. "Baby, you're about as good a liar as Pinocchio. Besides, poor Tavo's eyes about popped out of his head when you claimed him."

The endearment hit me right in the chest. This moment was everything I'd always wanted. Normal. Steady. Almost domestic.

"He's hiding from a possessive lover. A *married*, possessive lover who doesn't like the word no and has the power to make Tavo's life difficult."

"A judge." He nodded like he was remembering what the guy at the farmer's market said. "In San Francisco."

"Yeah. So you can imagine the kind of resources the man has. If Tavo's name turns up on any tax form or banking transaction—"

"Or fire investigation report," he muttered, finally understanding.

"Yeah," I sighed. "The judge might find him."

Judd parked the truck in his driveway and turned off the ignition. "What's the plan, though? Because he's been in Legacy for months."

"I have an uncle in the security business," I explained. "He's trying to dig up dirt on the judge or find someone else he's done this to. Otherwise, the plan is to wait him out. Uncle Joel says there are still people asking around about Tavo, which means the judge has definitely not given up yet. But eventually, he's going to have to move on. Hopefully, Joel will get evidence of a new love interest, and Tavo will be off the hook. I don't think he'll go back to San Francisco at this point, but he could at least get a real job. Right now, he's too afraid of pinging something in a government database."

We hopped out of the truck and made our way into his house. I loved his place. It was homey and snug, unlike my drafty rabbit warren above Timber.

"Come in. I made cookies," Judd said, shocking the hell out of me.

"You? *You* made cookies?"

His eyebrows dipped together. "Why do you sound so shocked? Yes, I made cookies. Sugar cookies, actually."

"I would have been less surprised if you'd said you changed the oil on your truck."

"My truck doesn't need an oil change for another three thousand miles," he said, still obviously confused. "Why would I change the oil on my truck when it doesn't need it?"

"You know how to change the oil on your truck?"

He let out a breath. "Is this like the *Costco run* thing? Is making cookies a euphemism? Or changing the oil?"

I walked up to him and wrapped my arms around his waist, leaning in for a kiss. Judd immediately stopped talking and kissed me as if it had been months since we'd last seen each other instead of hours.

When I finally pulled away to catch my breath, he was smiling. "I'd like to feed you my cookies."

"Now you're the one making it dirty," I said with a laugh.

We teased and flirted as he pulled out the cookies, still warm from the oven. "What were you doing out in your truck if you just made these tonight?" I asked. When he'd pulled into the Timber lot, I'd assumed he'd been on a call or running errands.

"It was nine thirty, and you still weren't here. I came looking for you."

My stomach flipped. "Really?"

He nodded. "I missed you. And I wanted to see you in person so I could make it official. I'd like to take you out on a date. A real one."

I stared at him. Judd Kincaid was seriously asking me out? And calling it a real date?

"I would invite you to my sister's wedding in Napa the weekend after next, but I would imagine a Marian family wedding weekend as a first date would kill any chance at a second date."

He laughed as he propped himself on the edge of the kitchen counter. "I think you're right. Baby steps. I was thinking maybe we could head up to Billings and check out the deals at a big-box store I know."

I moved between his legs and put my hands on his chest. "You could always take me to the Palomino. Make all those other boys jealous."

He leaned in and kissed me. "They'd be jealous, alright. I'd be there with the most beautiful man in Montana on my arm."

All of this was a dream. One I didn't want to wake from.

"Maybe we could just go see a movie," I suggested. "I've never gotten to hold hands in a movie with a guy."

He nodded. "Dinner and a movie it is. Also, I'm headed to a conference that weekend, so even if I was brave enough for a Marian wedding, I wouldn't be available. But I'm counting on you regaling me with tales of flammable decorations, the venue exceeding capacity, and unsafe storage of alcohol. It's the Marians, after all."

I tickled him in retaliation, which led to the sexiest wrestling competition of my life and ended in a shouted orgasm with my head hanging off one side of the bed while Judd finger-fucked me into oblivion.

"Anything else I can do for you, Firebug?" he teased breathlessly after he fed me his cock while I was still high from my own orgasm.

"Need my special effects permit reinstated," I croaked, my voice still wrecked from the abuse of my throat.

Instead of killing the mood, my words made his deep laugh echo around the room.

"I reinstated it three weeks ago. Don't you ever check your email?"

Sure enough, the next day at work, I found an email from early October.

Dear Mr. Marian,

Following review of the incident and confirmation of your compliance with fire safety protocols, the suspension of Timber's special effects permit has been lifted effective immediately.

Your establishment is once again authorized to use approved special effects in accordance with Legacy Fire Department regula-tions. Please ensure continued adherence to all safety measures in place, including staff training, proper equipment use, and routine inspections.

We appreciate your cooperation and look forward to main-taining a safe environment for both your staff and patrons.

Respectfully,

Judd Kincaid

Fire Chief

Legacy Fire Department

I closed my eyes and pictured Judd Kincaid's face the way it looked when he'd barked at me to come a few hours earlier in the shower. His eyes dark as pitch, his jaw clenched, and his entire focus on my pleasure.

Respectfully, my ass. Knowing Judd the way I did now, I knew he wished he could revoke that permit permanently, if only to keep me safe. It had most likely taken all of his self-control and professionalism to write that email.

While he knew now that it was a twenty-year-old who'd made the mistake that had led to the bar top fire, he still hated anything that put people in danger.

And I understood now the reason for his vigilance.

I hoped he understood that I wasn't a shot-slinging bartender at a club in a big city, trying to impress people for tips. I cared deeply for Timber and its people, and that included feeling responsible for the historic building it was in.

I hit Reply on the email.

Dear Chief Kincaid,

I know how hard that was for you to send, and I appreciate it.

Timber and its people will take the utmost care to make sure we continue to serve the people of Legacy with strict adherence to all such safety measures and concerns. Thank you for your trust in us.

Sincerely,

Alexander Marian

Owner

Timber - Artisanal Pizza & Curated Wines

A few minutes later, my phone buzzed with a text.

SMOKEY THE OVERBEAR

I can't decide if your email was snarky or sincere.

It said sincerely, didn't it?

SMOKEY THE OVERBEAR

I need you in my bed when I get home tonight. It will be after midnight because of another late training session. I left a key under the mat. Tell me you'll be there.

You're very bossy.

SMOKEY THE OVERBEAR

Huh. That explains why people keep calling me Chief around here.

Go back to work, Chief. I'll see you tonight.

All I got in return was a fire emoji.

"You're checking your phone again," Lennon said without looking up from his burger.

My sister and cousins had convinced me to come out for a late dinner at Frank's, and now they were giving me hell. I slipped the phone back in my sweatshirt pocket.

"What's new at the ranch?" I asked.

He shrugged and kept eating, so I turned to Rosie. "What's new at the ranch?"

"Boosters and tags, mostly," she said, dipping a fry in ketchup. "All the stock is off summer range, and we're staging hay for winter. The hands are working on equipment maintenance. Checking the plows and stuff."

Ella leaned in and lowered her voice. "I heard the fire chief is seeing someone up in Billings."

My ears perked up, and my heart started beating harder. "Where'd you hear that?"

"One of the servers at the Pinecone said she heard it directly from the horse's mouth. The chief said he was visiting his special friend up in Billings. She didn't know who the woman was, though."

I hid a wince. Hadn't I promised Ella I'd keep my hands off the chief since she liked him, too? I was a shit brother.

"What would you do if he asked you out?" I asked.

"I'd say hell yeah. Why?"

I huffed out a laugh. It was like that, was it? Good. "No reason." Maybe she'd forgotten our little agreement.

"What about you, Alex the Grape?" Rosie asked. "Tavo said you haven't been around much. In fact... he kind of implied you've been spending the night out."

Ella turned to me with red laser eyeballs. "Spill. Everything. Right fucking now."

I was a terrible liar. Judd had been right when he'd accused me of that. I swallowed and loosened my muscles so that I didn't stiffen up like people do when they get put on the spot.

"Yeah, so. Yeah," I said.

And then blinked. What? What even was that?

Ella's eyebrows shot into her bangs. "Oh my fucking god. Who the fuck are you seeing?"

Rosie blinked rapidly, her lips opening but not letting any sound out. Even Lennon leaned forward.

"No," I corrected. "I mean, yeah, but no."

Was that worse? I had a feeling that was worse.

Just then, Legacy's sexiest fire chief walked in to pick up a large to-go order for his crew. As he caught sight of the four of us sitting at a nearby table, he up-nodded casually and said, "Marians," and then continued to the counter as if nothing was amiss.

As if my body part hadn't been inside of his body part early this morning.

I swallowed. "I have a lover in Spokane."

My sister and cousins' heads swiveled toward me, and I could have sworn the chief's head tilted.

"Spo... kane," Ella said. "That's an eight-and-a-half-hour drive from here."

Lennon's face dipped into a thoughtful frown. "No wonder you look like shit. More driving than fucking."

Judd's shoulders crunched forward slightly like he was holding back a laugh.

"No, not Spokane," I snapped. "I always get them mixed up."

"Emigrant," the chief coughed.

"Emigrant," I said quickly. "*Emigrant.* Two hours over the mountains, that's all."

Ella stared at me. "You mix up Emigrant and Spokane?"

Rosie looked confused. "Doesn't Emigrant have like three people in it? How do I even know the name?"

Lennon was more generous. "Good barbecue in Emigrant. I can see the appeal."

I sat up and stretched my neck. "So anyway. Enough said.

What about your love life, Ella? Papa said he's planning on setting you up for the wedding. It's either that or he's inviting Britt Schmidt. Your choice."

That was enough to change the subject. My sister's pompous ex was always good for a healthy rant session, and there was nothing Ella was more hypocritical about than the family messing in her own love life. She'd do anything to avoid talking about the guy who'd been an on-again, off-again rollercoaster of drama.

When we were finally finished and we all went our separate ways, I made a beeline for Kincaid's place. After I got there and let myself in with the key he left, I sent Tavo a quick text.

> I'm out for the night and if my nosy family wants to know my comings and goings, tell them I'm in Emigrant.

TAVO

> I feel like this is a racial joke which is unexpected coming from you.

> It's a town on the other side of the Absarokas.

TAVO

> Why are you going there?

> I'll tell you when you get a little older.

Tavo sent me back a laughing emoji and an eggplant emoji.

I took a long, hot shower in Kincaid's bathroom, reveling in the fact that I was done with work for the day and had the entire house to myself.

We didn't know each other well enough for me to even consider poking around in his things. Kincaid had trusted me with access to his place, and I didn't want to fuck up that trust by being nosy. So after the shower, I grabbed a pair of his pajama pants from the dresser where I'd already seen they lived and slid into his big bed. The sheets and pillowcases smelled like his citrus body-wash, and the familiar scent lulled me half to sleep right away.

From my spot on the bed, I could see into the partly open closet, where a well-worn ball cap sat on a shelf. The words were hard to make out, but it looked like it said *Summer Song*. There was something familiar about that.

It reminded me of a poem I'd read... and something else. But I was already half-asleep, cradled and comforted by the scent and warmth of Judd Kincaid. And the rest of my efforts to remember were lost to slumber.

22

KINCAID

DrunkenPoet: *What would you do to me first if you had me naked and at your mercy?*

IndexEcho: *Stare. Then touch.*

I WAS A SELFISH MAN; I knew this. But when I saw Alex, sleep-warm and irresistible, I had to have him. First, I washed the mountain off me and used the shower spray to warm my skin so I didn't freeze him with my touch.

When I slipped naked into bed and wrapped myself around him, I started with gentle kisses under his ear, down his neck. Across his shoulders and down to his nipples. The skin tightened against my tongue as he let out a breathy noise.

"Shh," I murmured. "It's just the man from Spokane."

Low laughter rumbled through his chest to my lips. "I hate you."

"I adore you. You're about the most adorable thing I've ever seen."

His fingers moved into my damp hair. "Who are you, and where did you put my grumpy fire chief?"

I continued kissing a path down his stomach to the hair above the waistband of his borrowed pajamas.

"You smell like my shower stuff," I said gruffly. That scent, especially after finding him in my clothes, was bringing out the same possessive feelings I always had when getting naked with Alex Marian.

"Mmm. It's funny because grapefruit tastes like dirt and disappointment, but somehow, I've started thinking it smells delicious and sexy, and—oh, god, I need to stop talking," he babbled, trying to push my head lower.

Though he sounded half-asleep, his dick was already hard enough to tent the pajama fabric. I pulled them down and revealed his cock, warm and stiff with a bead of precum at the tip.

I kissed the salty fluid off and yanked down the pants until he was completely bare. Then I moved to the bedside table and grabbed the lube and a condom.

"Grab your knees, baby," I murmured. "Show me that tight little hole."

There was still a little moonlight coming through the window, enough to make out the puckered skin squeezing tight when he pulled his knees up. I leaned in to lick a stripe across the musky skin. "Stay just like that."

I licked and sucked and nipped until Alex was pleading for my fingers. "You want my cock tonight?" I asked, moving up so I could see his reaction.

"Yes," he breathed. "Fucking finally."

He'd begged me to fuck him during previous hookup sessions, but I'd held back. It wasn't because I didn't think he was ready. If he said he was ready, he was ready. The problem was me. I hadn't been sure *I* was ready.

I'd talked a big game about this only being physical, but from the first time our lips had touched, part of me had known it would go like this. That when I took him, when I buried myself balls-deep inside him, I wouldn't be able to walk away or treat Alex Marian like anything other than mine. Once we did this, it wouldn't be casual anymore by any stretch of the imagination.

And after seeing him flustered around his family tonight, willing to lie to keep this thing between us private, I'd wanted to claim him so badly. Tell his family, put all of Legacy on notice that Alexander Marian was *mine*... and would be for a very long time.

"This isn't a lesson," I told him. "Tell me you know that."

His eyes widened. "Okay."

"It's you and me." I opened the condom and rolled it on. "Something real."

Alex's smile was wide, even though it was still sleepy, too. "Who knew you were soft under all those fire codes, Chief."

I leaned up and kissed him while I slid two slick fingers inside him to help with the stretch. "Not soft," I murmured against his lips. "Just happy."

Alex's soft gasps filled my cock, making me ache for him. I moved him onto his side and slid in behind him, notching his knee up to give me easier access and make it more comfortable. He was still relaxed and pliant from sleep and let me move him exactly where I wanted him.

"Tell me to stop or slow down, okay?" I murmured against the side of his face as I moved my cock between his cheeks to his hole.

Alex's hands came up to hold the arm I had banded around his chest. My hand gripped his opposite shoulder as I worked hard not to go too fast.

As I began working my dick into his tight hole, he sucked in a gasp.

"Relax, baby," I reminded him. "Take a breath, push out. Just like that."

The tight heat of his body made my eyes roll back and my balls tighten. Fuck, he felt good. "So fucking tight for me," I breathed. "You feel amazing."

After a minute of my shallow thrusts, Alex's butt moved back toward me, seeking more. "Judd," he whimpered.

"You want me inside you, Firebug? Want to feel me fucking into your tight hole?" I squeezed his ass cheek with my free hand. "Fuck, you're making me lose my mind. Squeeze my cock." I let out a filthy groan as I pushed through the squeeze and bottomed out, my pubic hair brushing his ass and my balls resting on his inner thigh.

Alex moved his arm back to thread his fingers into my hair and hold my face next to his. His breath came in shallow pants. "You're fucking huge."

I pulled back and thrust gently forward again. Now it was his turn to groan.

Alex's fingers tightened in my hair. "Oh god. Judd, fuck. Please move."

My hips moved on their own, sliding back and pushing forward over and over until I was fucking him in a steady rhythm. I pulled back enough to look down at where my cock was stretching him, at his rim, which was sloppy-slick and shiny with lube. I moved my fingers down to rub my thumb across the taut, sensitive skin, and he whimpered.

"You're so fucking hot like this, spread out on my cock." My voice was rough with want, and I wondered how much longer I would last. He felt so fucking good.

I swiped some of the lube off my dick and pressed against his back again. When I wrapped my slick hand around Alex's cock, he arched back into me before bucking his hips and pushing himself into my fist.

I jacked him quickly with the help of his own thrusting. He was out of his mind with pleasure, crying out and gasping, clutching at my hair and hand until he came with a shout and a shiver.

He was so fucking hot, so beautiful, and knowing I was the only person he'd allowed this close to him was just the cherry on top. As soon as I felt his hot release on my fingers and smelled it in the air, I thrust deep inside him one final time and came.

My orgasm shot white-hot from the base of my spine to my toes and fingers, leaving me a grunting, shuddering mess.

We were plastered together as close as two people can get. Our sweat-damp skin was touching from knees to neck, and I reached around him with both arms to hold him tightly, pressing kisses to the side of his face and neck.

"You're so fucking sexy," I said. "So gorgeous."

I couldn't stop praising him for his submission and surrender. For trusting me. For letting me have that experience with him.

"Stay right here. I'll be back."

I held the condom and pulled out, wincing at his discomfort and the mess until I could hustle into the bathroom and clean myself up. Once I'd brought out a wet cloth to clean him up, too, I moved in next to him and pulled the covers back up over us. "C'mere."

I moved him so his head was on my shoulder and his arm wrapped around my middle, while my arm curled protectively over his shoulders. "You okay?"

He shuddered again. "God, yes. I can still feel you. But I also feel empty. It's weird."

"Mm."

"Have you ever bottomed?"

"Yeah. And if you want me to bottom for you, I absolutely will."

Alex moved up to rest his chin on my chest so he could look at me. "You were so closed off at first. It's strange hearing you suddenly be so open."

I brushed the wild hair off his forehead. "I didn't want to let go of the man I still had feelings for."

"What made you change your mind?"

"I caught feelings for another man," I said with a smile. "Either that or I've decided you need a full-time fire-safety officer to make sure you don't get into trouble. One of the two."

His laughing eyes flashed in the darkness. "Is that what I am? Your pet project?"

I nodded. "Someone has to keep you safe, baby, and it's clearly going to take expert-level care."

We fell asleep exchanging soft teases and kisses. And in the morning, he was gone. Off to a family thing and then straight into work.

I made my way to the station house, where things were already heating up with more calls than we had crew for. I spent the rest of the day in resource-management mode, coordinating with nearby counties and state agencies. Just before I was set to head out, another call came in. This time, there was a railcar derailment in nearby Roscoe requiring as many volunteers as possible.

I grabbed my gear, along with McMasters and Sujo, and headed out.

The following ten days were another batch of heavy-load workdays either for Alex or me so that we only had a few more late nights together before we both headed out to our respective trips, he to his sister's wedding and me to the conference in Spokane.

Believe me, I teased the fuck out of him for *actually* sleeping with someone in Spokane.

Once we were a couple of states away from each other, we were left with only a few text exchanges here and there as we could each catch a free moment.

Which was why I was shocked to get an invitation to join the Flint app from *TimberAlex* one night.

I clicked to download the app, quickly created a login, and checked out the message waiting for me. If Alex wanted to send me racy pics, all he'd need to do was text them to me.

When I opened the first message, there was a photo of a naked torso from the base of the neck down to the top of the man's pubic hair, showing the barest hint of a dick tip.

But I knew Alex Marian's body like the back of my hand by now, and that was not my Alex in the photos.

The message read, "Hey Chief, I've got a hot fire for you to put out right here."

Then there was another photo. This one was of a man's hand holding a hard cock. While it was plenty hot, it wasn't Alex. Although now that I looked at both photos, I could see the man was similar to Alex in body type and coloring.

I typed back.

HotChief: *Who is this?*

The next photo that came through was a snapshot of my Alex dancing at a wedding. He looked so hot in his tux, my gut immediately tightened with heat and desire. The way the pants curved along his delicious ass. His white shirt pulled around his biceps. The jacket was gone, and the bow tie was loose enough to allow an open button at the base of his neck.

He was dancing with a woman in a wedding gown, and I zoomed in to look for similarities in the sister I hadn't met yet.

TimberAlex: *I want you.*

I quickly typed back in an effort to figure out what was going on.

HotChief: *If I tell you Josh and I go way back, which Josh am I referring to?*

TimberAlex: *Stop playing silly games and ask me out on a date. Feuding makes the best foreplay.*

Whoever was pretending to be Alex was at Mattie's wedding but didn't know the two of us were no longer feuding. It had to be Ella or one of his Legacy cousins.

HotChief: *Why would I go out with someone who's reckless and careless?*

TimberAlex: *Because I'm amazing in bed.*

No shit.

HotChief: *Send me another dick pic. This time I want to see those black and white socks in the pic, too.*

Unsurprisingly, I didn't hear back from *TimberAlex*.

I waited until I got a text from him a couple of hours later, asking if I was still up, before video calling him.

"Hey," he said with a wide grin as his image appeared on my larger laptop screen. "God, it's good to see you. Fuck."

I noticed his glassy eyes and soft grin. "You're drunk."

He grinned. "Shakespeare said, 'So long as men can breathe or eyes can see, So long lives this, and this gives life to thee.' I think I finally get it. So long as these eyes can see..." He stopped on a sigh. "Good shit. Can always count on the Bard, can't we? Ignore me. I get poetic when I drink." His snicker of laughter was adorable.

"I take it you had a nice time at the wedding?"

"Woulda had a better time if you'd been here, Chief. How's the convention? I feel like I haven't seen you in days."

My eyes roved over him, taking in every detail. "Because you haven't seen me in days," I said with a smile. "I miss you, too."

"Take off your clothes," he said in a sexy voice.

"First, I need to ask you to do a search on your phone for the Flint app."

His forehead crinkled. "I don't have the Flint app."

"Just check and see. Can you think of anyone who might have had access to your phone tonight?"

I saw his jaw drop as he stared down at his phone screen. "What the fuck? Oh shit, I'm going to kill her!"

"Was it Ella?"

"No! It was my great-great-aunt Tilly! She does shit like this all the fucking time. I can't believe she... Whose dick is this?"

He took a minute to read through the messages, murmuring, "The wine," to the Josh question. Then his expression became thoughtful. "She's not wrong. Feuding does make the best foreplay. I'm kinda bummed we didn't get to have angry sex when we were still enemies."

"Our relationship is young, Firebug. Give it time."

His eyes lit up. "Yeah? You gonna stay with me long enough for us to have makeup sex?"

I grinned. "Expert-level care, remember?"

Alex's alcohol-flushed cheeks went even pinker, but he looked pleased... at least until he glanced back at his phone. "I'm so annoyed that Tilly did this. What was her goal? Humiliating me?"

"I think she was trying to matchmake us."

He frowned. "By telling you I'm amazing in bed? Gross! Why not tell *HotChief* what a nice man I am or how smart I am?"

I let out a laugh. "That's... not what men usually share on Flint, baby."

Alex's eyes narrowed. "Oh yeah? You familiar with the app?"

"It was created by firefighters for firefighters," I explained.

"Answer the implied question, Chief."

"You said something about me getting naked," I said, moving to pull up my shirt.

Thankfully, that got a laugh out of him. "Fine, change the subject with a strip show. I'll allow it."

He was so fucking fun. So sweet and interesting. And he *was* nice and smart... as well as amazing in bed.

By the time we were both on the verge of coming on camera, he begged. "I need to come. Please."

"Slide your fingers inside your hole, baby," I urged. "Find that good spot for me and stroke it."

The camera angle was a little off, but I could see the pink flush of his skin, the hard shaft of his cock, and the tight skin squeezing around his fingers.

"Fuck, baby, coming," I gritted out just as I heard his cry. After we both came down from our orgasms, he moved the camera up so I could see his ruddy face and bright eyes.

"My parents probably heard that," he said sheepishly.

"It's late, and their first child just got married. Maybe they're having their own noisy celebration. Ever think of that?"

Alex's face fell. "That's disgusting. How dare you harsh my vibe like that."

"I love that you have gay dads. My parents were definitely not accepting. Don't get me wrong, I loved them. But I'm not sure they would have been supportive if I'd been old enough and ready to come out to them."

"Half my family's gay," he said. "The poor straights like my sisters always feel left out. My cousin Cami even dated a girl because she was convinced that she was probably at least bi. No dice. Couldn't even fake it."

We continued talking for another half hour until I noticed his eyes beginning to droop. "Get some sleep, Firebug," I murmured. "Talk tomorrow?"

His smile was sweet. "Yeah. Night, Chief."

I ended the call and sighed happily. When I closed the video app window, my email app was open behind it, showing a new email from Max's private investigator friend. I assumed it was my final statement, so I opened it... and found something else entirely.

> *Judd,*
>
> *You said to stop the investigation, but I already had several irons in the fire. One lead came back tonight. Don't know if you still want it or not?*
>
> *I tracked down the IP address of the target to Napa, CA. Specifically to a place called Alexander Vineyards. The same IP address showed up on quite a lot of social media traffic this evening, including Grindr, Flint, IG, FB, and TikTok. Unsure if the target works there, lives there, or attended an event there, although the idea he was carrying on regular conversations with you over a long period of time would indicate he lived or worked here.*
>
> *The vineyard is owned by the Marian family. During the year*

you were in regular contact with DrunkenPoet, the legal residents of that property included Bartholomew (aka, Blue), Tristan, and Alexander Marian, as well as a live-in caretaker named Angie Rousseau. The only one of the four who took any fire certification classes during that time was Alexander. According to online records, he attained his ICS-100 during that time.

Let me know if you have further questions or would like me to re-open the search to get confirmation.

I stared at the screen, trying to make sense of what I was seeing.

Yes, Alex Marian was at his family's vineyard in Napa. Yes, he and his friends and family had probably been using a ton of apps there tonight. But the connection to *DrunkenPoet*, to the investigator...

I thought back to the moment Alex picked up the call.

So long as men can breathe or eyes can see...

What the actual fuck?

Ignore me. I get poetic when I drink.

My head spun as memories came flooding in. Of *DrunkenPoet* saying he was expected to take over the family farm. *Farm.*

But wasn't a vineyard essentially a farm? And had he even been the one to call it a farm, or had I misunderstood?

I thought back through almost a year of messages between me and *DrunkenPoet*, a year of getting to know someone who I was... now sleeping with? How was that possible? It wasn't. It just fucking wasn't.

I opened the forum where we'd originally met and had all of our conversations. They were still there, but his messages showed as sent from [Deleted User].

It took me hours to go through them all, looking for proof that

Alex Marian and *DrunkenPoet* couldn't possibly be the same person.

Instead, I heard Alex's voice in every single one of them. The same sweet, teasing tone, the sometimes naive take on things like relationships and sex. The love of pizza and dislike of grapefruit.

I also saw my messages encouraging him to leave his family and pursue his own dreams.

Which he'd done.

He'd moved to Montana three years ago to open Timber. *Three years ago.*

I couldn't even wrap my head around this. How was it possible?

I had to tell him. What would his reaction be?

Since I was here in Spokane for an important conference, I had to force myself to try and get some sleep. But when I finally fell asleep, it was to thoughts of what Alex had said about his ex. He'd been a firefighter who'd died.

I fell for him, hard. It's silly because we didn't know each other that well, but... we had an amazing connection.

Was it possible that *I* was Alex's dead firefighter? And that he'd had real feelings for me even then, the way I had for him?

23

ALEX

IndexEcho: *Three weeks, Poet. Three weeks and I'm flying home to you. There will be no more restrictions on what we can share. Your address is the first thing I'm asking for.*

DrunkenPoet: *I'm making a list of all the things I want to show you. Fair warning: it's getting long.*

IndexEcho: *I've got time. We've got time.*

THE NEXT MORNING AT BREAKFAST, I laid into Aunt Tilly. "You think you're hilarious, but you're not. And you could have seriously screwed up my professional reputation," I snapped as I sat down.

Papa's eyes grew large from where he sat next to her. "Woah, hold on. What's happening?"

I pointed at Tilly. "Manage your attack dog. She stole my

phone, downloaded a hookup app, and then sent a dick pic from me to a professional colleague."

So what if that wasn't the entire truth? Chief Kincaid was definitely a professional colleague of mine; he just happened to be one whose inner thigh I'd tasted.

"Colleague, my ass," she said. "The two of you have hate burning so hot, there's bound to be a conflagration soon enough."

My cheeks were a conflagration at the knowledge of how right she was. But from the way she was talking, it sounded like she hadn't had time to scroll my actual text messages. "That's my business, not yours. Stay out of my damned phone *and* my business."

I gathered my things and went to sit at another table. Unfortunately, this one had my cousin Jett at it. I'd been avoiding him all weekend.

"Well, well," he began. "If it isn't my harasser. Tell me, did you get to enjoy my castoffs? That was a long time ago; I'm surprised the guy remembered. Who can remember one random hookup from three years ago? Christ."

I put my middle finger in his face. "You blowing him off caused me a lot of grief. Stop doing rude shit if you're going to walk around with my face and last name."

He laughed and sat back, resting his coffee cup on his chest. "Not my fault we have the same biological parents."

Our aunt Simone flicked Jett behind the ear. "Watch it. Alex, I would claim. You, not so much."

Papa's sister, Simone, had donated her eggs when my dads had decided to have another child with a gestational carrier. The carrier got pregnant on the first try, which left several embryos leftover, so when my uncles decided to start their family the following year, Dad, Papa, and Simone had donated the embryos to them.

Jett and I shared the same DNA. Aunt Simone's and my

dad's. We rarely talked about it because it simply wasn't important, but at times like this, I wished Uncle Mav and Uncle Beau had gotten their own damned genetic material instead of using mine.

It was true what I'd told Judd: Jett didn't take anything seriously, and he loved sex. He'd practically made a career out of sleeping with as many people as possible, always claiming he was planning on growing his body count until the moment he stepped off this mortal coil.

Simone's son JJ always teased Jett that he was going to be like one of those retirees in the Villages in Florida, having to get treated for an STI from all the old-man sex.

"At least I'll die happy," Jett always responded with a grin.

"My family's going to be the death of me," I murmured into my coffee. "First you, now Tilly."

"What did she do?" Simone asked. I told everyone at the table about Tilly's Flint app extravaganza.

Jett barked out a laugh. "That explains why she asked me to take a dick pic in the men's room last night. She told me to borrow your socks."

"Tell me that wasn't your dick in my phone," I groaned.

"Fuck no. Even I have my limits, and sending my great-great-aunt a picture of my junk is one of them." Jett shrugged. "Besides, I was too busy hooking up with the lead singer of the band. Worth every flirty look, let me tell you."

I held up a hand. "Save the raunchy escapade stories for someone who gives a shit."

"Agreed," Simone said with a nod. Then she pinned Jett with a look. "One day, a man is going to knock you over with his special sauce, and you're not going to know what hit you."

I pointed at him. "And then he's going to say, 'No, thanks,' and leave you wanting."

Simone nodded, and my cousin Cami's big doe eyes flicked back and forth between all of us.

"And then," my cousin Wolfe added softly, "you're going to spend the rest of your life wanting someone you can't have."

"Harsh," I said, clapping Wolfe on the shoulder. I tried to lighten the mood, if only to distract everyone from his comment. Most of us knew that Wolfe had fostered a crush on Trace Bishop for years. But Trace was one of Wolfe's father's best friends and at least twenty years Wolfe's senior. That dream wasn't ever going to come to fruition. "But Jett would deserve it from all the poor boys whose hearts he's probably inadvertently stomped on over the years. Right, Jett?"

"Hey, they know the deal when they invite me up, right?" He winked at me, but I could see the understanding in his expression for our sweet cousin.

We continued to joke around until Mattie and her new husband finally showed up. And then our family did what we were best at—giving people love and hell at the same time.

Judd was strangely quiet the rest of the weekend, but I assumed the conference had taken more of his time and attention than he'd expected. I remembered one of his early rules: work came first.

Which made sense. Not only did I never want to come between him and his career, but I also didn't want him to come between me and mine. And while I cared a hell of a lot about Judd Kincaid, Timber was my priority. I was proud of the work I was doing there and eager to get back to it.

But when I did get back to Legacy and found Judd Kincaid standing in the back lot of Timber, waiting for me, all of those thoughts about priorities went out the window.

"Ask me up to your place, Firebug."

My heart took flight in my chest. "What about Tavo?"

"Tell Tavo you'll keep his secret if he'll keep yours."

There was something odd in his expression. His words were teasing, but his eyes weren't. He looked bothered by something. Or maybe just tired.

"Yeah. Come on up," I said.

Thankfully, Tavo wasn't home. He'd been over at Lennon's place to help with some ranch work, and chances were, he was staying over anyway. Rosie had started keeping a guest room ready for him anytime he wanted a hot meal and a quiet night at their place.

After a quick tour, I led Judd into my bedroom and closed the door.

"How was your conf—*nngh*!"

His mouth crushed mine as his arms came around me, holding me tighter than he ever had before. My back hit the door with a thump, and I nearly tripped over my heels.

I sucked in a breath and let it happen. Being mauled by Judd Kincaid was no hardship, and I was here for it in every way.

And what followed was *definitely* a mauling. Within moments, I was naked and face down on my bed with Judd's cock buried inside me.

It was hot as fuck.

I could barely catch my breath. My dick was so hard I couldn't think. And Kincaid's voice in my ear mumbling *mine*, along with various expletives, like a rough, growly chant, tipped me over the edge.

I came embarrassingly fast, and as soon as I cried out, Judd pulled out and flipped me over, shoving back inside of me while kissing me hungrily on the lips.

He whimpered into my mouth as he came but never stopped kissing me. By the time we were done, I felt like I was a Mentos dropped into a bottle of soda and shaken.

"I missed you so fucking much," he said, tucking his face into my neck. The words sounded desperate and strange.

I hugged him. "It's okay. I'm here. We're back."

Even though we were both now covered in a variety of ick, I continued to hold him close and rub his back until I felt his body relax further.

"You okay?" I asked.

He pulled back and met my eyes, except he seemed to be looking into my fucking soul. "I am now, yeah."

Was this how Judd was after a weeklong break from someone he cared about, or were these remnants of fear left from the man who broke his heart?

Either way, my plan was to reassure him and be there for him without pressing him to tell me more. We'd only just started this thing between us—hell, we hadn't even had our real date yet— and I didn't want to do anything to fuck it up.

"Come shower with me," I said. "And then you're going right to sleep. You look like hell."

"I need to tell you about this weekend—"

"And you will. Later. Right now, you need to clean up and catch up on some zzz's."

It turned out Judd wasn't the only one who wanted to give expert-level care. Part of me wanted nothing more than to protect and soothe the bear of a man.

And that wasn't the only surprising revelation of the evening. Because for the ten minutes it took us to shower, brush our teeth, and get back in bed, Judd Kincaid—my grumpy, standoffish fire chief—was clingy.

24

KINCAID

DrunkenPoet: *BBQ chicken or pork for pizza? Testing ideas for my sister's birthday dinner.*

IndexEcho: *[No response]*

DrunkenPoet: *Index, you there? Get caught up on a long shift?*

IndexEcho: *[No response]*

WHEN I WOKE up in Alex's bed, he wasn't there. Since there was a giant tractor-trailer in the back lot, I assumed he was getting an early morning delivery of some kind.

Unfortunately, Tavo *was* there, and I surprised him.

"Dios mio!" he yelped, jumping back and slapping a hand over his heart. "Chief Kincaid? What are you doing here?"

I'd been all ballsy last night, saying if we could keep Tavo's secret, he could keep ours, but now in the bright light of morning, I didn't feel nearly as in control.

In fact, everything in my life felt wildly out of control right about now.

"Uh, Alex said I could test his smoke detector," I said stupidly.

Tavo looked unsure. "Okay?"

I stared at him. He stared back. Finally, he spoke. "Need me to show you where it is?"

I nodded.

He pointed up.

Sure enough, it was exactly where you would expect it to be. I reached up and pressed the Test button. It made a god-awful chirp that left a ringing in my ears despite the fact that I'd heard that sound hundreds of thousands of times.

"Works great," I mumbled before getting the hell out of there.

I found my vehicle two streets over where I'd parked it and took off for the station house. When I arrived, things were already hopping. Thankfully, work stayed busy for the first half of the day, and by the time it slowed down, I'd chilled out a little.

I could figure this out. I'd think of a way to bring up our online history with Alex, we'd talk it through, and then we'd get past it. No problem.

My quasi-chill only lasted until I was called to the corporate office of Untrace for another small incident.

Once again, Will Wascomb had accidentally set his desk on fire.

"To be fair," Hazel Marian said, staring at the twice-burned desk, "I did say he could still use a mug warmer at his desk."

"Did you advise him to stop using paper at his desk while he used it?" I asked.

Ella Marian snorted from the doorway of her office, which was next to Will's. "Critical oversight," she murmured.

Will himself looked horrified and guilty. "I'm so, so sorry! What can I do to make it up to you, Ms. Marian?"

Hazel's eyes widened. "Well, for one, you can stop calling me that. Since when do we do last names around here?"

Ella snickered and crooked her finger at me. "Now that the danger is gone, do you have a minute?"

I glanced at Sujo, who indicated he had everything under control, and then I followed Ella into her office. When she closed the door, I was surprised.

"How can I help?" I asked politely, reminding myself she had no idea I was in a relationship with her brother.

As far as she was concerned, I was the fire chief who gave her brother grief... not the fire chief who gave her brother dick.

I blew out a breath and tried to find my chill again, but it was gone.

"Who is my brother sleeping with?" she asked, folding her arms over her chest.

"Um, what?" I'd been wrong before when I thought I had no chill. Now I had actual negative amounts of it.

I had... what was the opposite of chill?

I had hellfire.

"I know you know who my brother is hooking up with. The other night at Frank's, you corrected him." Ella's intelligent eyes bored into me. "Who's the guy in Emigrant? I need to know, and he's not talking."

"Why do you need to know?" I asked, stalling for time.

"Okay, you don't know this about my brother, but he's actually very sweet. And naive. I don't think he has as much experience as he claims to have, and I worry about him getting hurt."

I opened my mouth to say something, but I didn't even know where to begin.

Which was fine because Ella kept talking. "Look, I'm going to tell you something in confidence, okay? And only because I'm genuinely worried."

I nodded, throat tight, and she continued.

"He was talking to this guy online a few years ago and really fell for him. Only the guy ended up ghosting him. Alex totally believed this guy's story—that he had a dangerous job and he couldn't meet up in person because he was stationed overseas at a 'mystery location' and blah blah," she said with air quotes and an eyeball. "He even thinks the guy died and that's why he suddenly disappeared. That's how naive he is."

"Or maybe the guy was exactly who he said he was," I tried. "Maybe Alex wasn't naive at all. Maybe something really did happen to him. Maybe he... maybe he's been desperate to get back in touch with Alex all this time but hasn't found a way yet."

"In several years?" Ella snorted. "At this point, I hope the asshole stays gone because no good could come of them getting in touch again. The whole experience... it broke Alex, Chief. *Crushed* him. He spent years grieving someone who might never have existed, and he's avoided getting close to anyone romantically ever since. It's like he's almost expecting to get his heart broken again." Her eyes met mine. "So if Alex finally *has* put himself out there again, I need to make sure whoever he's hooking up with isn't another asshole user who's going to fuck him over or saddle him with more pain and confusion." She blew out a breath. "My brother deserves happiness. Simple, uncomplicated happiness."

I stared at her.

She was right that Alex deserved nothing but happiness. But she was wrong about wanting the past to stay buried. Alex would want to know who I'd been to him. Who *we'd* been to each other. That wasn't a complication; it was the truth. A part of our story.

Ella firmed her jaw in a way that was very familiar. "So tell me who the guy is," she said.

I wanted to tell her it was me. And that I was sorry for what Alex went through. And that I cared more for him than any ten more perfect men ever could.

But I wasn't about to tell her before I told him.

I shook my head. "I don't know anyone in Emigrant, I'm sorry."

Ella was kind of cute when she was stymied. "Well, hell. How can that be? How did you know he was seeing someone in Emigrant, then?"

"I didn't. It was all a big misunderstanding. Sorry, I need to get back to the station. Talk to your brother, Ella. If he wants you to know who he's seeing, he'll tell you. He's a big boy. Give him credit for making his own decisions."

I didn't wait for her response. After telling Sujo I was heading out, I left... feeling ten times worse than I had this morning or last night.

Halfway back to the station, a call came in for a barn fire clear on the east side of town. I threw on lights and sirens and pulled onto the highway right behind one of our trucks.

I spent the rest of the afternoon dealing with a multi-structure fire that decimated three outbuildings and a quarter of the Hilldales' largest barn.

When I finally got a break just long enough to take a leak and down a bottle of water, I shot off a text to Alex.

I stared at the screen. We needed to talk. God only knew how long this shit could eat at me before I became physically sick from carrying it around.

> I have a crew dinner, but I'll duck out early. My place, eight tomorrow night?

FIREBUG

> Sounds perfect 🖤

I stared at the hearts as my own did a flip-flop in my chest. This man was it for me. Done. End of discussion.

I'd thought I was falling for him before, when I only knew him as *DrunkenPoet*. But that was nothing compared to the feelings I had for Alexander Marian.

I would do anything to keep him...

Even if it meant sitting on this news for thirty more hours.

25

ALEX

DrunkenPoet: *Please just tell me you're alive. I don't care if you changed your mind about us. I don't care if you want me to fuck off. Just tell me you're breathing somewhere.*

IndexEcho: *[No response]*

DrunkenPoet: *I love you. I love you and I'm sorry for whatever I did wrong.*

IndexEcho: *[No response]*

KINCAID WAS OFFICIALLY BEING WEIRD. I was half-tempted to duck out of work early and surprise him at his house, but I'd heard from Javi Sujo's girlfriend that the fire crew had been out battling a big barn fire all afternoon. The man probably needed hydration and rest after that.

"The fire chief's a tasty treat," someone said as I placed another pizza on the large row of tables pushed together for the SERA instructors. "We should've invited him."

"Forget about his ass," Monroe said with a shake of his head. "You should ask him about his work experience, man. Guy's hardcore."

I moved back to the kitchen, even though I was desperate to hear what he was saying about Judd. We still had several pizzas to get out in addition to the extra appetizers Trace had ordered when the original ones had run out.

After bringing more food out, I did a round of drink refills and helped two of my servers bus a few tables. Juni and Karim were beginning to clean up in the kitchen, and I was eager to stay caught up, on the slim chance the SERA group would make it an early-ish night.

Make that a *very* slim chance, considering they usually celebrated the end of another cohort session with a long night of craft brews and cocktails. I'd already had three orders of the Slingshot Flame tonight, and they seemed to be just getting started.

Judd would have been proud of me for my responsible fire-making.

"Hey, Alex, can I get another Get Lost Pale Ale?" Tommy asked as I moved behind him.

"Absolutely. What about Foster?" I glanced at my cousin with my eyebrow raised toward his boyfriend.

"Bourbon, but this is the last one since I'm not strong enough to carry the bastard."

Their dog, Chickie, lifted her head up from her spot under Tommy's chair. I leaned over and gave her long ears a little bit of love. "Good girl," I murmured. "And a treat for you, hm?"

Just as I was headed back with their drinks and a dog biscuit tucked in my apron pocket, I overheard Monroe say something about Kincaid again.

"And he's ARFF. So I asked him, what the fuck are you doing working here instead of on an airfield someplace? He used to work with big planes, like index E–level shit."

I stopped and stared. Then I carefully set down the drinks and asked Monroe to repeat what he'd said. I probably sounded deranged, but I didn't care. "What's ARFF, and what's index E?"

"Oh, aircraft rescue and firefighting. And index E means big planes. That's the indicator that an airport serves mostly planes longer than two hundred feet. Like 747s and 777s and MD-11s. It means the airport has to have at least three big-ass trucks with over six thousand gallons of water for foam production."

I already knew this, of course. I'd asked IndexEcho the origin of his username at one point and had gotten an explanation very similar to this one.

"How do you know all of that?" I asked, like I was just making casual conversation. "I thought you were mostly a helicopter pilot."

"I am." Monroe took a quick sip of his beer. "But my brother's a United pilot out of Denver. He's super-nerdy about all this stuff and bragged like a bitch when he got rated to fly MD-11s."

My stomach felt hollow, and my toes tingled with a strange kind of numbness. "That's cool," I said. "How do you know all of that about Chief Kincaid?"

"He told me about it one night last summer. And, honestly, I got the feeling he was probably just taking a break before finding another big ARFF job somewhere. Sounds like he needed a temporary gig until jumping back in the fray." Monroe grinned and winked. "Why the interest in the chief?"

I felt like my face was made of stone. "No reason. I just didn't realize that about him."

Tommy shot me a look, like he heard the strain in my voice, but he cleared his throat and summoned a smile. "Alex is probably fishing for some dirt on the chief. Guy's been a total pain in Alex's ass with inspections every week and shit."

The chief had definitely been a pain in my ass.

But he'd quickly become something else—the man I was falling for.

And now, it seemed, he was something way, way worse.

A fraud.

I didn't have the brainpower right now to figure out what this all meant, but I could feel in my bones it wasn't good.

"You guys need anything else?" I asked.

Tommy's smile dropped, and so did his voice. "Hey, you okay?"

I nodded and tried to smile. "Amazing."

And then I walked back to the kitchen like I was going to fetch something, found Karim and begged him to take over, raced up to my bedroom to crawl into my bed, and cried for two straight hours over the mess that Monroe's simple words had made of my love life.

Was it possible Judd Kincaid was *IndexEcho*?

If he was, then he wasn't dead, which was a miracle...

Except it also meant my sisters were right and he'd ghosted me four years ago, which would rip my heart out all over again.

And... *oh, fuck*. Did Judd know I was *DrunkenPoet*? Had he known all along and hidden it from me?

Months of our exchanged conversations flowed through my memories as I fought the temptation to pick up the phone and call him to clear all this up. That would be reactionary and foolish. Accusing Judd of being *IndexEcho*—even asking him if they might be the same person—would damage our relationship if it wasn't true. What would that say about my trust in him?

And if I made the accusation and it *was* true...

I closed my eyes and tried not to cry again because I'd already cried enough for this fucking man. But it was hard not to feel like fate had it out for me. I'd had something amazing at my fingertips, and it had been yanked away four years ago. And now here I was again, on the verge of losing the very next man I'd let myself fall for...

Either that or I'd been screwed twice by the same man.

I curled on my side, mashing my face into my pillow, and despite—or maybe because of—all this uncertainty, I found myself missing the citrus scent of Judd's sheets. The comfort I'd felt falling asleep in his arms, in his bed—

I lifted my head as a memory came freewheeling into my thoughts.

The ball cap I'd seen in Judd's closet before falling asleep weeks ago.

Summer Song.

At the time, I'd been half-asleep and hadn't processed why it seemed familiar. Why it had given me an extra level of comfort. Now I realized it wasn't just the words on the cap that were familiar but the *logo*.

Summer Song was a pale ale. *IndexEcho*'s favorite. From a brewery near his hometown, he'd said. And we'd joked about how I liked the name because it reminded me of a poem.

Like a lovesick idiot, I'd looked it up online after he'd mentioned it, desperate to get my hands on some just so I could drink his favorite beer and have an additional connection with him. I'd memorized the logo so I could look for it at the store. And when I hadn't been able to find it locally, I'd gone back online to see where it was brewed and where I could find it. It was a craft brew made and bottled in West Virginia. And it wasn't distributed anywhere outside of the mid-Atlantic.

Which, last I checked, was where Philadelphia was.

IndexEcho was Judd Kincaid. It was becoming obvious, and I could no longer deny it.

Did I even *want* to deny it? For so long, it had been my greatest wish that *IndexEcho* was alive and well in the world, even if he didn't want to be with me. Now, not only was he alive, but he was in my life. He'd made love to me. He'd held me for hours. He wanted to date me.

But another thing Monroe said also echoed in my head. *I got the feeling he was probably just taking a break before finding another big ARFF job somewhere.*

Judd and I had never talked about the possibility of him leaving Legacy, but *IndexEcho* had talked about what he wanted his future to look like. His job had been important to him. Part of his identity. Surely, he'd want to go back to aviation firefighting at some point.

And, hell, even if that had changed in the past few years, Judd was an active firefighter. He didn't just hassle small businesses about code violations. I'd seen him injured once already from a wildfire. I'd seen the burn scars on his body. I knew how often he was in the shit with his crew—situations that often led to serious injuries...

Or worse.

I'd lost *IndexEcho* once when he'd only been a dream, a fantasy. Could I handle losing him again now that I knew he was Judd Kincaid, the man I'd surrendered my body and my trust to?

No. Absolutely not. Not a chance.

And I was angry that he'd even consider putting me in that situation.

Again.

We were barely into... whatever this was. Hell, we hadn't even had a real date yet. And already I felt betrayed and heartbroken.

My tears came again, cooling the worst of my anger, hardening it like volcanic rock.

The next day, I woke up feeling hungover. I was dehydrated and sleep-deprived. My head pounded to the rhythm of my heartbeat until it felt like contractors were hammering around me all day.

Work was excruciating. We had a moms' group for lunch who'd brought a motley collection of babies and toddlers and stayed for two hours. Usually, I loved having this group on a weekday, especially now that tourist season was behind us. But today, it was torture.

By the time I went upstairs to shower and change before heading to Kincaid's house, I was low-key nauseous.

Tavo looked up from his spot playing video games in the living room. "You look like shit."

"Mm, you're the best kind of friend. Don't ever change."

"For real, man. You want me to call Ella? She gives you hell, but you know she'll come baby you if you're sick."

I shook my head carefully. "No. I'm going to hop in the shower, then I'm headed out."

As I turned, Tavo started to say something and stopped.

"What?" I asked, turning back to him.

"Remember that guy at the farmer's market who said he remembered me and the judge from back in San Francisco?"

I tried to think of what he was referring to, but I had no idea. "The guy in the ball cap?" I asked in surprise. "Wait, he said he knew Judge Miller?"

He hesitated. "Not really. He knew who he was, but it wasn't like he *knew him*-knew him. He was a server at Pinch, a club Kirk and I used to go to. I told him it wasn't me, and then Chief Kincaid made a joke about doppelgängers. That's when you walked up."

"Oh, right. And the chief told the story of mistaking me for my cousin because we look alike." That part I remembered.

He nodded. "Yeah, exactly. And the ball cap guy was super nice after that, moved on quickly and ended up buying a steel and flint from me. I just... I keep wondering if I should have been more worried about it than I was."

I considered this for a moment. "I wonder how he knew who the judge was? I own a restaurant in a tiny town, and I still don't know all my customers."

"Yeah. I think that's why it's bothering me." Tavo scooted sideways on the sofa so he could see me better. "The judge is a regular at Pinch. And this guy said the judge had been flashing money around to keep an eye on me. That's why it stood out for him. But you don't think...? I mean, it's not like this guy is going to go back to the judge and tell him he saw someone who looked like me, right?"

The chances of the judge asking some random server at a club if he'd seen a guy he was supposed to remember from a year earlier were unheard of. "I think you're okay," I said. "Besides, the judge has to drop this eventually. Maybe we should have asked the server if Judge Miller had been back with any other guys."

Tavo's eyebrows winged up. "Oh shit. Good call. That would have been sweet. Except then he would know I was the guy instead of someone who just looked like the guy."

He was right. Better to claim not to know anything about anything. "I'll tell Joel to have one of his investigators stop by and question people at the club. What club was it?"

"Pinch on Valencia."

I nodded and reassured him before heading back to my room to get ready. After showering, dressing, and shooting off an email to my uncle about Tavo's case, I headed to Kincaid's.

And tried not to vomit from nerves.

26

KINCAID

DrunkenPoet: *I have to stop looking for you. It's been four months and I'm losing myself.*

DrunkenPoet: *I'll never forget you, Index. You changed my life.*

DrunkenPoet: *I hope wherever you are, you're happy.*

WHEN I HEARD the crunch of tires on my driveway, I steeled myself.

After a long, sleepless night, this was finally it. I needed to confess the truth. Talk to Alex about our shared past. The forum messages. My accident.

My palms were damp, and my stomach was in knots. The last thing I wanted to do was cause him more pain.

I opened the door before he could knock. "Hey, Firebug."

He looked as awful as I felt. His eyes were red and scratchy-looking, his hair stood in all directions like he'd been yanking at it, his skin was pale and dull, and there was absolutely no life in his expression. Only exhaustion and resignation.

I stepped forward to pull him into my arms, but his words froze me in place.

"How long have you known?" He didn't even come in. Simply stood on my front porch and looked up at me. "I need to know how long you've known that I was *DrunkenPoet*."

Hearing that name in Alex's own voice was somehow still shocking. But whatever he saw on my face must have given away the fact that it wasn't *entirely* a shock. His nostrils flared, and his eyes hardened.

"Since the night of Mattie's wedding," I said quickly. "Since Spokane. And I was going to tell you immediately, but you—"

He closed his eyes and rocked back on his feet. "How did you find out?"

I hesitated. Somehow, despite spending thirty hours over-thinking this, I hadn't considered this part. Did I admit to him that I'd hired an investigator to find my long-lost love while I was already hooking up with Alex, or did I tell him—

"You have two seconds to tell me the fucking truth," he hissed. "Or I am out of here."

"Please come in," I urged gently. "We can talk about it."

Alex shook his head. "That would be a mistake. Just answer me."

"I... I hired someone. An investigator. To look for you. I mean, *DrunkenPoet*. But then..." I stopped. *Keep it simple, stupid.* "He told me the same IP address used in *DrunkenPoet*'s posts was being used at Alexander Vineyards. And that the only person who'd lived there during that time who also got an Incident Command certification was you. Alexander Marian."

His face fell. "You came back from that trip and had sex with me without saying a word."

Made love to you, I wanted to bark. But I kept myself calm and regulated for fear of making him bolt.

"I wanted to tell you," I began. "I tried to tell you, but you—"

"Me?" he snapped. "Are you seriously getting ready to tell me *I* was the reason you didn't tell me that my dead lover was alive and *oh by the way* his cock was already inside of me?" His voice had gone ragged until he was croaking out the last part. Tears fell down his face, and I tried reaching for him again.

He pulled away and took a big step back. "No," he said, swiping angrily at his face. "Do not touch me. Because I can't... I... Just don't."

"I'm sorry," I said. "I'm so fucking sorry. I don't even know where to start."

"Start by telling me what happened! I thought you were dead! I thought... I thought only death would make you leave me like that. Without a word. Without a single fucking sign."

Alex's arms folded over his chest, his fists tucked into his armpits.

I clenched my own hands into fists to keep from reaching for him again. "Baby, please—"

"Do *not* call me baby!" he wailed. "Please do not act like you care about me when you let me mourn your *fucking* death for four *fucking* years." Tears spilled down his face and dripped off his chin as he swiped at his nose. "I waited for you, for any word. And then I searched desperately for anything that might explain it. And I learned about the mortar strike in Iraq. Was that it?"

I nodded.

"And were you hurt?"

I nodded again. "Bad concussion. Head injury. They kept me

under for a long time, and then I was out of it for a while after that, Alex. For months. I'd been transported to another country. No cell phone or computer. No access to anything. They contacted my next of kin, which is my friend Max in Philly. He... he didn't know about you."

Alex winced like that was yet another blow. "I guess I wasn't that important."

He was tearing my heart into shreds. "You were! You are. When I got back, I was desperate to find you. But you told me your family had a farm! I had no idea what part of California or what kind of farm. Alex, I told Max all about you, once I got home. I hired an investigator, for fuck's sake—"

"After you were dating someone else."

I stared at him, unsure whether he was mad at me for cheating on him with him, or what. "I... I don't know what to say right now to make this right," I confessed. "Please tell me what to say to make this right."

"Do you have any idea how long I waited for you? It took me months of therapy before I agreed to delete my message board accounts. Nearly a year of it before I could consider moving on and doing something meaningful with my life. And even then, *even then*, I saved myself for you. It took two more years before I could wrap my head around having sex with someone who *wasn't* you. And now here you are, fucking me while carrying around the knowledge that the man I thought was dead was alive this whole time!"

Alex clenched his jaw, sucked in a breath through his nose, and dropped the next words like a killing blow. "And lying to my face while telling me you gave a single shit about me."

The emotional storm settled low in my gut like a lead weight. This wasn't a catharsis meant to help him move past the painful past and into a new future together. No... this was... this was starting to sound like the end.

Like forgiveness wasn't even something he was considering.

"Please, Alex. Please, I am begging you. I fell for you twice. Please don't throw that away without letting me tell you... Just come inside so we can talk."

"Talk about what? How can I ever trust you again? I can't. I can't, Judd. It... it almost killed me getting over you, and I can't do it again. Just ask my family. They're the ones who had to pick up the pieces."

His sister's words echoed through my head like the clang of a cell door being locked. *The whole experience... it broke Alex, Chief. Crushed him. It's like he's expecting to get his heart broken again.*

At this point, I hope the asshole stays gone because no good could come of them getting in touch again.

My own heart was shattered for Alex, for the hollow grief in his eyes. But the look on his face, the one that said I was losing him, made me desperate and stupid. Made me want to lash out.

"So that's it, then?" My own eyes were burning. "You got over me once, so now you're just going to run back to your perfect family and your fancy therapist and get over me again? How nice for you. How nice that it's that easy, Alex. How nice for you that you have that kind of love and support. Go ahead."

I regretted the words the second they were out of my mouth. The last fucking thing I wanted was to hurt Alex. All I wanted was to protect him, dammit.

But it was clear by the way Alex's jaw dropped and his eyes widened, by his single punched-out "*wow,*" that my outburst had put the final nail in the coffin.

"I'm sorry," I said quickly. "Fuck, I'm sorry. I didn't mean that."

"Obviously, you did because you said it. I've had an easy life with no challenges, and all I have to do is go confess to my giant fucking family with their giant fucking opinions that I fucking failed at something they do as if by fucking magic. *Twice.* That I trusted the wrong person. *Twice.* That I thought that person actually cared about me. *Twice.*"

Every time he said *twice*, his voice broke a little more until he was crying again.

I felt my own tears soaking the front of my collar. "Alex, please."

"No. This... I can't do it. Maybe it's a good thing we figured it out now. Maybe we were never meant to have a first real date." He took a shuddering breath. "Because if this had happened after we were already officially together?" His face fell, and his voice became nearly impossible to hear. "I wouldn't survive it."

Then he turned around and left.

By the very next day, it was as if the past six months had never happened. Alex Marian treated me like nothing more than the annoying fire marshal who hassled him for no good reason.

And after a week of trying everything I could think of to get him to give me another chance...

That's exactly what I became.

27

—————

ALEX

Ella: *How did you like the new therapist?*

Alex: *She wants me to practice meditation.*

Ella: *Fuck that. Let's burn some shit.*

—————

"ALEX, THE CHIEF'S HERE AGAIN!" Mali called back to my office. As chipper as my hostess was, even she was getting sick of this.

"You have to be fucking kidding," I snapped, closing my eyes and counting to ten.

Is he out of his mind? This was his third visit in the past six days.

Ella sighed from her spot in my office's "visitor's chair," which was really just a stack of Rubbermaid bins at the moment. We'd decorated for Thanksgiving last week, and the empty bins apparently lived in my office until it was time to swap them with the Christmas stuff next week.

"Why is he like this?" she demanded. "I thought the two of you were getting along better and then, boom! More inspections and feuding. Make it make sense."

Despite Judd's awful accusation of my running straight to my family, I hadn't told them anything. Which was honestly making the quasi-breakup ten times worse. I was screaming in pain on the inside and had to act completely normal on the outside.

And it was all Kincaid's fault.

"What do you want?" I asked when I got out to the front of the house.

He tilted his chin at my string of turkey lights hanging over the bar. "Those aren't to code. They need to be eighteen inches below the sprinkler deflectors."

I stared at him and tried not to notice how jaw-droppingly beautiful he was. Judd Kincaid was a gorgeous man. If he didn't scowl most of the time, people would be all over him like white on rice. Hell, they already were.

"And how many inches are they, Chief?" I asked, because if he was threatening to cite me, he already knew he was in the right.

He met my eyes. "Seventeen and a quarter."

"This is harassment," I hissed. "You know it, and I know it, and — Hi, Mrs. Carilla! Yes, it's good to see you, too. Oh, the mah-jongg group today, hm? Well, that's wonderful. Welcome to Timber. We're happy to have you. Mali, here, will find you a couple of tables in a nice, private corner."

"Verbal warning," Judd said, after the older lady and her friends walked away. "And when you put up the next set of holiday decorations, remember the Four F's."

I glanced at him in pleasant surprise. "Oh, believe me, Chief. I can remember some effs right fucking now."

His eyes never wavered from mine. "Flame, fixtures, flow, and food zones. Use only flame-retardant or -resistant decorations, plug fixtures into rated outlets and avoid daisy chaining, keep exits and sprinklers clear, and keep decor away from cooking grease or grill flames."

"Think you forgot an eff-word, Kincaid," I growled.

He tapped his chin, then snapped his fingers. "Yes. You're correct. *Fuse.* Use lights with built-in fuses. Thank you. You're ever so helpful when it comes to fire safety, Marian."

By the time I finished holding back a shout of frustration, he was gone.

"That man is a stickler for fire safety," one of the older ladies at Mrs. Carilla's table said with a bright smile. "Isn't that nice having someone like him here in Legacy? He's such a dear."

I inhaled deeply and held the breath in my lungs for as long as possible before letting it out slowly and silently.

"Such a dear," I exclaimed. "Just a dear, dear, *dear* man. Yes he is."

Later that evening, I concocted an email in response to a "Fire Safety For the Holidays!" leaflet he'd left on the bar.

To: His Excellency, the Earl of Overreach

I wanted to thank you for your most recent seasonally appropriate reminder that twinkle lights, wreaths, and anything made of pine needles apparently qualify as "potential death traps." Your festive leaflet really puts the "bah" in "humbug."

While my staff has dutifully removed the three strands of "metrically inadequate" turkey lights (RIP, gobbling ambiance), I feel confident that Timber can safely handle holiday décor without turning into a yuletide bonfire. After all, our extinguishers, sprinklers, and staff training remain—as you so often remind me—at acceptable levels.

That said, I am throwing myself on His Excellency's mercy to request official approval for our upcoming holiday dessert feature: Cherries Jubilee. Yes, it involves a small table-side flambé. Yes, it involves fire. And yes, before you choke on your Nomex, I will ensure:

Only trained staff handle the torch.

A fire extinguisher is within arm's reach.

Patrons are warned that their Instagram stories may spontaneously combust with delight.

If it eases your professional conscience, you are welcome to come by for a live demonstration. I'll even set aside a seat at the chef's table so you can glower from an optimal angle.

Most neutral of holiday wishes,

Alexander Marian

Owner, Timber

As soon as I shot it off, I rubbed my face with both hands and tried to mentally saddle up for tomorrow. Marian Thanksgiving.

Marian Thanksgiving was at my grandparents' lodge. Thankfully, not everyone was coming to Legacy for it since we were having a huge family Christmas here in just a few weeks. But Thanksgiving still included my dads, my uncles Jude and Derek, and all of the Legacy resident cousins. There were most likely a few other Marians or Marian-adjacent people coming as well.

It was going to suck.

My parents' generation tended to invite stragglers to any family event, which meant you never knew who would be there. While that was great because it meant Tavo was obviously welcome, it also meant Papa and/or Ella sometimes took the opportunity to invite a friend who just so happened to be gay or bi and just so happened to be single and *oh-by-the-way* also happened to have something in common with me.

I pulled out my phone and sent a pre-excuse prep text to the small family chain of just Papa, Dad, Ella, Mattie, and me.

> I'm not feeling well. Think I'm coming down with something.

PAPA

> Ooh! I'm really good at diagnosing from afar. Hang on… Wait for it… I think… you're coming down with an excuse to skip family Thanksgiving.

DAD

> Nailed it.

ELLA

> You are literally in your office with a half-eaten order of mozzarella sticks next to your face.

I glanced up and saw her standing in the hallway outside my office.

"I hate you," I said without any feeling.

"Mfh. Tell me what else is new."

She typed on her phone, and another text came through on the family chain.

ELLA

> Hey, I tried this great red the other day. Alex, can you pick up some…what was it called… Woodbridge Cab Sauv?

DAD

> You mock me, daughter.

She snickered and put her phone away. "Tell him you've decided to make sangria with Sutter Home because Tastings says it has hints of Fig Newton."

"Why are you here?" I asked. "You were here earlier today. I'm starting to feel like there's something going on."

"Fine. I was elected to 'Make Sure He Doesn't Bail.' My job is to pick up you and Tavo and bring you to the lodge tonight. Mandatory family fun starts at o'dark thirty tomorrow."

I glared at her. "No. I reject your interfering ways. I will come to the lodge when I get up in the morning and not a minute sooner."

She gave me a mock-pitying look. "'Fraid that's not an option, Alexander the Grape. It's my way or the highway. Actually, it's my way, or Uncle Derek said he was bringing the stun gun. Apparently, you owe him a game of Sequence, and he intends to get you to pay up tonight."

I groaned. The last thing I needed was Marian interference in what had become my nightly pity-party ritual.

"Make concessions," I insisted. "If I go tonight, I can leave right after the meal tomorrow."

She held out her hands in an "I don't know, I don't make the family's stupid rules" shrug. We both knew once I was under the tractor-beam-like powers of our fathers, there was no way I was leaving before midnight tomorrow. We also both knew if I didn't come tonight, our parents would just turn up here, wondering what was wrong.

And there was absolutely nothing wrong.

"Fine. I need to tell Tavo and pack a bag."

She hopped up and followed me out to the front of the house so I could tell Mali to stop seating people if she hadn't already.

But when I got as far as the bar area, I stopped and stared.

"Hey, Alex," Kaidee greeted me with a friendly smile. "How are you? I'm just here grabbing pizza since I got in too late to cook, and Judd had to work late."

Her words struck like boulders to the chest. "Oh. You're here for Thanksgiving? With Judd?"

I hoped my voice sounded breathy and high only to me and not to everyone else. Unfortunately, I felt my sister's eyes on the side of my face.

"Yeah, but he said your family invited us to Thanksgiving out at their place. A historic inn, I think? Is that right?"

This couldn't be happening.

"Oh," I managed to say. "Yes, well."

Thankfully, Ella sensed my freak-out and took over.

"I'm Ella, Alex's sister. My grandparents own the old Legacy Inn and Lodge, only now it's a private family residence. We usually host holidays there and invite whoever needs a place to be. You're very welcome to join us tomorrow. I look forward to sharing the day with you."

Somehow, I managed to introduce the two of them, and then Karim came out with Kaidee's food order, and I made a beeline for the back door.

Ella raced behind me. "Alex, what's going on? Why are you upset that Judd and his girlfriend are coming to—"

"She's not his girlfriend!" I snapped. "They're just friends."

Ella's eyes rounded. "Okay, sorry. Why are you mad that Judd and his *friend* are coming to Thanksgiving? I know he gives you a hard time, but you did agree to extra inspec—"

"It's not about the inspections," I said. "It's not. I just... It's fine. I'm tired, El. Okay? That's all. I'm being moody and unfair. I was already in a bad mood, and now Papa and Dad are insisting I come over there and probably stay up too late and get woken up too early."

Her mention of the extra inspections reminded me that they were done. According to our agreement, they should have been over after the one today. So at least that was something. He would no longer have an excuse for his bullshit appearances any old time he wanted to.

I thought about Kaidee. Why was she here? Had he called and invited her? Had he finagled an invitation to Thanksgiving on purpose, or had he been roped into it by one of my well-meaning family members?

Did it matter?

Did I care?

Of course I cared.

I blew out a breath and went upstairs to find Tavo. When I entered the living room, he and my barback jumped apart on the sofa, and I stared at them for a beat.

"Hello, Drew," I began. "Tavo. I see you two finally met?"

Tavo began to blink like eyelids had gone on deep discount and he'd bought out the store. "Yeah, so, uh, yeah."

Ella snorted and turned her back to the room so she could close her eyes in glee.

"Right. Well, carry on," I said. "Wait. Except... we're headed to the lodge for Thanksgiving, and my family wanted you to come."

Tavo's cheeks were deep red. "Oh, er. It's just that..."

Drew blurted, "Mom invited him to our place for Thanksgiving. I-if that's okay."

"You two know that I'm not your parents, right? And that you're both over twenty? Because I'm feeling like I'm expected to set curfews or listen for the telltale sound of a window sliding open later tonight."

Tavo groaned and threw himself back on the sofa. "I didn't know how to tell you I wanted to go to Drew's for Thanksgiving. I didn't want you to think I didn't—"

"Tavo," I said, dropping a hand on his shoulder to squeeze. "If I could go to Drew's with you, I would. I don't begrudge you a normal holiday tomorrow. You two have fun, okay?"

They both grinned. God only knew what the two of them would get up to once Ella and I were gone. Suddenly, I was glad I was getting out of Dodge.

Once we were in Ella's car on the way out to the lodge, she turned to me and asked if I was feeling better now.

"Yeah," I lied, flashing her a smile. "I'm great. It's going to be fine."

It was not, in fact, fine.

28

KINCAID

To: *OpSec Director, Sillar, Johns, and Covey*
Re: *Request Replacement Device/Online Access*
Judd Kincaid: *Due to the accident that led to my evacuation to Ramstein, my personal phone was lost/unusable. Please advise if a replacement device can be issued or if I have authorization to procure one locally in order to reestablish secure online access. Respectfully, Judd Kincaid*

THE GROCERY STORE flowers shook in one hand as I reached the other out for the heavy brass knocker on the massive door to the Marian Lodge.

"You can do this," Kaidee said under her breath. "I got your back."

I swallowed a lump of nerves in my throat. She'd told me about seeing Alex last night on her way into town from Colorado and how he'd acted strangely. After two glasses of wine, I'd confessed the whole thing. *DrunkenPoet, IndexEcho*, the time it took me between learning the truth and confessing it to him, everything.

And she'd been amazing.

When Hazel and Avery Marian had stopped into the firehouse a few days ago to personally invite me to their family's house for Thanksgiving, I'd assumed I would be having the meal with the two women and their new baby. Never in a million years did I realize it was a giant Marian gathering at the lodge until after I'd already committed to coming.

But then it was like some other part of me—the part that had spurred me to keep showing up at Timber every other day for no good reason, the part that refused to give up on Alex, on *us*—had stubbornly insisted on going, if only to force Alex to bear witness to the fact that I was still here. I existed in the world despite his efforts to pretend nothing between us had ever happened.

"Hi, welcome! Come on in," an older man with graying strawberry-blond hair said as he waved us inside. "I'm Blue Marian, and this is my husband, Tristan. And you are...?"

Just my luck Alex's own parents were the ones who opened the door. "Judd Kincaid," I said, handing Blue the flowers. "And this is my friend Kaidee Driscoll."

After all of the friendly greetings, shaken hands, and offers to hang up coats, we were led into a large half-commercial kitchen, where the family was gathered around a huge island filled with various platters, pie plates, and dishes on trivets.

"What can I get you two to drink? Our family prides itself on our wine selections, but we also have—"

"He likes a craft brew called Summer Song," Alex said from a hallway behind me. As soon as he came fully into the room, I was struck stupid. He was wearing my favorite color on him—a heather green sweater over wash-worn blue jeans. "It's similar to the Get Lost Pale Ale in the fridge."

"What about you?" Blue asked Kaidee. I didn't hear what she said because I was still listening out for Alex's voice.

He glared at me.

"Happy Thanksgiving," I murmured.

"Is it?"

I turned, wondering if I should just collect my coat and get the hell out, but I caught Blue's eye, and he nodded me over to a second fridge off to the side. "Pale ale's in here. There's a bunch of other stuff, too, since my parents will have people here pretty much nonstop from now through New Year's."

I glanced back at Kaidee and saw someone hand her a glass of wine. She was happily chatting with several people and looked perfectly at ease.

I walked to the fridge and tried to select a beer, but the entire contents of the fridge became a colorful blur. My brain kept giddily reminding me that Alex was nearby, and my entire consciousness was stubbornly focused on him.

After a moment, Blue grabbed one and shut the door, handing the cold can to me. "This one."

The beer in my hand was the one Alex had recommended. A local Montana brew he carried at Timber. "This is great, thanks."

"So, Chief Kincaid," Blue began. "Tell us about yourself. Ella said you've been working in Legacy since the spring?"

I cleared my throat. "Yes, sir."

He barked out a laugh that startled me, mostly because I was wound up tight from the stress of the situation. "No *sirs*, please. I save those for my husband during special moments."

I felt my face flush. "I'm not sure how to answer that, to be honest."

He laughed. "How old are you? You're acting like you're one of my kids' ages, but I hope you don't take offense when I tell you I don't think I'm old enough to be your father."

"Forty."

"Phew. Was afraid for a minute that I'd offended a guest in record time."

I liked the guy. Which made me feel even more like an ass for the spiteful, untrue things I'd said about Alex's family. "No offense taken. I promise."

"So, I hear you take a keen interest in my son's safety. At Timber, I mean."

"I do," I said cautiously, bracing myself for a lecture or to be hassled by a protective father, but it didn't come.

"I appreciate that. Tristan and I both do. Our children are the most important people in our lives, obviously, and anyone who wants to keep them safe is okay in our book."

I ground my back teeth together, glanced around for a sign of Alex, and focused back on his Papa when I didn't find it. "I would do anything to keep your son safe."

The man's eyes widened in surprise and then immediately, maybe out of habit, sought out his husband's. Tristan noticed Blue's expression like he was as attuned to Blue as I was to their son, and he quickly made his way over to us.

"What exactly is your relationship with Alex?" Blue asked.

I gave him a half smile. "Let's just say I never knew a love-hate relationship was a real thing until I met Alexander Marian."

The two of them exchanged a look before Tristan said, "Maybe you should go check on him and find out where he went. He probably snuck off to avoid being social. He's been in a strange mood today."

After directing me to a bedroom, they left me to converge around Kaidee, obviously making sure she was taken care of while I went searching for their wayward son.

I found him exactly where they directed me, only he wasn't just hiding; he was punching something.

A heavy bag hung from a two-by-four mounted on the ceiling in an alcove in one corner of a small collection of rooms that looked like it was half guest suite and half home gym.

"Hi," I said carefully.

He shook out his hand from the punch but didn't turn to look at me. "Why are you here?"

"Here in this room? Your dads sent me up here to stand in for the heavy bag, I think."

His nostrils flared in annoyance.

"Hazel and Avery invited me," I admitted. "I thought I was attending a simple affair at their house."

Alex's shoulders dropped as he exhaled. "Well, there's that picture-perfect family you talked about, Kincaid. Making sure everyone feels fucking welcome all the fucking time."

Guilt stabbed at me. "Do you want me to go?" I asked in as steady a voice as I could.

He finally turned around and looked at me, and his expression was full of emotion. Anger, resentment, guilt, exhaustion. "You know what I *really* want? I really want you to get on your knees and suck my dick, Chief. I want you to give me what I need without any of this... this... emotional fucking *bullshit* that I can't fucking get out from under!"

That "emotional fucking bullshit" was exactly what I wanted from him. But I knew he didn't want that from me right now. So, okay. I'd give him what he *did* want.

What we both wanted.

I kept my eyes on him as I took a step toward him. Then another. And another.

And I sank to my knees at his feet.

Alex sucked in a breath, and I could tell he was trying to decide whether to retract his words or not.

But he didn't.

I reached for the button on his jeans and flicked it open. The sound of his zipper lowering filled the room.

"What about Kaidee?" he asked in a low voice.

I shook my head slowly. I was pretty sure he knew the answer to that. At least I hoped he did. But I answered anyway. "Still just a friend."

"This doesn't mean anything," he snapped as I pulled his pants and underwear down to mid-thigh, releasing his already hard cock and the scent of my favorite human.

I leaned forward and inhaled at the spot where his leg met his body. That warm crease of skin. Then I tasted it.

It means something to me, Alex. And it always will.

"Okay," I murmured, keeping the rest of my thoughts to myself.

Alex's fingers threaded into my hair. "Stop dicking around," he said through clenched teeth, moving my head closer to his cock.

I obeyed him by taking the base of his cock in my hand and bathing his shaft and tip with my tongue. Then I dropped down over his cock and took him as deep as I could, wrapping my tongue around him and going for it.

He grunted and curled over me, arching into me. The tiniest whimper sound came from him as if he was trying to hold back.

I heard you, sweetheart. You need me. You need me to make you feel good the same way I need you right here, right now.

I sucked him off like I was in a fellatio competition, bobbing and sucking and teasing until his breaths were coming out in uneven, ragged pulls.

Neither of us said a word. Him because he was too busy sending all of his available brain cells out to lunch and me because I didn't want to miss a moment of having his body as close to mine as he would let me.

I snuck my hands onto the firm globes of his ass and squeezed, pulling him even deeper into my throat until both of his hands were in my hair and he was whimpering again.

Come for me, beautiful.

Alex made a choking noise, and it took me a minute to realize it was because he was trying so hard not to express his pleasure to me.

I pulled off to bark at him to let go of his rigid control just as his release came jetting out. His spunk hit me hot on the nose, cheek, and chin.

Had anyone ever come on my face before? *Absolutely not.*

And maybe I would have been annoyed by the bad timing if I hadn't seen the look on his face when he caught sight of me. Alex's eyes widened before they darkened with heat. His ruddy cheeks turned darker, and pink splotches appeared on his neck as his mouth dropped open.

He quickly closed it and clenched his jaw. "We done here?"

I opened my mouth to tell him to go right to hell when I saw the tremble in his hands.

My sweet Alex was pretending. He was every bit as affected by this encounter as I was. And he wasn't nearly as heartless as he was trying to seem.

I stood up, hard and aching enough that I needed to do a hip wiggle to readjust my dick in my pants before I gave the Marians a show downstairs.

"Guess so," I said softly, reaching to swipe some of the cum off my face with a finger before making a slow production of sliding that digit into my mouth and sucking his flavor off it.

I let my eyelids drift closed for a split second as the salty tang hit my tongue. Then I opened my eyes and enjoyed every moment of his blown pupils from watching me.

He tilted his chin toward an adjoining bathroom.

"Clean up before you embarrass both of us," he grumbled. Then he left.

I looked around the room, wishing for additional insight into his personality, but then I remembered he hadn't grown up here. There were, however, a ton of family photos on a wide built-in bookshelf, along with a selection of popular novels and several books on Montana and Yellowstone National Park.

There were framed photos of Alex at various ages with his dads and sisters. Photos of what I assumed was their family dog. A picture of Alex as a teenager with a group of other kids his age at a backyard barbecue.

The images in the photos dripped with wealth and privilege, but they also showed a large, loving family full of different person-alities.

I noticed a photo of Alex and Tristan standing among vines heavy with grapes. Tristan's arm was around Alex's shoulders, and they both wore button-down shirts with an Alexander Vineyards logo over the pocket.

DrunkenPoet's old messages ran through my head.

I love my family, but I don't think this is the life I want.

Now that I'd met his parents, I was even more proud of him for leaving. It was one thing to leave your home when you had no family, no ties, as I had. It was another thing entirely to turn your back on a future that had been laid out for you and decide to forge your own path like Alex.

After finally moving to the bathroom, I cleaned up and ran fingers through my hair, trying to calm it down from the nest it had been after Alex's greedy fingers had yanked at it.

When I finally rejoined everyone, people were starting to make plates in a buffet line around the big island.

Alex very carefully ignored me, but he was a little less icy to Kaidee. It was a concession of sorts, and I appreciated it.

Blue and Tristan, on the other hand, treated me like family. Like they knew something everyone else didn't. I wondered if they were particularly perceptive, or maybe Alex had broken down and said something to them. Either way, I wasn't sure how to handle it. Alex himself clearly wanted to hate me, while his dads treated me like one of their own.

Every time one of them went out of his way to suggest a dish or ask if I needed another drink, Alex scowled. It became almost comical, honestly, because with every scowl, I realized that Alex Marian was anything but ambivalent toward me.

It wasn't that he didn't care about me at all. He clearly *did*. It was that his care was focused on the negative right now while he processed his anger and grief.

What he didn't know was that I had time. With age came wisdom, and I was wise enough to wait him out.

Because I wasn't going anywhere.

And Alexander Marian was mine.

29

ALEX

To: *Judd Kincaid*
Re: *Device/Access Request*
We have requisitioned a replacement. Please allow 4-6 weeks for delivery.

DECEMBER BLEW in like a son of a bitch. I was angry all the time, and the only thing that seemed to open the pressure valve was taking sexual pleasure in my biggest enemy.

I knew exactly what Judd Kincaid was doing. He was waiting me out. Like I was going to change my mind eventually and give him another chance.

He was wrong.

Our fight had been a gift. I'd made the mistake of falling for a thrill-seeker once. Now I was preventing myself from making that mistake again.

It was the weirdest possible coincidence that Judd had been put in my path twice, but now I could do what I should have done in the first place: look at things logically and rationally, and realize that I didn't want to develop real feelings for someone whose job put his life in danger regularly.

I couldn't handle it. It was as simple as that.

But sleeping with the man without letting myself fall for him? No problem. In fact, yes please. Sign me up.

The first week in December, I'd shown up at his place and insisted on sucking his dick. Not because I cared about him, obviously. But because I wanted more practice sucking a man off for when the time came that I was ready to jump back into the dating or hookup pool.

Did I get immense satisfaction from seeing his eyes roll back in his head and hearing his fists pound the wall behind him while I drove him quickly to orgasm? Yes, yes I did.

But again—and this was crucial—not because I cared about him at all. Only because it meant I was good enough to go out there and hook up with other guys without feeling like such a green newbie anymore.

Because I wasn't. Thanks to Judd Kincaid, I was no longer a virgin or inexperienced. I was a regular guy who wasn't intimidated by sex.

In fact, the more I thought about it, the more I realized I didn't need Judd to get off with. I could get off with anyone.

I could plan a motherfucking *Costco run* up to Billings if I wanted.

So when an opportunity for a date with someone else practically landed in my lap, I took it.

Maddox was apparently working with a social media influencer from out of town, and the guy needed a date for an event he was filming. The guy was hot. His Instagram was straight fire, and I was 100 percent here for it.

Probably.

I'd quickly agreed, reveling in my new life as a single guy who was absolutely up for dating new people.

And then my cousin Rosie had caught wind of it and had quickly shot off a bunch of texts while I was in the middle of my personal grocery shopping on a weekday afternoon.

ROSIE

Say no to the InstaGay.

Why? And how do you even know about this?

ROSIE

I heard it from Maya who heard it from her brother.

Maddox asked me for a favor. And you have to admit it's not a bad favor.

I linked her to his Insta.

ROSIE

So the man has abs that are more visible than other people's. So what? What would your crush say if he saw you on a very public date with a beautiful influencer?

I stood motionless as the blood drained from my head and face.

What crush?

ROSIE

Fine, we'll play it like that. Let's say you had a crush on… Oh, let's say the sheriff.

That is abhorrent. Guy's a total snooze.

ROSIE

Oh, really? Fine. Then let's say it's the
FIRE CHIEF. Anyway, imagine if he caught
wind of you carrying on with the pretty
boy from out of town and it made him feel
some kind of way. How would that make
YOU feel?

I stared at the screen of my phone long enough to get bumped by Mrs. Hoffman's cart. "Sorry," I murmured, moving further off to the side by the endcap, where bags of beef jerky tried hard to jump into my cart uninvited.

She was right. If Judd Kincaid accepted one of these dates with Adrian Hayes, I would lose my fucking mind. Which meant it would be mean and hypocritical if I did it.

Did my sister put you up to this?

ROSIE

No, but Uncle Blue knows this guy is into
you and asked me at Thanksgiving what
the deal was. I told him the truth, that I
had no idea. But between you and me,
Grape? The two of you look at each other
like something's going up in flames.

I took a deep breath and shot off a text to my father.

You're a meddler who needs an
intervention.

PAPA

Your sister asked for those classes, I
swear!

What are you talking about?

PAPA

Her WSET classes… Why? What are YOU
talking about?

Ella is taking wine classes?

PAPA

Can we pretend this entire exchange
never happened?

Someone else tried to squeeze past me in the narrow aisle, so after texting Maddox and Adrian with a lie about why I couldn't go on the date, I slipped my phone into my pocket and got back to shopping.

Five minutes later, Karim called me about a food delivery at work, and I sighed. Who was I kidding?

I didn't have time to date. I was too busy at work to even do a Costco run, let alone a *Costco run*.

"Juni, I need you guys to pick up the pace," I said, rushing into the kitchen two nights later to check on an order a customer was asking about for the third time.

"How do you expect me to cook with this thing here?" she cried, shooting an evil eye at the fire extinguisher mounted next to her elbow. "Move it to the other side."

We'd had this conversation too many times to count. "I can't move it to the other side because the other side has the eye rinse thing and the first aid kit," I explained for the millionth time. "The pizza oven takes up most of our wall space, Juni. You know that."

"Take your pasta and go," she barked, nodding toward the order she'd just completed.

I slid the dishes onto a large tray and carried it out into the dining room, apologizing to the customers and throwing in a gratis dessert for their wait time.

Unfortunately for Juni but fortunately for my holiday bank

account, the place got busier as the night wore on. We'd already been busy from two office holiday parties, and now it was a group of ice hockey kids and their parents coming to celebrate a win from the looks of things.

We managed to keep up with the flow once Tavo came down to pitch in. I appreciated the assist, and Karim even shot me a quick *Thank fuck* as I showed him a few simple tasks he could do in the kitchen.

Too bad it wasn't enough.

At ten past 8:00 p.m., the kitchen's Class-K fire extinguisher lost its months-long battle with Juni Song.

I heard a crash, quickly followed by the sound of broken glass and a collective gasp from the kitchen staff and a grunt from one of the booths in the back.

A familiar grunt.

How Judd Kincaid was in my restaurant without me knowing was beyond me. But it was a zoo in there, and his back was to me in a tall booth. On the other side of the booth was an older woman I didn't recognize. But I definitely recognized the air of authority in her and the firefighter-looking patch on her black sweater.

Fuck.

I raced into the kitchen to see a giant hole in the single window over the sink. Juni had gone right back to cooking, but I could see from the flush on her face and the slight satisfaction in her eyes—and the lack of fire extinguisher on the wall—that she'd finally taken aggressive action.

"You could have just taken it down and slid it under the table," I cried. "Juni, what the hell?"

"I will pay for the window," she said calmly.

"Damned straight you're paying for the window," I snapped. "And you're paying the fine I'm going to get from the—"

"What exactly is going on in here?" the woman from Judd's table asked, standing just inside the door to the kitchen from the front of the house.

"Nothing," I said quickly. "It's fine. Just one of those busy Friday nights during the holiday season."

Unfortunately, that was when the inspection tag on the buckle that normally held the extinguisher to the wall fell off with a little *plink* onto the floor.

We all stared at it. And then the woman glanced up at the empty extinguisher mount.

She looked from me to the man who'd come up behind her. "Chief Kincaid, is there a problem here? It seems the restaurant which just came off a permit suspension is already back to regrettable standards."

The chief was clearly annoyed. "Looks that way," he said in his gruff voice. "But looks can be deceiving. There's probably an explanation, right, Mr. Marian?"

Maybe it was my own personal hang-ups that caused me to shoot myself in the foot, but I refused to accept his kindness. "Nope. Just a simple decision to yeet the extinguisher during a busy shift."

Kincaid's eyes closed, and the woman sighed. "Judd, I trust you will write this up appropriately?"

"Yes, ma'am. Of course."

She turned to leave while Kincaid glared at me. "You had to be a smart-ass in front of the state fire marshal? Really, Alex? Christ."

Then he turned his glare to Juni. "You want to tell me what you'd do if the kitchen caught on fire right now? And don't tell me it won't because we both know shit happens."

Surprisingly, my head chef looked a little remorseful. "There are other extinguishers."

He sighed and pinched the bridge of his nose. "The citation will be in your email in the morning, and today's your lucky day. It comes with more inspections. How fun for both of us."

And then he was gone.

And Juni Song was lucky I didn't have homicidal tendencies.

30

KINCAID

IndexEcho: *Baby, I'm here.*

[Deleted User]: *[No response]*

I COULD HAVE KILLED HIM. Moreover, I was mad at myself for choosing to take Fire Marshal Houle to Timber. I'd thought it would help Alex out during the winter slow season, but as soon as we'd sat down and other groups started flooding the place, I'd realized how wrong I'd been.

While I was happy for Alex that his business was doing so well, it was a reminder of how difficult it had been for the two of us to find time together.

It had been hard enough finding that time when we both wanted it, but now that only one of us wanted it, it was near impossible. And sometimes I just wanted an excuse to look at him.

Unfortunately, Marshal Houle had taken the seat in the booth that would have given me a view of him, and it had also given her a better view to see when something went wrong.

Now, here we were.

Two nights after the fire extinguisher yeeting, I saw Alex across the square at Legacy's Mistletoe Ceremony. I was still angry at him for the immature way he'd handled the situation at Timber when I'd even tried to spare him the official consequences of Juni's actions.

But now, watching him as he gazed longingly at the two men kissing under the lights of the giant mistletoe ball, my anger blew away like tiny snowflakes caught in a gale.

He was so fucking beautiful. Pink-nosed and bright-eyed. His neck was covered in a thick cranberry-red scarf, but his hands were bare. I knew because I'd caught him shoving them deep into his pockets every time he began gesticulating with them and then remembered they were cold.

I wanted to go over there and talk to him, but he was surrounded by his cousins and sister, and I was there with a few members of my crew and their family members. As soon as it was acceptable to beg off and head home, I politely excused myself and said my goodbyes.

The house was quiet but cozy. I warmed up with a hot shower and headed to bed with plans to get up early and catch up on some expense reports first thing in the morning, but as soon as my head hit the pillow, there was an angry knock on the door.

It was Alex.

"Alex," I said hesitantly, waiting for him to lash out.

He didn't make eye contact with me. "I'm still angry. I just need to get some sleep, okay?"

"Okayyy?"

His jaw muscles moved before he spoke again in a rush. "I can't sleep, and I need to sleep here. With you. But it doesn't mean anything, and we're not having sex. Just sleep. No talking."

And then he pushed past me and headed straight for my bedroom.

I watched him go, the stiff set of his shoulders mixed with the overall slump of exhaustion. Then I turned back to lock the door and turn out the lights before joining him in bed.

He'd brought in the smell of snow and the almost-metallic scent of winter air, but as soon as he settled into my sheets and warmed up, he smelled like himself again. Yeast and woodsmoke mixed with red wine.

I didn't dare touch him, only laid my head on my own pillow and pulled the covers back over me. After about four minutes, he began moving toward me comically slowly, as if he thought I wouldn't notice.

"Jesus fuck," I muttered, reaching out to yank him onto his side so I could move up behind him and hold him as the little spoon, the way I knew he wanted. "Go to sleep, Firebug."

After a minute, his entire body finally relaxed against me. He reached for my hand and threaded his fingers through mine before sighing and settling for good.

I inhaled the scent of him—his shampoo and the warm spot behind his ear I couldn't get enough of. I loved that he'd shown up here. That he'd needed me like this and took comfort in sleeping in my bed.

But I also recognized it was a slippery slope. His being here, sleeping in my bed and in my arms, wasn't protecting anyone from future heartbreak. In fact, it was prolonging the agony if he wasn't going to change his mind about being with me.

For tonight, though, I would take it. As soon as I was sure he was asleep with his rhythmic exhales and complete relaxation, I pressed a kiss to that spot behind his ear and murmured the words.

"I love you so fucking much."

In the morning, he was gone, as I'd known he would be, and I was back to my lonely existence, completely at the mercy of his mercurial moods.

Which was why I decided to shake it up a little.

And accepted a date with the pretty outsider who'd shown up in Legacy for his hashtag holidates.

Unfortunately, before I could enjoy my bonfire date with Adrian Hayes—which I knew wasn't really a date—the state fire marshal called to inform me in the politest of terms that I should pop into "that restaurant" for an inspection focused on their holiday decorations.

Since I was in the mood to needle him—and make sure Juni had replaced the K-class fire extinguisher—I headed to Timber during the lunch rush.

"Hi, Mali," I said in a cheerful voice. "Happy holidays. How are you?"

She flashed me an uncertain smile. "Uh, okay? You here for lunch, Chief?" she asked hopefully.

"Nope. Here to check on Juni and her beloved fire extinguisher."

She let out a little puff of air. "I don't suppose I could convince you to come back in two hours when Alex is at a dentist appointment, could I?"

I grinned at her. "Not a chance."

She hesitated. "Wait here." And then she hustled to the back.

I waited patiently, waving hellos to people I knew and thanking several others who wished me a happy holiday. By the time Mali returned with Alex, I was actually feeling the holiday spirit.

"No," he said upon greeting me.

"Ah, you've chosen to be the Grinch today, I see," I said with a big grin. "Come on, why not embrace our new season of fire safety inspections? After all, I gave you an out, and you chose not to take it. I actually think you like getting… *inspected* from time to time."

His eyes blinked rapidly as his lungs filled with hot air, ready to spew vitriol at me. "W-what? I most certainly do not!"

I shrugged. "Welp, might as well get it over with. I want this even less than you do, so let's go."

Alex followed me into the kitchen, still sputtering. Thankfully, the fire extinguisher was back where it belonged, even if it did have a framed photo of me above it with devil horns and a goatee scribbled on it in black Sharpie marker.

I took a similar marker out of my bag and leaned in to autograph it over the glass without saying a word. Juni actually let out a snort of laughter, so I winked at her.

Alex was not amused by any of it.

"Show me clear egress," I said. "And I'll be out of your hair."

When we got to the back door, which was clear and passed the inspection, Alex poked a finger into my chest. "Stop coming here."

I leaned in and brushed my lips over his ear. "Did you wake up hard and aching in my bed this morning, Firebug?"

His body shuddered. "N-no."

I brushed my nose across his cheek and noticed he didn't pull away. "Liar. I'll bet you woke up with my morning wood pressed against your hole, and you thought about it. Thought about stripping us down and backing up onto my cock, didn't you?"

His eyes fluttered closed. "I didn't."

"Didn't do it or didn't think about it?" I teased softly. "Either way, it's too bad. I would have enjoyed waking up buried in your hot, tight ass."

Two could play at the torture game.

And when I left Timber a minute later, I felt like I'd finally at least gotten myself on the board.

31

ALEX

Support Ticket 82199723
Username: *IndexEcho*
Support requested: *Need help tracking down deleted user DrunkenPoet.*
Resolution: *Request Denied. For security purposes, user information cannot be shared.*

TWO DAYS after the random fucking fire inspection—which had honestly become even more of a pain in my ass than the dental cleaning that came right after it—one of my beer taps broke and sprayed expensive IPA all over me.

I headed to Sullivan Hardware in hopes of finding what I needed to fix it without having to call the equipment company up in Billings.

As the bell over the hardware store door tinkled, I spotted Maddox's sister chatting with the usual contingent of Legacy gossips... which apparently now included Adrian Hayes, the influencer I'd skipped out on "dating." We'd met finally, and I had to admit I liked the guy. But not like that. He was nice, but a little too fancy for me.

"Maya," I pleaded, throwing myself on her mercy, "please tell me you have something that can fix a broken beer tap."

"O-rings and gaskets are right over there, plumbing section," she said, pointing toward an aisle.

Adrian threw out a friendly smile. "Alex, what's your favorite Christmas movie?"

I paused. "Uh... *Die Hard*? What about you?"

"Never seen it," he said. "But I remember liking the Snoopy one."

Maya and I, along with Mrs. Hoffman, gasped.

Adrian blinked at us in mock confusion. "You guys don't like Snoopy?"

I stared at him. "You've never seen *Die Hard*?"

I shook my head and headed to the plumbing section, remembering I had a restaurant full of people waiting for me. "It's true what they say about people from LA," I teased over my shoulder.

Maya laughed and said. "You're from Napa. Don't go acting all local on us just yet. You've been here five minutes."

I found what I was looking for quickly and returned to the counter. "I've been here full-time for three years, and that's after a decade of summers in Legacy, little lady."

As I pulled out my debit card, Mrs. Hoffman asked Adrian something I didn't hear.

"Oh, uh... Actually, I'm going to a holiday bonfire and s'mores tonight with, um..." Adrian frowned. "The fire marshal? I can't remember his name."

Hot rage flooded my system. I could have sworn Maddox had

counted Kincaid out of the mix when he was putting together all of these video dates... or so Rosie had led me to believe.

"Oh my god, Maddox set you up with Kincaid after all? For real?" I shook my head in disgust. "Good luck, I guess. He's the grumpiest human you've ever met. Makes Maddox look like a happy ray of sunshine in comparison."

Adrian shrugged. "My business manager hooked me up with a small sponsorship to create fire safety content and just sent me the information this morning. He arranged it with the people at the search and rescue training program who are putting on the bonfire—"

"SERA," Maya supplied with a nod.

"Right," Adrian agreed. "So we're going to film out there tonight."

I headed toward the door, waving a hand over my shoulder. "Like I said, good luck. Chief Kincaid's an ass and ten times more stubborn than one. Enjoy!"

I stormed back to Timber in an even worse mood than before. The fire chief was ruining my life. And now he'd accepted a date with the town's prettiest newcomer.

Great.

No problem.

It was fine.

But like... I obviously needed to go to that bonfire. I had spent quite a bit of time in the past year being schooled on proper fire safety technique, so it only made sense for me to attend the town's holiday bonfire, where there would necessarily be quite a bit of fire danger. I also liked s'mores, and it wasn't like Timber would ever get a permit to make them.

So I *had* to go to the SERA bonfire.

It was downright obligatory, honestly.

Later that night, I turned up at SERA and watched as Judd

Kincaid stood up in front of everyone and lectured them on fire safety rules. It seemed to be part of whatever Adrian was filming, and I had to admit it was a little bit of a relief to see Judd more interested in fire safety than in the model-pretty influencer beside him.

I quickly learned from the excited chatter surrounding me that the two of them were filming public safety for the forest service or something. It seemed like our grumpy fire chief was taking his job way too seriously, as usual.

In fact, only a short time later, he seemed to become annoyed at his "date" when Adrian accidentally set his marshmallow on fire.

"What the hell is going on over here?" Judd asked, moving swiftly to remove the flailing marshmallow skewer from Adrian's hand and stick it in an empty tin can on the ground. "Did you even listen to a word I said? Are you demonstrating what *not* to do?"

Adrian didn't look sorry, but he apologized anyway in his charming way. "Sorry, Chief. I got carried away."

Kincaid narrowed his eyes at the guy like he was ready to string him up for improper marshmallow-toasting safety behavior. "You're putting people at risk because you can't put your phone down."

This was unusually grumpy, even for Kincaid.

I stepped forward and grabbed Judd's arm, trying to pull him away. No one needed the local fire chief to ruin the mood of a holiday gathering. "Hey! He was just trying to film content like *you* asked him to. Take it easy on the guy. It's not his fault you're impossible to please."

The chief's eyes snapped to me and narrowed, causing my heart to flicker with more heat than the flames in the giant bonfire nearby. "Not sure you're the one who should be giving safety advice, Firebug," he growled.

"You need to calm down," I said, mentally owing Ella a shot of alcohol for the inadvertent Taylor Swift lyrics. "You need to just stop." Dammit. Two shots.

I let out a breath and regrouped. "Listen. It was a flaming marshmallow. We all get them from time to time. Do you want all these little kids so scared of you that they run away from the helpers during a fire? Think about it."

He folded his arms over his broad chest and glared. "This helpful advice coming from the same man who—"

I couldn't help interrupting him. The words had been waiting hours to spill out. At least I had the decency to lower my voice. "Also? Why the hell are you on a date with Adrian fucking Hayes? And did you know that he asked me out first and I said no? I said no because I thought it wouldn't be very nice to you! And I worried that if you saw me out with him, it might cause you pain. Ha! I guess not! Because here you are—"

Judd clamped a large hand over my mouth to stop my rant and then grabbed my hand and yanked me away from the fire and deep into the shadows behind a nearby building. As soon as I opened my mouth to say, "And another thing," he slammed his mouth down on mine.

The little baby-bird-like noise that came out of my nose wasn't attractive, but I couldn't help but melt into him. The commanding kiss was feral but also familiar. Controlling but also caressing.

Judd's hands moved into my hair to clasp my head as if I would ever for any reason want to pull away or stop.

I didn't. I *wouldn't*.

Instead, I let him kiss me for as long as he wanted. Unfortunately, that wasn't very long. He pulled back and glared at me. "Stop coming to my house if you're not going to treat me like someone who deserves more than just your body. Now, go home."

Before I could say anything—rage or complain or beg him for

more kisses—he was gone. Back to the bonfire and back to his supposed date.

I blew out a breath and put my fingers to my lips.

I was never getting over Judd Kincaid, was I?

"Fuck that," I said into the freezing cold night. "There's nothing to get over! I stopped that in its tracks before it could get started. I am perfectly capable of enjoying my life without him. Watch me."

I spent the following week forcing myself to put the chief out of my mind and have fun. I worked hard, but I also played hard. Rosie invited me to the town snowball fight, and I agreed on the condition we wouldn't talk about "other" subjects.

And it *was* fun. Honestly.

Things were good.

Until three days after that, when Timber had another random fire inspection. And I lost my fucking mind.

32

———

KINCAID

Max: *No offense but you need to get laid, man. Take advantage of that bitch of a layover in Amsterdam. I'll see you in two days.*

———

WHEN THE SYSTEM popped up a reminder to revisit Timber again since I'd forgotten to inspect the decorations the last time, I groaned.

"Problem, Chief?" McMasters called out from down the hall.

I opened my mouth to ask him to take this inspection visit, but then I remembered just how happy Alex had seemed lately. I resented the hell out of him for acting like he was suddenly over our... whatever it was... and I also still resented him calling me out while I was just doing my job at the bonfire.

So. Fuck him. He was getting the full heat of my focus for his inspection visit, and he could fuck right off if he didn't like it.

Part of me knew I would unleash another shitstorm when I showed up, so I put it off until the last possible moment. I waited until I was done for the day and headed out. Instead of pulling up in front of Timber, I passed it and went to Frank's instead for a beer.

Sujo and his girlfriend Tiffany were there, but they seemed to be in an argument about their Christmas holiday plans with various family commitments, so I stayed well away from them, tucking into my own little corner and pulling out my phone to answer a recent text from Max I hadn't responded to yet.

I'd finally told him about Alex, but only because I hadn't wanted him to hear about it from Kaidee or to ask her to keep it a secret. He was pissed. *How dare that fucker not give you a chance. You? You're a catch. Fuck him.*

It was his role as my best friend to be protective, but I still hated hearing him speak spitefully about someone I truly cared for.

MAX

You still haven't told me if you'll come for Christmas. Say yes, bro. Make it happen.

I stared at the text.

Think I'm gonna stay here.

MAX

You staying for the kid?

Max had thought the thirteen-year age difference between Alex and me was a problem, but I'd told him the truth: I honestly never thought about our ages anymore when Alex and I were together.

Lay off, brother. I know you're in my corner and I love you for it. But Alex isn't a kid. And I don't blame him for feeling hurt and confused.

And *scared*, I didn't add.

I remembered Alex confessing to me months ago that he was afraid he might fall for someone and have things ripped away again. And I was pretty sure that, in Alex's mind, that's exactly what had happened.

I just didn't know how to get through to him. How to make him realize this second chance was a freaking *gift*, and the only thing keeping us apart was him.

When Frank yelled out of his little kitchen window to ask if I needed another beer, I realized I'd been sitting there too long.

"No, thanks. I'm heading out."

It was time for one last stop before heading home... where the only things waiting for me were a frozen Italian dish and the second half of an old mystery novel I was rereading.

Timber's front door opened with enough force to rattle the windows. I walked in annoyed as fuck that we were back in a situation that required goddamned inspections every two seconds after the six-month shitshow we'd finally gotten through.

But here we were.

Alex looked just as pleased about it as I was.

"Oh, for the love of fucking Christ," he murmured.

Maddox Sullivan and Adrian the influencer guy were there filming—probably another one of their holidates—and Maddox made a snarky comment under his breath.

"By complicated, you mean Kincaid's about to make my night a living hell with another ridiculous inspection to make sure Timber's living up to his impossible standards," Alex said, not bothering to lower his voice as I approached the bar.

I made my way toward him, taking my time and nodding to a few people along the way.

"Evening, Firebug," I called, also not bothering to lower my voice. "Hope you're not burning anything down, with all of these poor innocent townsfolk trying to enjoy the holiday season."

Alex cut me a look and inhaled sharply through his nose. The pain of seeing him stole my breath. He was so fucking beautiful and so fucking far away, though he was right in front of me.

"You know what? I actually expected you tonight, Kincaid. It's been a whole week since your last inspection," Alex shot back. "Figured you were due for another power trip."

If these stupid inspections were all we had right now, I was going to make the most of them. Get under his skin, the way he was still—and I was pretty sure would *always* be—under mine.

I reached the bar and pulled out my flashlight to inspect the paper Santa hats hanging precariously close to the string of holiday lights. "These lights properly secured? Electrical cords in good condition? You know what happens when bars get careless with their wiring."

"The lights are fine. The cords are fine. *Everything* is fine," he said through gritted teeth. "It was one time, Kincaid. And nothing fucking happened."

I tilted my head at him and pretended to be confused. "I'm sorry, you didn't just suggest lighting something on fire thanks to your carelessness was 'nothing,' did you?"

Alex closed his eyes. His jaw ticked. He took a breath before opening his eyes and plastering on a fake smile. "What can I do for you, Chief Kincaid? Would you like a holiday cocktail? It's on me. I'd love to help you celebrate the season with a *sedative*."

I wanted to provoke him, make a potshot comment about how he tended to light cocktails on fire, but I decided instead to stop antagonizing him. I was tired. One final tease, and I'd go. "Thanks for your kind offer, but I have to decline. I have a hot date tonight with my—"

"Great, have fun," he snapped, cheeks crimson and eyes wide. "Good night."

I stood there as Alex moved away to mix cocktails. His movements were forced and deliberate, as if he was having to pay extra attention to make sure he didn't fuck up the process.

"My book and a frozen pizza," I finished softly, but I wasn't sure he heard me.

I waited for a response, but none came.

On my way home, I considered texting Max back to tell him I'd changed my mind, that I would fly to Philly for the holiday weekend. But I was too depressed to even pull out my phone.

I didn't look at my phone again until hours later, when it buzzed with a text from an unknown number telling me they'd deposited their cousin in my yard and "good luck with that."

I threw on warm clothes and stomped into my boots before racing out the front door, where a very drunk Alex Marian was reciting poetry in my snowy front yard.

"O ruthless stars that grant me sight." He stopped to hiccup. "To see the man I dream each night. He glares, he stomps, he will not stay—And still my heart won't look away. If love be a wound, then let it burn—For every scar's a lesson learned!"

His arms were open, and he spun.

"Goddammit!" I shouted, thankful my neighbors were too far away to hear. "What the fuck are you doing here?"

"I held a flame I could not keep, A blaze that burned my nights of sleep," he continued, burping a little and weaving on his feet. "That's Rumi, you know."

"I can't keep doing this, Alex," I cried, throwing out my arms in frustration. "I love you, and it's killing me. You can't be with me because it took you too long to get over me? The grief was too much? You want to know who mourned, Alex? Me! I mourned! Except I kept looking for you for over three years!"

He blinked at me and squinted through the freezing night air. "You love me?"

Before I could answer him, he wobbled a little and then face-planted right into the snow.

By the time I got to him, he was snoring peacefully, as if none of this had happened. As if I hadn't poured my heart out to him. And yeah, that fucking hurt.

Instead of taking him inside, I shoved him in the back seat of my truck and drove him back to Timber, where I forced Tavo to help me get him into bed, prop him on his side with pillows and extra blankets, and leave an empty trash can nearby in case he woke up puking.

And then I went home and pulled out my laptop to search for last-minute plane fares to Pennsylvania for Christmas.

33

———————

ALEX

Papa: *I am so damned proud of you, Alex. Timber's Grand Opening was fantastic because you've worked hard to make it an amazing community gathering spot. Your dad and I couldn't be happier for you.*

Dad: *I made fun of Blue for bringing the travel pack of tissues to your opening night tonight. But he got the last laugh. I used every single one of them. You're where you're meant to be, Alex. And we are so proud. Love you.*

———————

I WOKE UP DEAD. Had to be death, anyway, because I couldn't imagine anything worse.

"Get your ass up, Grape," Ella muttered, smacking me on the leg through my bedcovers. "Grandma and Grandpa need our help out at the lodge and voluntold both of us. Apparently, Grandma and Aunt Ginger got it into their heads to do some last-minute holiday things, and we're the free labor."

I pulled the pillow over my face. "I'm happy to be disowned. Just tell them I can't make it on account of personal death."

Unfortunately, the death excuse didn't work on her, and she forced me into the bathroom for a hot shower. When I didn't come out, she threatened to come in and forcibly remove me. The thought of my sister intruding on my bodily privacy was enough to get me going.

The day turned out to be okay. I'd forced myself to put Mali in charge for the day since we were only open until four tonight to make up for how late last night had gone with the special tasting flights event. By noon, my hangover was under control, and by five, I was enjoying myself enough to be grateful I didn't need to race back to Timber for the dinner rush.

Just as I was beginning to think of heading home for the night, a call came in from my uncle Joel.

"Hey," I answered with a smile. "I heard you guys weren't getting in till tomorrow. You need a pickup from the airstrip?"

"Nah, Simone's got that worked out. Listen, my guys asked around at that club you told me about. Pinch?"

I frowned and headed to a corner of the lodge's kitchen for a little privacy. "Yeah?"

"We couldn't find the guy you guys met at the farmer's market. The one who recognized Tavo. From what we found out, he doesn't work at Pinch anymore. But my guy stuck around and partied, and in the past few weeks, he's seen the judge there with random guys. We were just about to declare Tavo in the clear when my guy overheard the judge say something about Montana. So then my guy tries to get chatty with him and says, 'Oh, I love Montana. I've spent a bunch of time there. Yellowstone and Glacier, right?' And the judge asks what he knows about a little town north of Yellowstone called Legacy."

I glanced across the kitchen, where Tavo was laughing and

bumping shoulders with my cousin Rosie. "Shit, Joel. Judge Miller knows where Tavo is."

"Yeah. But we don't know what he's planning to do about it. Until we can figure it out, tell Tavo to stay at the lodge, okay? I already called Derek, and he'll be keeping an eye on him, but that'll be easier if Tavo stays on Thomas and Rebecca's property."

Suddenly, the chipper mood I'd been forcing on myself all day faded away and left me disappointed and heartsick again. Nothing seemed to be going right.

I had a vague memory of spouting poetry in Judd's front yard, but then I'd passed out. Tavo had said the chief had driven me home, but I'd been too embarrassed to ask if he knew what had happened before that.

The entire thing was mortifying, and I'd hoped that pretending it hadn't happened would make it so.

It hadn't.

And now this shit with Tavo. The poor guy was going to have to move again. Maybe if he went back to South Carolina with Maverick and Beau after Christmas, he could start over there. My cousin Gabe still lived there, and he could help Tavo meet people and find a job.

After checking in with Tavo and saying goodbye, I found Ella in the living room, playing Sequence with Uncle Derek.

"I'm headed out. Big day at work tomorrow. But I'll see everyone at the Starlight Spectacular the day after."

Everyone sent me lazy goodbyes or waved from their spots on sofas and chairs until I was out the door and into the freezing cold night.

I considered swinging by Kincaid's place to apologize for last night but decided that probably wasn't a good idea.

God, I missed him.

I missed his laugh. I missed his scent. I missed the rumble of his voice and the glint in his eyes when he teased me. I missed the feel of him against me—and not just for sex, although, *fuck*, that too. I missed being held in his arms, comfortable and secure, with his heartbeat under my ear.

Over the past few weeks, my brain had been processing in the background all of the things I'd been too panicked and heartsick to consider when I'd first learned the truth about Judd being *IndexEcho*. I realized now that Judd hadn't actually been hiding it from me—not for longer than the day it took for him to tell me in person. I knew both of us had reacted in hurt and anger and had said things we didn't mean that night. I even understood that Judd's fire-code bullshit about my Christmas decorations was just like me pretending I only wanted him for sex or cuddles—a pretense to be together without *being together*.

I imagined Kincaid was really fucking angry about me showing up in his yard last night... and I didn't blame him. I'd been acting like a child.

But I didn't know what to do about it. I didn't think there was anything I *could* do, besides trying harder to stay away.

Because deep down, I was still afraid.

Hell, I was fucking *terrified*.

If I let myself fall for Judd, it wouldn't be a halfway thing. I'd be all-in, one-and-done, forever-and-ever. It would be the fairy-tale kind of love my parents, and grandparents, and uncles had found. The kind I'd always dreamed of finding. And we would be so damn happy...

And then one day, I'd lose him.

Maybe not tomorrow, maybe not for years or decades. But the fear would always be there. Haunting me.

If I truly let myself love Judd Kincaid and then lost him again, it would break me into such tiny pieces no therapist or well-meaning siblings would ever be able to put me back together.

So as much as I missed him, as much as I longed to be with him, it was simply safer to hold back. To stay away.

Halfway home, my phone rang with a call from Ella, and I answered it immediately, eager for the distraction.

"I hope you're calling to tell me you finally beat Derek at Sequence," I said with a laugh. "Because that man is spooky good, but he's not—"

"There's a fire at Timber," she said urgently. "Derek got a call from Trace, who heard it on the dispatch radio. Legacy FD is on the way."

"Gotta go, Ells," I said, disconnecting.

On the drive home, I forced myself not to put the pedal to the metal. No one in Legacy's emergency services community needed me causing two incidents tonight. Thankfully, I'd been close to home when her call had come in.

When I pulled up the side road that led to the back entrance, the top half of the back of the building was encased in an orange glow, and smoke poured out of one corner of the roof into the sky. My stomach dropped, thinking of all the work I'd put into Timber going up in flames.

But that was nothing compared to what I felt when Judd Kincaid screeched to a halt on the other side of the street, lunged out of his truck, and went running toward the back entrance of my building.

Without a helmet or mask. Without his heavy boots or Nomex clothing.

Without oxygen or heavy equipment.

Without waiting for backup.

In violation of at least five thousand of those fucking fire-safety protocols he could recite from memory.

I threw my door open and screamed, "No!" But there was no way he could hear me over the shriek of the sirens, the noise of the engines that arrived five seconds too late, and the shouting of his crew trying to call him back.

As soon as he disappeared into that burning building, my breath got stuck in my lungs. My entire body went cold.

And I knew without a single breath of hesitation that I'd rather my restaurant—my life's dream—burn to the ground than have one hair on Judd Kincaid's body harmed.

So I started running.

34

———————

KINCAID

Judd: *I got the job in Montana. I think I'm gonna take it.*

Max: *Damn, brother. I'm gonna miss the fuck out of you. But maybe a fresh start is what you need.*

———————

I'D BEEN ONLY a few blocks from Timber when the dispatch call had come over the radio.

All units, respond to a reported structure fire at Timber on Founder's Row. Witness reports smoke and flame visible from the roof. Repeat, smoke and flame.

Over the years, I'd heard thousands upon thousands of calls like that one, and each time—whether it was a hangar fire on a base overseas, or an office building back in Philly, or a wildfire here in Legacy—my stomach would drop. For just a heartbeat, I'd feel the panicked helplessness of a twelve-year-old who'd watched as his whole world was burned to ash.

It only ever lasted a second before my years of training would kick in. Before the haze of panic would recede in a wash of cool logic. I'd remember I wasn't a helpless kid anymore and that I knew what to do: follow the rules, stick to the procedures that had become second nature.

Rely on protocol.

But tonight was different.

I'd texted Tavo this morning to ask how Alex was, and he'd said Alex was glad Timber was closed tonight so he could get to bed early. It was already ten thirty, which meant they were probably both in bed by now.

Right under the roof that was now engulfed in flame.

As I wheeled my truck toward Founder's Row, my stomach dropped and kept dropping. Panic gripped me with long claws and stuck. And once again, it felt like my whole world might burn to ash...

Because somehow, Alex Marian had become my world.

Though I was already close to Timber, I felt like I lived a hundred lifetimes in the time it took me to get there. A hundred lives without Alex Marian's sweet smile, without his laughter, without his stubborn affection, without his pleasured cries ringing in my ear. A hundred lifetimes I had no interest in experiencing.

So when I saw the fire licking out from under the eaves, a living thing crawling fast through the attic toward the room where Alex was sleeping, I didn't stop to assess. I didn't set up a command. I didn't wait for my crew to run line, or handle the scene like the damn textbook rules I'd drilled into rookies a hundred times—*two in, two out. Wait for backup. Don't risk collapse with attic fire.*

What did the rules matter if Alex was up there burning alive?

I took off running for the building as soon as my feet hit the ground. My crew shouted after me, but I was already inside, smoke wafting down the hall and out the door I'd opened.

"Alex!" My panicked voice cracked in the thick smoke, nothing like the calm command I usually kept on scene. I swept my light hard across the ceiling, up the narrow stairs, heart hammering.

Every instinct screamed that this was wrong. *Reckless.* The kind of choice that could cost me my life. But I didn't want my life if Alex wasn't in it, plain and simple.

I battled my way up the stairs one at a time, through air so thick it choked me. It was so dense, I knew it was more burn-off than flame, but smoke was the killer in most house fires. And if Alex and Tavo were up there with no gear, dammit, I had to reach them.

I heard a scream from outside and a radio crackle behind me. I reached for the handset on my turnout coat to respond—but I wasn't wearing my turnouts, so of course it wasn't there.

Suddenly, I felt a hand clamp on my shoulder and yank me back.

Sujo was in full gear with his SCBA mask in place until he peeled it away. "Get the fuck out right now," he shouted. "Alex is outside. Says the building is empty. Tavo isn't home."

It was too good to be true. "Are you sure?" I croaked through the billowing haze.

The roar of the flames above us and the sound of debris falling made Sujo yank me down the stairs toward the door. "I'll clear it. Save us both by going now!"

I did as he said, realizing he was right. I was putting his life and the lives of the rest of my crew in jeopardy by staying there without the proper gear. After quickly making my way out, I passed McMasters going in.

I stumbled down the stairs, lightheaded from the smoke. My eyes burned, and my nostrils stung.

But the pain faded when Alex tackled me outside, nearly knocking me over.

"Judd! Oh, fuck, Judd. Why? Why did you run in there?" he shouted and cried, all while practically strangling me with his arms wrapped tightly around my neck. "Why would you do that, you asshole! I can't believe you! Don't you care about me at all?"

He wouldn't loosen his death grip around my neck even long enough for me to pull back and kiss him. So I hitched him up until he wrapped his legs around my waist, and then I walked toward my truck. Pope gave me an up-nod of understanding, and I knew she'd taken command of the scene.

I opened the back door of my truck and sat sideways on the seat, propping my boots on the running board. "Baby, are you sure the building is clear? Is there any chance someone's in there?"

"I can't think of who. Tavo's at my grandparents' for the night. It's Juni's son's birthday, so she's at home celebrating." He went through the major players at Timber before shuddering. "Judd, what if they'd all been there? What if we hadn't been closed?"

I glanced at the building while smoothing a hand over his hair and rubbing his back. "From what I can tell right now, the restaurant itself doesn't seem to have taken damage. The fire seems to have originated in the farthest corner of your apartment or maybe the attic. At most, the restaurant's bathrooms and food storage rooms might have smoke damage. If the crew can get the blaze under control, I can get back in there. We'll assess the damage. Then I can grab your things. Your clothes. Your... your wine key—"

"Stop! Judd, I don't care about the wine key. I don't even care about the building," he sniffed. "I care about you."

He finally pulled back so I could see his face. His eyes were red, and tears had soaked his cheeks.

"I love you," he croaked. "I love you, I love you, I love you. And

I'm so damn sorry. I don't want to be mad at you anymore. I want to be with you. I want to be *with* you."

I reached up and cupped his cheeks, swiping the tears away gently with my thumbs.

"Baby. Fuck. I love you, too." I leaned forward, pressing our foreheads together. "All I could think about when I saw the flames was getting to you and getting you out. You're my person, Alex. The most important person in the world to me, and nothing is going to change that."

I kissed him softly before the kiss turned deeper.

The radio squawked from the front seat, letting me know McMasters and Sujo were safely out, and they were opening the lines to attack the blaze.

Alex and I turned to watch.

Sujo aimed his line at the windows in the back room of the apartment while Pope and McMasters swept the stream of water up through the attic vents, pounding the flames until the orange glow dimmed to a darkened gray. Steam rolled out in gusts, hissing like an angry cat, while the crackle of burning lumber dulled to a wet sputter.

Alex leaned his head on my shoulder. He was still able to see his building from his position in my lap, and we watched it together.

The weight of him against me was the most profound relief. One I'd never take for granted. But while I had everything I needed in my arms, I knew he was watching one of his dreams literally go up in smoke.

I pressed a kiss to his temple. "I'm so sorry, baby."

He shook his head, then said in a small voice, "What if I did something wrong? What if... what if I left a stove on or had something wired wrong in my apartment, and it's my fault?"

I kissed the top of his head. "Well, if that's the case, we'll learn some lessons. And one of those lessons will be that nobody's perfect."

He lifted his head up and stared at me. "Who the fuck are you right now? Is this a side effect of smoke inhalation? Does it cause personality changes? Where's my grumpy fire chief?"

I leaned in and kissed him again. "He's right here. By your side, where he belongs. And I don't think you did anything wrong, Alex. In fact..." I hesitated, then added, "I think I smelled lighter fluid in there. I don't want to speculate before we have a chance to investigate, but—"

"I don't use lighter fluid," he said, his eyes wide enough for me to see white all the way around in the dark parking lot. "I swear, Judd."

"Baby, I know. Remember when this building was inspected after your original renovations a couple of years ago? I wasn't here, but I went through the inspection notes. At that time, the previous chief noted that the only accelerants on the property were the ones in the restaurant that were known and regulated."

"I remember making a joke that I didn't even keep a lighter or matches to light birthday candles upstairs, because if I was going to celebrate, it would be in the restaurant or at my family's place," he murmured.

"Mm," I said. "Or in the back lot with a cake and twenty-something candles."

He snorted lightly and tucked his head under my chin again to watch the building. "I had to grab a lighter at the checkout counter when I picked up the cake," he murmured. "I wasn't about to take my lame-ass birthday cake into the Timber kitchen and have Juni rat me out to my family."

"It would have ruined your nefarious seduction plans," I teased softly, keeping my eye on my crew as they went through their process methodically.

Alex's voice was a whisper. "Judd... will you give me another chance? I promise I'll try to be braver."

My heart clenched. "We'll each give each other another chance. But you're already plenty brave. I don't even know what you mean by that."

His hand came up to fiddle with the collar of my coat. "I thought... I thought if I told myself I hadn't fallen in love with you, if I didn't *let* myself fall, that I'd be able to keep my heart safe. That I wouldn't have to l-lose you again." His fingers threaded into the back of my hair and gripped tight, like he'd try to keep me there by force if I attempted to escape him.

Like that would ever happen.

"But that was stupid," he whispered. "Because when I saw you running in there without any gear, I realized it didn't matter whether we were in a relationship or not. If you were hurt, I would want to be there for you. If you were killed, I'd want to lie down and die, too. I fell for you a long time ago. First when you were *IndexEcho*. And then again when you first called me Firebug." He sniffled. "Letting my fear keep me from being honest about that wouldn't protect me from having my heart broken; all it would do was prevent us from being happy together right now. I... I don't want to live afraid anymore."

God, this man was so fucking strong. So beautiful.

I brushed his messy hair back and kissed him firmly on the forehead. "You were brave enough to move away and follow your dream. I know you're brave enough to do this with me. If I need to promise you that I will not be as stupid again as I was tonight, I'll do it. On one condition." I tilted his chin up until he met my eyes. "That it's never you in a burning building. Because apparently, I'm shit at the rules when it comes to you, Firebug."

Alex threw his arms around me again and kissed me again.

When I finally pulled away, it was time for us to break out of our little bubble and face reality.

While we may have figured things out between the two of us, we still needed to figure out what the hell happened to his home.

I wasn't going to rest until I got to the bottom of the damn fire... and made sure the man I loved was safe.

35

ALEX

Alex: *You know I'd walk through fire for you, right?*

Judd: *Like I'd ever let that happen.*

AFTER WATCHING the man I loved race into a burning building—*my* burning building—then having him confess that he loved me as much as I loved him, I was an exhausted, emotional mess. My eyes still stung a little from the smoke, and I seemed physically incapable of detaching myself from Judd Kincaid's person.

And both of us seemed to be okay with that.

When the blaze was mostly out and Judd's crew confirmed that the fire, smoke, and water damage had been confined to the attics and the rooms in the back on the second floor, I was relieved... and also beyond ready to have the nightmare portion of the day be over so I could enjoy the wonderful bits.

Specifically, I wanted to head back to Judd's comfortable little cabin, shower the ash off both of us, climb into his warm bed, breathe in his scent into my lungs like oxygen, and then hold him as close to me as physically possible for at least twelve hours.

Possibly twenty-four.

However long it took for a person's heart rate to return to normal after a night like this one.

Unfortunately, while I might've been done with the day, the day wasn't done with me... which became clear when Sheriff Westland hurried over to us.

"Kincaid—" he began. His expression softened when he saw me doing my human limpet impression as Judd and I stood bundled together, using his truck's back door as a windbreak.

Judd didn't move away even a fraction at the sheriff's approach but kept me curled against his chest as he shook the other man's hand. "Elias."

"And Alex," the sheriff said, turning to me. "Sorry about Timber. Glad you're okay, though."

"I'm fine," I assured him. "Just... really lucky we were closed tonight so no one got hurt."

"Actually, I think it might have been more than luck." His eyes met Judd's. "Don't suppose either of you knows a Steve Hinton?"

Judd and I exchanged a look, and both of us shook our heads.

"Should I?" Judd asked.

The sheriff shook his head. "I had three of my officers canvass the neighborhood," he said. "They found a rental car parked by the entrance to the back lot. Your fire crew actually blocked it in with their rigs when they arrived." He hooked a thumb at the far side of the building, where the fire trucks were still parked at an odd angle to the street. "Now, ordinarily, I wouldn't think anything of it, considering how many tourists we have in town for the holidays... but then my uncle Folger called."

"Folger, the Grumpy Bear?" I asked. I nodded toward the small hotel at the other end of the street, where the old hotel's ursine logo looked more cuddly than grumpy.

"That's him. He named the place for himself, according to family legend," the sheriff said with a small smile. "So, you can imagine he wasn't thrilled when he got woken up by an out-of-towner needing a room a little over an hour ago. And he was even less impressed when the guy started complaining about being unable to get a ride to the airport right then and there."

"From Legacy? In the middle of the night? In winter?" Judd demanded.

The sheriff's laugh came out as puffs of white vapor. "Exactly what Folger told him. Then Folger noticed the guy didn't have a car, a suitcase, or a proper winter parka, which made him more than a little suspicious, so he called me. I'll give you two guesses what the name on this out-of-towner's credit card was."

"Steve Hinton?" I guessed. But then I shook my head. "I don't follow, though. He accidentally parked his car back here and got blocked in? Why wouldn't he tell someone so they could unblock him?"

"A great question." The sheriff and Judd exchanged another look, and Judd's arms squeezed me more tightly. "But Folger was right that something seemed off, so I did a little digging. Turns out Hinton just did a stint in Salinas Valley State Prison in California for aggravated arson, and he's out on parole. Which means he shouldn't have left the state without permission from a judge."

The word *California* made my eyes widen, and *judge* made my jaw drop.

Tavo.

My eyes met Judd's and I saw he'd made the same connection. His big hand was warm and soothing as he caressed my jaw. "Tell me you've got this guy in custody, Elias."

The sheriff nodded. "I sent a couple of my people over to the Grumpy Bear just to have a word. And wouldn't you know it, Mr. Hinton started bleating about how we couldn't prove anything, and he only, quote, 'set a little fire to scare him and flush the kid out,' and he 'made sure the bar was closed first.' Then he told us we should call a..." He consulted a note on his phone. "A Judge Kirk Miller in San Francisco, who supposedly told Mr. Hinton he would 'make all this bullshit go away' if Steve just 'did Judge Miller a little favor.'" His eyes met mine. "The name Kirk Miller ring any bells, Alex?"

I swallowed hard. I knew Judd wouldn't approve of my decision to keep quiet. He'd want me to cooperate fully and immediately, by the book, and I understood why. But I couldn't bring myself to tell the sheriff anything until I knew Tavo was safe and had agreed to make a statement.

"I'm sorry," I blurted. "I don't... um... I can't really..."

Judd's boots scraped along the pavement as he twisted slightly, blocking me with his body. "Alex has been through a lot tonight, Elias." He spoke the words softly, but there was a distinct thread of steel beneath them. "Why don't you let him have a minute to think about it, and we'll both come talk to you first thing in the morning?"

The sheriff glanced between us and nodded slowly. "Alright. Alex, I have enough with the parole violation to keep this guy locked up till morning. But I'm going to need you to come in first thing and help me out with some of this, okay?"

"Absolutely. Thank you, Sheriff."

"Welcome. Tomorrow, then," he said, raising an eyebrow at Judd.

Judd inclined his head.

When he was gone, I looked up at Judd's face. Streaks of soot marred his brow and collected in the creases at the corner of his eyes. Under the bright lights the crew had set up while battling the blaze, he looked as tired as I felt. And still, he hadn't hesitated to back me up.

Fuck, he was a good man. *Fuck*, I loved him.

"You didn't tell him." The words came out like an accusation. "You didn't say anything about Tavo to the sheriff."

Judd cupped my cheek and ran his thumb along the skin there. "Of course not. I figure you can call and talk to Tavo in the morning, let him know what's happening, and ask your family to help you find an attorney to protect his interests and identity. The sheriff's going to want him to make a statement, if his lawyer agrees, baby." He took a deep breath and added, "And I think that would be a good idea if he wants this judge to stop coming after him. But that's his call."

Warmth and love swamped me. "You're willing to protect Tavo, even if it means causing the sheriff a harder time with his case?"

"Family comes first, Alex," Judd said, like it was the most obvious thing in the world. "My friend *DrunkenPoet* told me that."

I remembered a night when I'd messaged him about spending hours working alongside family, to haul in the harvest a few days early due to an unexpected frost. I'd missed a concert, and I was pretty sure my sisters had both canceled dates to stay and help, but even at the time, I'd recognized there was something wonderful about being part of a team.

It had been part of my explanation about how deciding to leave the family fold wasn't an easy one. I loved my family. They were everything.

But I loved the man in front of me every bit as much.

"I love you," I sighed, pushing myself against him. "Thank you."

Judd lowered his head so his cold nose rubbed against mine. "Always, Alex. Now, how about I check in with the crew to make sure everything's under control. Then we can head back to my house, and—"

"Yes," I said quickly.

His eyebrow rose. "Just like that? You're supposed to hear the whole offer before you—"

"Yes," I repeated.

Judd laughed out loud. "I might have been saying 'Let's head back to my house and read some fire code manuals,' you know."

"And I'd be okay with that." I wrapped my arms around his neck, burying my fingers in his hair. "I have this strange new kink where I find fire codes sexy," I confessed. After a brief kiss to his lips, I added, "Or maybe it's just that I'm wildly in love with this grumpy fire chief who likes to *ignore* them."

He pushed me into the back seat of his truck and kissed me so hard my lips tingled. "What are you going to do when your fire chief isn't so grumpy anymore, Firebug?" he demanded against my lips.

My words were a whisper against his skin. A promise. "I'll keep finding new ways to light your fire."

The following morning, after we'd showered and managed a little sleep, we met up with Tavo and my uncles Joel and Pete. While Joel owned a security firm that also did investigations, Pete —Tommy's father—was an attorney in the Bay Area. He was fired up to protect Tavo's best interests, no matter what happened next.

It took a couple of hours to work through everything, but since Steve Whatshisname, the man in custody, was cooperating fully, it looked like there was plenty of evidence of Judge Miller's involvement. The judge had told Steve flat out—via text, no less—that he wanted Tavo "retrieved" for him. Steve produced evidence showing the money trail, too. From what Joel had provided, it seemed clear that there were witnesses at Pinch who could provide corroborating testimony about the judge's inquiries into

Tavo's whereabouts. And as of this morning, the soon-to-be ex-judge was the subject of an SFPD investigation.

"I can't believe it's over," Tavo kept saying as we joined the rest of my family at the lodge for a late lunch. "Is it really over?"

Pete clapped his hand on Tavo's shoulder. "Foster said he knows a judge in Wyoming who would process a name change for you and seal the records if you'd like. You know we'd be proud to make you a Marian."

Everyone around the pair of long tables in the kitchen nodded and added their approval as Tavo looked around in shock. Then he burst into tears.

Tavo's friend Drew rushed breathlessly into the room from the direction of the front door. "Tavo, I'm here! The car wouldn't start, and I—"

Tavo crashed into him, tucking his face in Drew's neck. Drew's arms went around him as his eyes slid closed. "Sorry I wasn't there, baby. I'm here now. It's going to be okay."

I blinked at the two of them. While I'd known they'd messed around and had been spending a lot of time together over the past several months, I hadn't realized things had become serious.

Ella clutched her chest and made an *aww* face, and so did almost everyone else in the room.

One thing you could say about us Marians is that we were unapologetically in love with love.

I glanced at Judd, and the second our eyes met, he mouthed, "I love you." My cheeks flushed, and my stomach went floaty.

Papa noticed because he nudged Judd in my direction. "Careful, Chief," he said with a warm smile. "Once we start making Marians, there's no telling who else might get swept up."

Judd took my face in his hands before kissing me full on the lips in front of everyone. I threw my arms around him and held him tight. When he finally let go, everyone was staring, some in shock and some with zero visible surprise.

"Oh, right. Turns out I don't hate him," I announced with a shrug. "Surprise."

The room broke out in laughter.

I slid my hand into Judd's. "And... we've known each other longer than you think."

Judd stood up straighter. "I met Alex online over five years ago. We became close, but then I was in an accident—"

"*IndexEcho*?" Ella's eyes went comically wide, and Mattie's jaw dropped.

He nodded once. "It's a long story, but now we're here and we're together... and I can't thank you enough for loving and supporting Alex during everything. I'm so glad he had you."

Tavo leaned against Drew's chest, smiling through his tears. "And I really thought you were at Alex's apartment to inspect the smoke detector."

Judd's cheeks turned crimson, but before he could say anything, one of my cousins said, "He was there to inspect something, Tavo, but it wasn't the smoke detector."

Considering my grandparents were in the room, I was officially mortified.

"Alright, alright," my uncle Derek said, waving everyone to calm down. "No one needs to hear about their child's... or grand-child's... inspections."

Grandpa shot him a wink. "Promise? Because you're one to talk, Derek Marian."

As everyone began laughing and joking around tables filled with sandwiches and side dishes, I grabbed Judd's hand again, and we went to check on Tavo.

"You okay?" I asked.

Tavo smiled. "God, yes. I can't thank you enough for everything. After my parents left, I thought I was on my own. Then your family just... just appeared like a miracle."

"No miracle. Just helping others and giving back," I explained. "And I'm sure you'll do the same to someone else someday."

He nodded.

"Now that you can work legally without worrying about being tracked down," I said, "I'd like to offer you an assistant manager job at Timber. But only if you'd like that. If you have another dream you'd rather pursue—"

Tavo's eyes got wide. "Are you kidding?" he interrupted. "Working for you at Timber *would* be a dream. But you don't need to do that for me."

I glanced at Judd, squeezing his hand tighter. "I'm not just doing it for you. When Judd and I started seeing each other, we learned that it was really hard to find time together with our work schedules. I'd like more freedom to be home when Judd has time off. Being devoted to Timber for the past three years was necessary, but it's time for me to dial back and find better balance."

"Hear, hear," Judd murmured. "I'll try to do the same."

I glanced at him. "I know it's not as easy for you as it is for me."

The determined look on Judd's face suggested that *easy* didn't matter. My grumpy fire chief would prioritize us, even over his work.

I'd already confronted him about Monroe's suggestion that Legacy was just a temporary stop on his career trajectory, and he'd spent a significant amount of time in the shower this morning convincing me that he was here in Legacy to stay. "Or wherever you are, Firebug," he'd added with whispered words against the back of my neck.

I'd been thoroughly convinced he'd meant it.

Judd slid his arm around me but turned to look at Tavo. "And maybe you want to rent Alex's rabbit warren once the fire damage is fixed up because it's going to be available. He's staying with me from here on out."

My chest was so full of contentment, I hardly knew what to do with it.

I could see domestic fantasies of living together swirling through both Tavo's and Drew's heads, but there would be plenty of time for that while Timber's upstairs apartment went through the long process of insurance assessment and cleanup. In the meantime, Tavo was planning on staying with Lennon and Rosie out at the ranch.

The four of us found spots at the tables and sat down to lunch, and the rest of the day passed like a dream that was too good to be true.

It wasn't until the following day that it sank in.

I was back at Timber, working behind the bar, when Maddox called. "I need you to make up an excuse to keep Adrian distracted today. Everyone's been helping out, and now it's your turn."

"I don't know what that means," I said. "And I'm leaving here in a bit to serve hot drinks at the Starlight Spectacular. Our food truck is doing hot cocoa, cider, and these cinnamon stick things—"

"Just give me an hour. Please?"

I blew out a breath. Thankfully, Tavo had already taken charge of prepping the truck for the event with Karim's help. "What exactly am I supposed to do?"

"Doesn't matter. Just get him to Timber and keep him occupied."

Since Judd was back to work at the firehouse, which was particularly busy today as they helped prepare the holiday light display on Slingshot Mountain's ski slope, I was honestly happy to have my own distraction.

What could I say to get him to Timber that he would believe?

"Adrian!" I said when he answered his phone. "Thank god you answered. I need backup. Legacy's asshole fire chief just called in another 'random inspection,' and I'm about to lose my fucking mind. Can you come keep me company while he's here and help me not commit homicide?"

Thankfully, he didn't particularly care that when he showed up, there was no inspection or any chief.

My bad.

Instead, he drowned his sorrows in my spiked hot cocoa and told me the story of the miscommunication between him and Maddox. Poor Adrian was completely twisted up about it.

"It's going to be okay," I said firmly.

He stood up. "What do you mean? Do you know something?"

I nodded. "I do. And I have a question for you. Have you told Maddox how you feel? Like, specifically?"

Adrian dropped back down on his stool. "I've told him I want him. That I... that I have..." He hesitated, but I could tell he had strong feelings for our grumpy hardware store owner.

I smiled at him in understanding. Why did it always seem so much clearer when it was someone else experiencing it? "Have you said the words 'I love you, I want to stay here, I choose you over everything else'?"

Adrian's eyes widened. "Not exactly."

"Uh-huh." I leaned against the bar. "You know what's not complicated? Telling someone you love them. Everything else is just noise."

"But..."

"And if you love him, Adrian," I said softly, "then trust him."

Before he could respond, Tommy appeared beside us.

"Adrian! Perfect. I need you to—"

Adrian shook his head. "No. I'm sorry. If someone needs cookies or a ride or to be saved from a rogue fire inspection, you're gonna need to find someone else. I have to find Foster. I have to get to—"

"Slingshot Mountain?" Tommy finished. His smile was suspiciously bright. "Good, 'cause I'm here to drive you. To make sure you get there safely."

I hid my own smile. Maddox had roped in another Marian for whatever grand gesture he was planning for Adrian.

As soon as they left, I raced to the kitchen, gathered my crew, and headed to the mountain.

Even though I'd attended the Starlight Spectacular for the past three Christmases, this one was different. As I passed out hot cups and paper envelopes of warm treats, I finally felt like a true local.

"Thanks, Alex!" Mrs. Hoffman called as she hurried away with her drinks.

"Alex, thank god you're here," Tim, a regular customer at Timber, said, rushing up and yanking out his wallet. "I promised my niece one of those cinnamon things she got last time. She's been talking about them for literally an entire year."

We stayed busy until the lights went on in an exciting reveal, and everyone's attention was pulled away by the display.

The moon shone down on the snowy slope as the colored lights danced and flickered to the sound of synchronized holiday music. Everyone stood around in clusters of happy couples, families, and friends.

As I watched my community and hundreds of tourists enjoy the festive moment, I remembered another conversation I'd had with *IndexEcho* all those years ago. About spotlight moments.

His voice came warm and smooth from behind me as Judd's arms snaked around my middle, and his lips found his favorite spot below my ear.

"Sometimes in life, we have those spotlight moments, don't

we?" he murmured. "When all the world seems just right, and we're caught between wanting to live it and wanting to capture it."

"Which one are you going to do?" I whispered, leaning back against his solid frame and enjoying this perfect moment as fully as I could.

"Live in the moment and capture the man," he said softly.

We stood there together like that, watching the faces of our family and friends turn all the colors of the rainbow while the hushed, white winter around us lay thick and clean like a blanket full of promise.

This was our fresh start. Here, together.

DrunkenPoet and *IndexEcho*.

Alex and Judd.

The names we carried didn't matter as much as the connection. And I'd never felt more connected to anyone before.

I'd thought it was coincidence that had drawn us together twice... but now I knew it was fate. There was a part of me I knew would thrive now that my heart was safe in Judd's keeping, and I was determined to make sure the same was true for him.

After our "spotlight moment," when the cold started seeping in, the cinnamon stick warmer began to beep, and a few people lined up for more refreshments, Judd let me go so I could get back to work. But after a minute, I felt his eyes on me.

"Firebug, tell me you have a fire extinguisher in this thing."

I glanced to the spot where the fire extinguisher lived...

Or was supposed to.

But tonight, in its place was a note in Juni's handwriting.

I borrowed this one to replace the one I yeeted. Replacement hasn't come yet.

In the time I spent composing shrieking, ranting text messages to Juni that ranged from *WTF* to *you're fired* to *bring me a fire extin-*

guisher asap, the warming oven began to let out a distinct burning smell.

I looked up at the Chief in horror as his eyes narrowed at me.

"You know I have to write you up for this, right?"

Instead of being angry, though, he looked downright thrilled.

I realized that the infraction meant another several months of random fire inspections from my very own Smokey the Overbear.

And I decided I was very okay with that.

EPILOGUE
KINCAID

Jett: *We don't really have to go to this thing, do we?*

Benji: *Tell Aunt Tilly you're not coming. I dare you.*

Wolfe: *We're all supposed to be there.*

Caspian: *Wait, can we skip it?*

Lennon: *If skipping is an option, I'm totally skipping.*

Gabe: *#TeamSkip*

JJ: *I'm married and straight. Why the fuck do I have to go to Dick Town with all the rest of you?*

Jett: *Wait. Dick Town? NVM. I'm in.*

Tilly: *You think I can't see your mf-ing group chat? You show up tonight or we're doing this again next month.*

———————

IN THE SIX months I'd been with Alex Marian, I'd been to plenty of Marian events, but I had to admit none of them were quite like this.

The dining room of the Fairmont Hotel in San Francisco gleamed like something out of a flashy lifestyle blog. Crystal sconces bathed the long table in golden light, catching the gleam of polished silver and the delicate shimmer of cut-glass goblets. Tilly had insisted on fresh roses in scandalous shades of crimson and violet, their fragrance mingling with the buttery aroma of homemade rolls drifting in from the kitchen. A string quartet played discreetly from the corner, the music just loud enough to soften awkward silences and cover any whispered asides.

And there were many whispered asides.

It hadn't taken long for Ella to spill the beans about what Alex's great-great-aunt Tilly was really up to with this dinner party. It was some kind of massive setup affair for all of the cousins in Alex's generation who didn't already have a partner. It was hard to express just how giddy Alex had been when he'd realized the bullet he'd dodged.

"I knew there was a reason I was dating you!" he'd declared one night while shimmying over to me with two glasses of wine from the kitchen. We'd been preparing to catch up on our favorite home renovation show when he was interrupted by a call from his sister.

"Ah, yes. The reason that's less about who I am as a human and more about how I can protect you from the meddlingest family on Earth."

"Precisely. So, get this." And then he'd proceeded to give me all the hot goss from his family, including this strange dinner party in San Francisco. I tried not to let on how much I enjoyed his overly large family and all their quirks, but he always saw through me. "We're invited, of course, but we're supposed to stay militantly monogamous. Tilly's words, not Ella's."

"Damn. No gang bangs at the fancy dinner party?" I'd asked dryly. "However will we cope?"

But now that I saw the collection of beautiful and successful men Tilly and her cronies had somehow managed to rope into this thing, I could understand the need for the warning.

"Shit," Alex said, moving closer to me. "I should've forced you into a sham marriage or something. At least gotten you a cheap wedding band."

His hand tightened subconsciously in mine, which made me love the sweet man even more. I leaned over and pressed a kiss to his cheek, inhaling his sexy cologne. "You have a wedding band on my heart, Firebug. Even if I don't have one on my finger yet."

Guests mingled with a blend of curiosity and suspicion while Alex's great-granny greeted each arrival from her perch near the large but cold fireplace like a benevolent monarch, wineglass in hand, and her wife, Irene, busied herself with introductions that somehow felt more like chess moves than polite conversation. The undercurrent of purpose was palpable, though cloaked in charm and candlelight.

"Yet," Alex said softly, as if he were tasting the word for possibility.

"Hm?" I murmured as we reached the open bar. "What do you want, baby? Wine or beer? Ginger ale?"

"You said you didn't have a wedding band *yet*."

I shrugged. "There's no rush. Whenever you're ready. White or red? I think I'm going to have a bourbon."

Alex yanked my hand and pulled me off to the side. I shot the bartender an apologetic smile and followed Alex to a secluded spot against the wall. "What is it? Oh, there's Jett. I still can't get over how much the two of you do *not* look alike at all. I blame the mistaken identity on my head injury." A point I'd made before, but every time I saw Jett now, it bore repeating.

When we'd met each other at Christmas, Jett had laughed his ass off. "Man, I should have scooped that silver fox!"

Alex had gone semi-feral. The possessive, claiming sex we'd had that night remained in my top five highlight reel. Maybe it was because it had been the first time I'd bottomed for him, but it might have also been because seeing Alexander Marian that hot and jealous at the same time had made me see fucking stars when I came. He never failed to light me up inside.

Case in point. At the edge of the mingling crowd, he gripped my necktie and pulled me close, which only served to make my dick hard.

"Baby, if you're trying to get me to focus, you're being too bossy," I murmured.

"Are we getting married?" His voice sounded breathy and strange.

"Uh, not today. But yes. Surely that's understood. Unless you don't want to? In which case, I'm going to still need a verbal life-long commitment from you of some kind. But there's no rush."

Alex's face broke out in a wide grin. "I love you."

I smiled back and looked around at all the men starting to take their seats at the various large round tables. "I know. And thank god because your great-aunt and great-granny scare the fuck out of me. They're ruthless. I don't think I would have made the cut for this thing."

"Can we leave early and have wild animal sex in our hotel room?"

I focused back on him in confusion. "I thought that was a given, too. That's how we celebrate things, remember?"

Alex laughed, but I was serious. It was how we'd celebrated when the asshole judge who'd harassed Tavo had ended up on the other side of a judge's bench, and when the Timber renovations had finally been completed, four months after the fire, so that Tavo and Drew could move in to the rabbit warren. It was also how we'd celebrated when Alex's beloved Diet Coke had gone on a two-for-one sale at the grocery store last week.

One of the things I loved best about life with my firebug was that we were committed to celebrating the hell out of every day we were together... and, let's be honest, we'd take any excuse to have wild animal sex.

We finally moved to the bar to order our drinks before finding our seats at a table off to the side. The name card placement—and the appearance of Tommy and Foster—had made it obvious we were at the boring couples' table instead of any of the many fun singles' tables.

"Welcome to the old folks' home," Foster said with a wide grin. "Aren't you glad you're not single?"

I reached out for a fist bump. "Fuck, yes."

Foster and Tommy had quickly become some of my closest friends. Alex and I got together with them regularly back home in Legacy, and Ella was usually part of that regular crew also. In fact, she'd recently brought my own Cody McMasters along to one of Tommy and Foster's backyard barbecues out at their cabin on the SERA campus.

I'd tried hard not to interrogate Cody about it, but I could tell he was goofy for Alex's big sister. Unfortunately, Ella herself was playing it close to the vest.

As the meal began, Foster leaned over and whispered made-up stories about several of the men in attendance.

"He's a bull rider," he said, tilting his head toward a clean-cut guy with tidy blond hair who was wearing an expensive suit. "Masquerading as a tech bro."

Alex leaned over from the other side. "He's actually a tech bro masquerading as a tech bro," he murmured. "Total douche, too. He dated a guy I went to college with."

"That one," Foster said, pointing with his butter knife at a man with a quirky smile and messy man bun. "Snuck in without an invitation. He's doing an exposé on dating in the twenty-first century. He's straight as an arrow."

Four minutes later, Man Bun snuck his hand onto the lap of the man next to him.

"*Whomp, whomp*," Tommy said. "Sorry, babe. You're not that good at this."

Foster met Tommy's eyes and winked at him. "You saying a straight man can't have his horizons broadened, Doc?"

Tommy's cheeks turned pink. "Touché. Who's next?"

Before Foster had a chance to make something up, a new man entered the room. Despite all the noise and myriad conversations around us, the man's commanding presence seemed to create a vacuum that sucked all the attention away from everyone else and onto him.

A screeching noise from someone shoving their chair back brought everyone's attention to Jett Marian, who looked at the newcomer with a shocked expression.

"Holy fuck," I breathed. "Who invited *that* guy?"

"Dunno," Alex murmured. "Why?"

"Because that's the man Jett left me for in Amsterdam."

Alex turned to stare at me. "You're joking? The guy from... what? Four years ago?"

I nodded, eyes fixed on the commanding guy whose decisive stride was eating up the ground between him and his target—Jett.

Jett stood up carefully from his pushed-back chair, darted a look around the room, licked his lips... and then bolted out of the room.

"What the fuck?" Tommy whispered.

"Holy shit," Alex said.

"Someone's in trou-ble," Foster sang with a shit-eating grin.

As I watched the man stride angrily after Jett, I blew out a breath. Thank god the stranger had claimed Jett back in Amsterdam because I wouldn't change a single thing about how my life had worked out. It made me wonder if maybe there was truly such a thing as fate.

Alex leaned into me and whispered in my ear, "How much longer do we have to stay before we can sneak out?"

I bounced my eyebrows at him. "Want me to pull the fire alarm?"

Want more of Alex and Judd? Sign up for my newsletter now to get The Cheaty Fire Bowl, *a* Burning for Alexander *bonus story, here* →
https://readerlinks.com/l/5028179

Up next in the Made Marian Legacy series is Owning Jett. *To find out what happened between Jett and his stranger from Amsterdam, grab your copy here* → *https://readerlinks.com/l/5028293*

A LETTER FROM LUCY

Dear Reader,

Thank you for reading *Burning for Alexander*. I am thrilled to be spending time in Legacy and with the Marians! Up next: find out what really happened that night in Amsterdam and why Jett's stranger came looking for him in *Owning Jett* → https://reader links.com/l/5028293

Be sure to sign up for my newsletter to get bonus content, sales announcements, and more, including discounts on the next releases!

You can also follow me on your favorite retailer site to be notified of new releases, and look for me on Facebook for sneak peeks of upcoming stories. You can also join me right now on Patreon for exclusive content and behind-the-scenes glimpses.

Please take a moment to write a review of *Burning for Alexander*.

Reviews can make all the difference in helping a book show up in searches.

Feel free to stop by www.LucyLennox.com and drop me a line or visit me on social media. To see inspiration photographs for all my novels, visit my Pinterest boards. The Pinterest board for *Burning for Alexander* can be found here → https://readerlinks.com/l/5028420

Finally, I have a fantastic reader group on Facebook. Join us for exclusive content, early cover reveals, hot pics, and a whole lotta fun. Lucy's Lair can be found here.

Happy reading!
Lucy

ABOUT LUCY LENNOX

Lucy Lennox is the USA Today bestselling author of over fifty gay romance titles including the GoodReads Hall of Fame winner Wilde Love. Born and raised in the southeast USA, she is finally putting good use to that English Lit degree she earned before the turn of the century.

Lucy enjoys naps, pizza, and procrastinating. She stays up way too late each night reading romance because it's simply the best.

For more information and to stay updated about future releases, sales and audio news and to grab some free and bonus reads, please sign up for Lucy's author newsletter on her website at Lucy-Lennox.com or to stay in the know, join her exciting reader group, Lucy's Lair on Facebook.

facebook.com/lucylennoxmm

instagram.com/lucylennoxmm

amazon.com/Lucy-Lennox/e/B01N0IOYPT

bookbub.com/authors/lucy-lennox

patreon.com/lucylennox

pinterest.com/lucy_lennox

ALSO BY LUCY LENNOX

Find me online → https://www.lucylennox.com/links/

Read my books:

Made Marian Series

Forever Wilde Series

Aster Valley Series

The Billionaire Brotherhood Series

Made Marian Legacy Series

After Oscar Series (with Molly Maddox)

Twist of Fate Series (with Sloane Kennedy)

Licking Thicket Series (with May Archer)

Champion Security Series (with May Archer)

Honeybridge Series (with May Archer)

Find a complete list of my stand alone romances and novellas at www.LucyLennox.com along with audio samples, freebies, suggested reading order, and more!